WINTER AND ROUGH WEATHER

The story of *Winter and Rough Weather* begins when James and Rhoda Johnstone have just been married and return from their honeymoon to the hill-farm of Boscath in the Scottish Borders. Rhoda has been used to a gay life in London, and she feels that if she had been translated to Mars she would not have found life upon that planet more utterly and completely different. Rhoda is a painter and has given up a promising career to marry James; sometimes she feels regretful—was it right when you had been dowered with an artistic talent to bury it in domesticity? As the story unfolds, Rhoda is able to find the answer to this question in an unexpected way.

There are various neighbours in whom Rhoda takes a keen interest: the Big Business Man and his sister, who have come to live at Tassieknowe and startle the law-abiding district with their goings-on; the young doctor Adam Forrester, whose love affair has such a very unexpected conclusion; the lovely Spanish lady who has lived most of her life in Scotland, but still retains her foreign flavour; and many more.

As is inevitable in any story of the Scottish Border country, the weather plays an important part. The hills are shrouded in mist, or bathed in golden sunshine; there are still, grey days and blizzards of snow, and the river which flows past Boscath Farm is sometimes a mere trickle in its rocky bed, and at other times a rushing, roaring torrent.

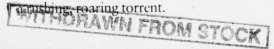

WINTER AND ROUGH WEATHER

By

D. E. STEVENSON

COLLINS
8 Grafton Street, London W1

William Collins Sons & Co Ltd
London · Glasgow · Sydney · Auckland
Toronto · Johannesburg

First published in 1951
This reprint 1988

ISBN 0 00 223390 8

Made and Printed in Great Britain by
William Collins Sons & Co Ltd, Glasgow

FOREWORD

Winter and Rough Weather is another story about Mureth Farm and Drumburly and the people who live there; it continues the theme of *Vittoria Cottage* and *Music in the Hills* but it is a complete novel in itself. The three books are merely strung together by the story of James and Rhoda and their friends.

Mureth and Drumburly are not *real* places in the geographical sense of the word. There is no metalled road that leads to Drumburly (the best road to take is an easy-chair before the fire on a winter's evening) but the picture represented is artistically true of the Scottish Border Country, of the rolling hills, the rivers and the burns, of the storms and the sunshine. So, in one sense, Drumburly is real and in another it is imaginary—and the same is true of the characters in the story; they are not real individuals and yet they are true to life. To me they are real and human for I have been living amongst them and sharing their joys and sorrows for months on end. Now the time has come for me to leave Drumburly and say good-bye.

D. E. STEVENSON

Who doth ambition shun,
And loves to live i' the sun,
Seeking the food he eats,
And pleas'd with what he gets,
Come hither, come hither, come hither;
Here shall he see
No enemy,
But winter and rough weather.

AS YOU LIKE IT

CHAPTER ONE

BOSCATH Farm House was a small two-storeyed building of grey stone with a snugly-fitting roof. It faced south, down the valley, and from its windows could be seen the silvery links of river, now dashing between black rocks in a frenzy of impatience, now dawdling along through green meadows in its journey to the far-off sea. The house stood on a slight eminence; behind it was the steading and the barns, beyond rose the rolling rounded hills of the Scottish Border Country dotted with Cheviot sheep.

Boscath belonged to Mr. Johnstone of Mureth Farm which lay upon the other side of the river; he had bought it some fifteen years ago when farms were going cheap and although it was a good little farm with a fine dry hirsel he had sometimes regretted his action. The river was the trouble. It was a beautiful river and he was extremely fond of it; he had lived beside it all his life, he had fished its pools and gone to sleep with the sound of it in his ears but as a farmer he found it inconvenient. When the river was low it was easy enough for Jock Johnstone to ride through the ford and visit Boscath, but in winter, or at other times when the river was in spate, the two farms were separated by a rushing roaring torrent and the only way to pass from Mureth to Boscath was to cross by Drumburly Bridge—five miles away. It was not very far of course but Jock Johnstone found the evagation very irritating. There lay Boscath before his eyes, he could have thrown a pebble across the river on to Boscath ground, but if he wanted to visit the place he was obliged to turn his back upon it, to drive five miles down the valley to the little town of Drumburly, to cross by the bridge and drive back another five miles upon a rough and rutty road.

" It's a daft road," Jock would say. " Goodness knows who planned it. I've spent pounds on that road and I might as well have poured the money into the river for all the good it's done."

Jock's description of the road to Boscath Farm was justified. It wound hither and thither for no conceivable reason, it climbed the shoulder of a hill when its obvious course was comparatively level. No sooner had a culvert been repaired than the ground shifted and the culvert fell in, no sooner had the surface been mended than the hill-burns rose and washed it away. The men declared Auld Hornie himself took an interest in the Boscath road and that their labours were in vain.

It must not be thought that the sensible, hard-working men really believed in their own assertion. They knew perfectly well that Auld Hornie was too busy finding work for idle hands to take pleasure in the destruction of a silly wee road. Their fathers might have believed it, their grandfathers would have believed it implicitly, but they themselves were less credulous than their forebears. All the same it was odd . . . one had to admit the fact. For instance they mended the road in the middle of a dry summer when the ground was hard as iron and the burns a mere trickle in their rocky beds; and then, before they had left the place, a small black cloud appeared in the cerulean sky and sitting down comfortably upon Crowthorne Hill it discharged a flash of lightning and a peal of thunder and emptied itself completely in less than half an hour. Down came the burns, roaring and rushing like a stampede of grey horses, carrying all before them in their stride.

It was a fine sight of course, but the men did not appreciate its grandeur. They stood and watched the outcome of two weeks' labour being swept away before their eyes. Auld Hornie or not, there was something uncanny about the road.

It was a fine afternoon in early autumn. The weather had

been dry and the river was low. Mr. and Mrs. Johnstone crossed it in a farm cart with the greatest of ease and, dismounting upon the other side, walked up the path to Boscath Farm. They were going to inspect the alterations which were in progress and to see if their instructions were being properly carried out by the workmen from Drumburly. The house was being renovated and thoroughly done up for their nephew and his bride who, at that very moment, were enjoying a honeymoon in Cornwall.

As far as the outside of the house was concerned the preparations were complete. Everything was tidy and clean. The chimneys had been whitewashed, the paths weeded and the clutter of broken barrows and old wheels and such-like rubbish which had disfigured the place for years had been gathered up and burnt.

" What a difference ! " Mamie Johnstone exclaimed.

" It's tidied up nicely," agreed her husband. " I told Willy Bell to get a move on. He knows how I like things kept."

" I hope they'll be happy here," said Mamie softly.

" Of course they'll be happy," declared Jock. " They've everything to make them happy. James is one of the best—and Rhoda—you said yourself he couldn't have found anybody nicer."

" I know," agreed Mamie.

" What are you worrying about, then ? "

" I'm not worrying, Jock. At least I'm not really *worrying* —but of course it's very isolated. Boscath is like an island in some ways."

" I see what you mean," nodded Jock.

" And Rhoda isn't used to islands."

" Very few people are," Jock pointed out.

Mamie was not listening. She said, " If only it was spring ! I mean it would break them in gradually, wouldn't it ? I like winter at Mureth myself; I like the snow and lovely big log fires—but it will be so awfully different for Rhoda after London . . . and marriage is always a risk."

" It's too late to think of that now," said Jock sensibly.
" They've taken the risk and it's up to them to make a success
of it. Come on, Mamie, we'd better go and see what Flockhart
is doing, hadn't we? "

" Mr. Flockhart is very nice but terribly slow," said Mamie
as they walked on. " It's such a bad mixture. I mean if he
weren't so nice you could be firmer with him and make him
hurry up."

" I'll be firm with him," said Jock, smiling.

" But not horrid," said Mamie quickly. " You won't be
horrid, will you? His wife has been ill and he's got such a
beautiful voice. . . ."

Jock laughed. He and Mamie understood one another very
well. There had not been much risk in their marriage.

The front door of Boscath stood wide open, revealing the
mess inside. Two ladders were set at an angle across the hall
and a plank was balanced upon them in a precarious manner.
Mr. Flockhart was sitting upon the plank with a paint-pot
beside him; he was splashing distemper upon the wall and
singing " Roaming in the Gloaming." As Mamie had said
his voice was beautiful, it was a full, rounded bass and seemed
to well up and flow out from his throat without the slightest
effort.

Incidentally his voice could be heard every Sunday morning
amongst others, less round and full and velvety, in Drumburly
Kirk.

" Don't speak to him! " whispered Mamie, clutching her
husband's arm. " If you give him a fright he'll fall! "

But there was no need to speak for Mr. Flockhart had seen
them and was not in the least alarmed. He stopped singing and
painting and ran down the ladder with the agility of long
practice, an agility which was remarkable in a man of his build.
Mr. Flockhart had a big round body and very short legs, his
face was large and round and he had very little hair. Mamie
always thought of Humpty Dumpty when she saw Mr. Flockhart
and the resemblance was accentuated by the fact that one so

often saw him sitting upon a plank with his tiny legs dangling in mid-air.

" What's all this, Flockhart? " inquired Jock.

Mr. Flockhart did not reply, but stood looking up at Mr. Johnstone with a seraphic smile. He had quite a long way to look up, for Mr. Johnstone was unusually tall and unusually broad-shouldered into the bargain.

" You promised to be out of here by Saturday," continued Jock. " You promised faithfully—and look at the mess! "

" I'll not let you down, Mr. Johnstone," said Mr. Flockhart earnestly. " Things have held me up a bit, that's all. When things hold you up you can't do nothing, but I'll not let you down."

" You have let me down," declared Jock. " The furniture is arriving. Mrs. Johnstone wants to get the place cleaned."

Mr. Flockhart gazed round the hall. " It looks worse nor it is," he said in comforting tones. " You'd be surprised how soon it'll be all ship-shape. Give me to-morrow, Mr. Johnstone. Just you give me to-morrow—that's all I ask. I'll not let you down nor Mrs. Johnstone neither."

Jock hid a smile. Mamie was right, you could not be angry with the little man, he was too nice. The absurdity of the whole affair struck Jock, for Jock had his own dry sense of humour. Firstly Mr. Flockhart's request was impossible to grant, for what human being could give to-morrow? Secondly, Jock had no alternative but to grant the request for the work could not be left unfinished and there was nobody else to finish it. Thirdly, to-morrow was obviously inadequate for the completion of the job . . . to-morrow and to-morrow and to-morrow, thought Jock, trying to master his amusement and to look as annoyed as he ought to feel.

" It's very disappointing," he said. " Mr. James and his wife are coming next week and we wanted the house ready for them. Where are all your men? Could you not put more men on to the job? "

" I will," nodded Mr. Flockhart. " I'll get them on to it

to-morrow. They'll maybe need to work overtime but I'll
not let you down. You see it's like this, Mr. Johnstone. Lady
Shaw wanted some painting in a hurry and you know what a
dominant lady she is."

Jock knew. So did Mamie for that matter. The Shaws of
Drumburly Tower had been lords of the district for countless
generations. Partly because of this and partly because the present
Lady Shaw had an exceedingly strong, though admittedly
benevolent personality, she invariably got her way.

" Oh, Lady Shaw . . ." began Mamie in doubtful tones and
then, remembering James and his bride, she pulled herself
together. " But, honestly, Mr. Flockhart," said Mamie. " It
will be dreadfully disappointing if the house isn't ready for
them when they come home from their honeymoon. You see
that, don't you? "

" It will be ready," declared Mr. Flockhart. " I'll be out on
Tuesday, that's flat. And I tell you what," he added, smiling
up at Mamie. " I tell you what, Mrs. Johnstone. You can
have Dorrie if you like."

Mamie gazed at him.

" It's my sister," he explained. " You were speiring about
a cook, they were telling me."

" Oh yes! " cried Mamie, who had indeed been speiring
about a cook or in fact about any kind of maid who would be
willing to brave the isolation of Boscath and help Rhoda in
the house. " Oh, yes—I *was*."

" Well then," said Mr. Flockhart.

" Do you mean your sister would come? " asked Mamie
incredulously.

" For a wee while anyway," said Mr. Flockhart with sudden
caution. " I'll not say she'll stay for long. It all depends.
Dorrie's a queer one. If she takes a fancy to a place she'll settle
down, but if she takes a scunner at it she'll be out at the end of
her month. That's Dorrie."

" Yes," said Mamie doubtfully. " Yes, but perhaps——"

" It's like this, you see. Dorrie's been stopping with us for the last year helping in the house—Mrs. Flockhart has been a wee bit under the weather as you might say—but now Dorrie's wanting another job. And to tell the truth we could do with her room," added Mr. Flockhart confidentially.

"But I wonder——" began Mamie, for so far she had heard nothing which could be taken as a good recommendation of Dorrie's character or capabilities.

"There's no need to wonder," interrupted Mr. Flockhart. "You take her, Mrs. Johnstone. You'll not regret it. She's a real good cook but she and Mrs. Flockhart . . . well the truth is they don't see eye to eye."

"Your sister was with old Mr. Brown, wasn't she?" asked Jock.

"That's so," nodded Mr. Flockhart. "She was up at Tassie-knowe with old Mr. Brown till he died and then she was in Peebles for a month but she didn't like it, so then she came to us."

"Oh, of course!" cried Mamie. "Miss Flockhart! How silly of me! It would be simply marvellous if she could come."

"She'll come," said her brother, who obviously was determined that she should. "She'll come next week—or whenever you're wanting her—and she'll see how she likes it."

Jock was a trifle shocked; he expected Mamie to be shocked too, but Jock had not been scouring the countryside for a cook. Mamie had been doing so for weeks and therefore was far too delighted at having a cook thrown at her head to mind the slightly unconventional gesture.

"How lovely!" Mamie exclaimed. "I'll come and see her to-morrow morning. Of course Miss Flockhart is the very person. She's a marvellous baker; I used to enjoy her scones when we went to tea with Mr. Brown . . . and I'm sure she'll like being here."

"I'm sure I hope so," said her brother. "She'll want out, of course. Dorrie's a great one for the Pictures, but I dare say her and Mrs. James can work it out."

" Of course they can! "

" About the money and that," continued Mr. Flockhart. " You see Dorrie has a wee bit of money of her own. Mr. Brown left her an annual-allity. She could live on it quietly by herself if she was sensible, but—but I tell you what, Dorrie would not *do* by herself. She's not just awful sensible."

As they walked back to the ford the Johnstones discussed the matter.

" Not sensible," said Jock in a worried tone. " Do you think it's wise, Mamie? "

" Nonsense," said Mamie cheerfully. " It doesn't matter a bit. I'm not awfully sensible myself and I could never live alone, but I'm quite a good housekeeper."

Jock laughed. He said, " I tell you what: you're fishing."

" It's infectious, isn't it? " nodded Mamie. " Not fishing, but telling people what. Jock, you can't imagine how light-hearted I feel . . . a real live cook! "

CHAPTER TWO

MR. FLOCKHART took a week of to-morrows to finish his job but at last he and his men vanished from Boscath taking with them their paints and brushes and ladders and planks. Mamie went over to see the results of their labours and decided that they had done well; but Oh, what a mess! The whole place needed scrubbing before the carpets could be laid; the furniture stood about, mournfully draped in dust-sheets and the crates of china and kitchen ware which had been sent from Rhoda's home at Ashbridge were piled one on the top of the other in the tiny hall.

" It's impossible," said Mamie to Jock as they were having supper together in the comfortable dining-room at Mureth House. " I simply don't know how to start. The floors can't be scrubbed until the furniture is unpacked and the furniture can't be unpacked until the floors are scrubbed."

" You'll have to leave it as it is then," said Jock after a moment's thought.

" Oh, Jock! " exclaimed Mamie, half laughing and half annoyed.

" Well, what about Miss Flockhart? You've engaged the woman. Could she not help? "

" No," said Mamie firmly. " No, that's *not* a good plan. It would be awful if she took a scunner at Boscath and it's enough to give anybody a scunner at the present moment. I'd rather she came when the house is reasonably straight."

" This is Monday and they're coming north on Friday."

" I know," sighed Mamie. " It's quite hopeless. They'll just have to come here for a few days, that's all."

" Does it matter? "

" I suppose it doesn't, really, but I *did* want to have it ready for them."

Jock saw she was disappointed. He decided something must be done. Mamie had said it was impossible to get Boscath ready by Friday but if he knew anything about her she would wear herself out in the attempt.

No more was said. Mamie was considering ways and means. She would go over to Boscath to-morrow and take Lizzie. She and Lizzie together could at least make a start. It would mean that Jock would have to have a cold meal in the middle of the day, for if she took Lizzie there would be nobody to cook for him ... but Jock would not mind. There was a piece of cold beef, he could have a salad, his coffee could be left in a Thermos flask.

Jock watched her. He knew exactly what Mamie was thinking; he usually knew. She'll wear herself out, I'll need to do something, thought Jock.

Early the following morning Mamie and Lizzie set off to Boscath. It was a beautiful day, the sun was shining in a cloudless sky, the hills were peaceful. As they walked down the gently-sloping track to the ford Mamie was struck afresh with the beauty of her surroundings. The river leapt and sparkled and swirled between black rocks, but at the ford it broadened into a quiet pool with a brown gravel bottom and to-day the water was scarcely ankle deep. Most people called it Mureth Ford but the ford had been there long before Mureth; it had been used by Roman legions (that was certain, for pieces of Roman pottery had been found buried in the shingle) and it had probably been used by Celtic tribes before the Roman occupation.

Mamie removed her shoes and waded in. The water was cold but after the first shock it was rather enjoyable. The fine rounded pebbles squelched between her toes. Looking down she saw her pink toes and the brown gravel, she felt the tug of the bright water as it swirled round her ankles.

Lizzie had donned Wellington boots for the passage but in spite of this she hesitated upon the brink for Lizzie was a towns-woman at heart. She had come to Mureth during the war as an evacuee from Glasgow and although she had been at Mureth ever since she had never got used to country ways. Lizzie had two children: Duggie who had been evacuated with her from the horrors of the Clydeside blitz and Greta who had been born soon after her arrival.

The children had grown up at Mureth and went in to Drumburly school daily in the school bus.

Mamie could not help smiling when she looked round and saw Lizzie standing upon the bank of the river. She looked so out of place. The wide rolling hills, the sparkling water— these were not the right setting for Lizzie Smith. She would have looked, and probably felt, more at home in Sauchiehall Street amongst the Glasgow crowds. Poor dear, I wonder why she has stayed, thought Mamie (not for the first time by any means). I suppose she must like us. Or perhaps it's because of the children.

"It's quite shallow," said Mamie encouragingly. "There's scarcely any current. Take my hand."

Lizzie's hand was trembling as she allowed herself to be piloted across.

" We'll get a cart to bring us back," said Mamie. " I never thought—I mean I didn't know you were frightened."

" I'm not," replied Lizzie, who had her pride. " It's just that I'm not wanting to get my skirt wet."

When at last they reached the little house and began to look about them and to decide upon a plan of action Mamie felt her heart sink. It was worse than she had thought, the task of cleaning it was Herculean, but Lizzie seemed undaunted at the prospect.

Lizzie took off her coat and donned an overall. " I'll light the boiler," she announced. " I'll need hot water to scrub the floors."

" It will take us weeks," said Mamie hopelessly.

" You'll not scrub," declared Lizzie.

" Of course I shall! "

" Not the floors. I'll do the floors myself and then I'll know they're properly done. You can get on with unpacking the china."

It was so like Lizzie to do a kind action ungraciously that Mamie almost smiled (she certainly would have smiled in normal circumstances) but smiles were out of the question to-day, she felt more like tears.

Lizzie disappeared into the kitchen and Mamie went upstairs and looked about her. The main bedroom was quite a good size, it faced west, looking across the river to Mureth. Rhoda had chosen pale turquoise paper for the walls and pale grey paint for the woodwork. It was unusual, of course, but Rhoda was an unusual person. Mamie decided it was a success. The furniture had been shoved in anyhow; the bed leant against the fireplace, the cupboard was in the middle of the room, the roll of carpet was standing in the corner. Everything was filthy, including the window.

I ought to do something, thought Mamie hopelessly. I ought to begin to do something. The question is what? She went to the window and looked out. There was Mureth, across the river, and there was the ford . . . and there was a farm cart coming up the track from the ford, a farm cart with four women in it!

For a moment Mamie did not understand and then, quite suddenly, she realised who they were and why they were coming. The female population of Mureth cottages was on its way to the rescue. It was almost too good to be true! She rubbed her eyes and looked again. Yes, it was a real cart with real women in it. She could see Mrs. Wilson, the wife of the under-shepherd; Mrs. Couper the wife of the ploughman; Mrs. Bell, the wife of the dairyman and, last but by no means least, Mrs. Dunne, whose husband, Willy Dunne, was Jock's right-hand man. Mamie waved to them joyfully. No watchman in a beleaguered city could have been more incredulously thrilled and delighted to see the approach of a relieving army than was Mamie as she beheld the approach of the farm cart, driven by Joseph Couper. Four women! Four able-bodied recruits!

This was Jock's doing of course; it was the sort of thing Jock enjoyed doing and, now that she thought of it, she remembered that Jock had been somewhat mysterious this morning at breakfast. She had caught him smiling to himself in a sphinx-like manner over his bacon and eggs and when she had asked to be allowed to share the joke he had replied, " I'll tell you the joke at dinner-time, or maybe you'll tell me," and had refused to say any more. Yes, it was Jock's doing, but how had he managed it? The women had husbands and children to feed and houses to look after. Mamie had never thought of asking them to come and help her.

She ran downstairs and met them at the door. " How kind of you! " she cried. " Goodness, I'm glad to see you! "

" Mr. Johnstone said you were needing help," explained Mrs. Bell.

" He just mentioned it," said Mrs. Couper.

" It would be a real pity if the house wasn't ready for Mr. James," added Mrs. Wilson.

" But the children! " cried Mamie.

" They'll be fine," Mrs. Couper assured her. " I kept Alice off school and Grandfer will be there. The wee Wilsons are spending the day with our ones."

" Daisy will look in and see to them," added Mrs. Bell.

Mrs. Dunne said nothing. She had no children; she had prepared a cold meal for her husband and left her cottage with an easy mind.

" Well, I do think it's kind," declared Mamie, who realised the amount of organisation which had been necessary. Every one of them must have been up at dawn preparing food and making arrangements so that her family could carry on in her absence.

The recruits had come armed with pails and scrubbing brushes—all except Mrs. Dunne who by reason of her superior position had armed herself with polishing materials instead. Mamie noticed this at once and laid her plans accordingly. She knew it was not going to be easy for although the denizens of Mureth cottages lived next door to one another they were not always friends. One day they would be as thick as thieves and the next, for some obscure reason, they would be scarcely upon speaking terms. Mamie regretted this tendency and she was all the more pleased and surprised to discover there had been so much co-operation amongst them and to note that for to-day at least all feuds seemed to have been forgotten. Even Mrs. Dunne who was usually at the bottom of any trouble in the cottages seemed amiably inclined.

" It seemed so hopeless that I didn't know where to begin," said Mamie as she led them into the hall.

" We'll sweep the floors and then scrub them," said Mrs. Couper cheerfully.

" Starting at the top," added Mrs. Bell.

" It'll not take long with four of us at it," declared Mrs. Wilson as she took off her coat.

They got down to it without more ado and soon the little house was full of the sound of scrubbing, of chinking pails and chattering voices. They were all happy. They were doing a kind deed and incidentally they were enjoying themselves, for it was a change from the dull routine of their daily work. They had come because they were fond of James and because all the world loves a newly-married couple. Perhaps they had been prompted by a slight feeling of inquisitive interest in the newly-decorated house and by an unwillingness to be left out of the picture (if Mrs. Bell were going to Boscath Mrs. Couper would not stay at home) but Mamie preferred to think it was all due to their innate goodness of heart and to the fact that they liked James.

Lizzie's face was the only glum one—and how odd that was! How odd that Lizzie should resent the coming of help! One would have thought that Lizzie's face would shine with pleasure to see the work being accomplished so easily. Lizzie had been willing to scrub every inch of the house with her own hands. Mamie could only suppose that Lizzie was jealous.

In some ways the day was even more wearing than Mamie had expected for instead of labouring herself she was now an organiser of other people's labour, directing, advising, smoothing out difficulties and keeping an eye upon everybody at once. She had to propitiate Lizzie, asking her opinion upon this and that, insinuating in a tactful manner that Lizzie was her lieutenant in the battle for cleanliness and order which was being waged at Boscath Farm. The management of Mrs. Dunne required even more tact for Mrs. Dunne might wreck everything if she became annoyed or offended.

"Perhaps you could help me to unpack the china," suggested Mamie.

Mrs. Dunne graciously agreed.

CHAPTER THREE

JAMES and Rhoda were spending a few days in London on their way home; they had intended to travel north on Friday, but on Thursday morning they suddenly changed their plan. It was breakfast-time and the newly-married couple were sitting at a small table in a London hotel endeavouring to satisfy their healthy appetites with the food provided for them. James had chosen porridge and had been offered a plate of curious grey pudding, flavoured with saccharine, he had turned from it in disgust and asked for a kipper. Rhoda, more used to London breakfasts or perhaps less optimistically inclined, had gone for cornflakes and fruit.

" Breakfast used to be so nice," said James sadly.

" I know," agreed Rhoda in sympathetic tones." I like a decent breakfast myself but lots of people eat nothing for breakfast so I suppose hotels don't think it's worth bothering."

" They make you pay for it," James pointed out. " If you have to pay for breakfast there ought to be something to eat. There's nothing on this kipper at all."

" Let's fly," suggested Rhoda.

" Fly?"

Rhoda nodded. " We could fly to Renfrew; we could get a train to Drumburly; we could be in our own house to-night!"

" Our own house!" cried James, looking at his wife with adoring eyes. " Oh Rhoda! But it won't be ready!"

" Who cares? I mean we could light a fire and make up a bed, couldn't we? How do you like the idea?"

James liked it immensely not only because he was a countryman at heart and detested the crowds and noise and bustle of London but also because he was longing to have Rhoda all to himself in their very own house with nobody to bother them.

Rhoda was aware of this. She had only been married to James for a month but she knew a good deal about him. She had known James when they were children and that helped, for James the man had developed quite naturally from James the little boy who had been her playmate. Even in those far-off days Rhoda had loved him; they had got into all sorts of scrapes together and had shared experiences, grave and gay. Then James had gone to Malaya and Rhoda had taken up painting in a big way so they had drifted apart. They had drifted so far apart that Rhoda had almost lost James, not because James had ceased to love her but because Rhoda had imagined—most foolishly as she now perceived—that painting was a more important career than marriage. If it had not been for James's aunt, Mamie Johnstone, Rhoda would most certainly have lost James. Rhoda shivered at the horrible thought.

" You're cold, darling! " exclaimed her husband.

" Cold! How could I be cold in this stuffy room? "

" Perhaps there's a draught."

" What nonsense," smiled Rhoda.

" It isn't nonsense," declared James earnestly. " The least draught might easily give you a chill. You don't wear enough warm clothes." He knew this quite definitely of course. For the last four weeks James had had the privilege of seeing his wife undress, of observing the diaphanous garments which were hidden from the rest of the world. There was no warmth in any of them—the whole of Rhoda's underwear could not have weighed more than half a pound—no wonder James was terrified of her getting a chill.

" Don't be silly," Rhoda said. " People never wear flannel petticoats nowadays. If you've finished picking at that piece of shoe leather we'll go and see if we can get seats on a plane."

It was late when James and Rhoda arrived at Boscath Farm.

They had flown to Renfrew, done some necessary shopping in Glasgow and having missed the last train to Drumburly had gone to a garage and engaged a car to drive them home. It was an expensive form of transport but Rhoda pointed out that it would cost no more than staying the night in a Glasgow hotel and, although James had a feeling that it would, he did not go into the financial aspect of the matter very thoroughly. He wanted to get home; Rhoda wanted to get home; the young man at the garage was ready and willing to take them.

The car went well on the smooth high-road to Drumburly but when they had crossed the bridge and turned on to the road to Boscath Farm they were obliged to slow down and proceed at a snail's crawl. Auld Hornie had been at his tricks again.

" Is this right? " inquired the young man from the Glasgow garage in anxious tones.

James assured him that it was.

" It's not very good for my springs."

" No," agreed James. " I'm sorry. It's an awful road."

" It's a daft road," declared the young man. " Look at the holes! Look at the turns! Jings, look at the bog! "

" It's better farther on," said James, hoping devoutly that his optimism was justified and that Auld Hornie had not any further tricks in store.

" It could hardly be wurrse," replied the young man sourly.

They bumped and slithered and twisted and turned but fortunately the young man was a careful driver and brought them to their destination without mishap. James paid him generously and they stood at their gate and watched him drive away. The lights receded into the twilit gloom and disappeared.

Now that they had reached their journey's end the impatience which had urged them forward and which had made the whole day a nightmare of haste and confusion vanished away. You could not feel impatient here for time did not matter. Clocks were an invention made for cities not for the everlasting hills.

It was very quiet, there was not a breath of wind, the only sound was the far-off murmur of the river. The sky was still bright with the reflection of the vanished day but the earth was dark and shadowy; the hills were dark, lying like sleeping monsters, their rounded backs outlined against the pale lemon and palest turquoise of the heavens.

" Peaceful," whispered Rhoda.

" Isn't it? " agreed James. " I feel as if there was only you and me in all the world."

She slipped her hand through his arm.

" I love this place," said James. " Boscath is part of Mureth, and to me Mureth is perfect—and you're perfect. Nobody has ever been so lucky before."

" I come second of course."

" You know that's not true. I would have given up all idea of farming if you had wanted me to. It was only when you said ' No ' that I came to Mureth to learn farming with Uncle Jock."

" And then I followed you here and threw myself at your head! "

" And I caught you," agreed James. " I wasn't wicket keeper in the first eleven at Stowe for nothing. I caught you and I'm never going to let you go. You're a farmer's wife, Rhoda."

" Your wife," she said, squeezing his arm. " It still sounds funny. I haven't got used to it yet. First of all it's so amazing to have a husband and secondly it's so absolutely staggering to be a wife. I dare say it sounds as if it were the same thing but it's two absolutely distinct things to me."

" Yes," said James doubtfully. " Well, I don't know. You couldn't have a husband without being a wife."

" And then there's that woman," continued Rhoda, chuckling. " That mysterious person who seems to haunt me. She's always cropping up at unexpected moments."

" A woman? "

" Yes, I've never seen her of course, but——"

" Who? " asked James, mystified.

" Mrs. James Dering Johnstone, of course."

" Oh, of course."

" People say, *Mrs. Dering Johnstone,* and I look round to see where she is."

James could sympathise with Rhoda's feelings for he too had changed his name, or at least he had taken the name of Johnstone in addition to his own. He had done so because Jock and Mamie, having no children, had made James their heir.

" It's a bit of a mouthful," James said. " And it's a frightful nuisance to sign, but I expect we shall get used to it in time."

" No doubt we shall," agreed Rhoda cheerfully.

Having settled this they turned and looked at their house. There it stood, a small solid building with a low roof fitting tightly upon its walls. It looked absolutely empty and deserted but that did not worry them for they had known it would be empty.

" Let's go in," said Rhoda. " It's getting cold and I'm famished. We can light the fire and make coffee and open that tin of tongue we got in Glasgow. It's just as well I remembered we should need food. Perhaps I'm going to be quite a good wife—a sensible, house-keeping farmer's wife. Wouldn't that be nice? "

It was then and only then that James remembered he had no key. The fact that he would need a key to open the door of his house had never crossed his mind for keys were not much used at Mureth. The front door of Mureth House usually stood open and even at night it was rarely locked . . . but this little house was empty so it was bound to be locked.

" Good Heavens, what a fool I am! " cried James.

" No key, I suppose? Aren't we mutts! "

" I'm the mutt, not you."

" We'll break in," Rhoda assured him. " I'm sure there's a window that somebody has forgotten to shut."

They went round the house examining the doors and windows but nobody had forgotten to fasten a window or to bolt a door.

Everything was safely locked and barred and bolted, no burglar could have made an illegal entry at Boscath Farm. Only upon the upper floor was there a window which had been opened a tiny crack—the smallest crack imaginable—from the top.

" It will have to be that one," declared James.

" No, James, you couldn't," objected his wife.

" I could. That's the window of the little back-bedroom, isn't it? I could get on to the roof of the coal-shed."

" We could go across to Mureth," suggested Rhoda who had uncomfortable visions of James falling off the coal-shed roof and breaking his neck.

James had thought of this, but he did not want to go to Mureth to-night. There were several reasons which made the idea distasteful but the principal reason was that he had been a fool to forget about the key and if he could break in it would restore his prestige. Having decided to do it James did not hesitate, he climbed on to the roof of the coal-shed and found that he could reach the window-sill. Fortunately there was a small staple let into the wall beneath the window and this made it easier than he had expected. He rested his weight upon it and was able to open the window from the bottom.

Rhoda watching with bated breath saw James draw himself up, throw a leg over the sill and disappear. She ran round to the front door where the luggage was stacked and waited for him to come. He was longer in coming down than she had expected but presently she heard the sound of bolts being drawn and the door swung open. The light was on in the hall and the brightness streamed out into the darkening night.

" Rhoda ! " said James breathlessly. " There's a woman——"

" A woman ! "

" Asleep in bed in that room—the room I got into. It's a strange woman. I never saw her before."

" James, what nonsense ! "

" It's true," declared James, half laughing. " A woman with a round flat face, with eyebrows like—like George Robey.

28

Her mouth was open and she had no teeth. I couldn't believe it! "

" I don't believe it either."

" Honestly, Rhoda. I lighted a match and gazed at her. She didn't move. She didn't stir. She's lying there asleep . . . not exactly snoring but breathing heavily through her mouth."

This wealth of detail convinced Rhoda. James might have made up the story of a woman in bed but not a woman with a flat face breathing heavily through a toothless mouth.

" It must be a cook! " exclaimed Rhoda in awed tones.

" Well, never mind who it is," said James. " I've opened the door so let's go in," and seizing his bride in his arms he carried her over the threshold with a masterful stride and set her down in the hall . . . and then, before relinquishing her, he kissed her.

In the last month James had practised this delicate art quite often and was now extremely proficient. No film star had anything on James when James really got down to kissing his wife.

" What was that? " exclaimed Rhoda, disengaging herself.

" What was what? "

" A sort of noise."

" What sort of noise? "

" A sort of—gasp," said Rhoda doubtfully.

" Couldn't have been."

" The cook! "

" The cook—if she is a cook—is asleep. She's as fast asleep as the Sleeping Beauty waiting for her Prince. I can assure you a bomb wouldn't have wakened her."

" A kiss might have," said Rhoda, giggling.

" Wait till you see her! " said James.

The house was ready. It was clean and orderly and shining. There were sheets upon the bed, there were towels upon the rail in the bathroom, soap in the soap-dish. The fire in the sitting-room was laid and blazed up brightly when James put a match to it. James went round his house gloating upon everything and seeing in every little detail the hand of Mamie —the hand of love. Meanwhile Rhoda had found what she

29

needed in the kitchen; she was opening up the box of provisions which they had bought in Glasgow and preparing a meal.

It was their first meal in their own home; they had it comfortably in front of the sitting-room fire and took their time over it. They talked quietly, remembering the cook—if she were a cook—and unwilling to disturb her slumbers. They had been in each other's company for a month but there was still plenty to say and somehow now that they were actually at home there was a new relationship—a tender relationship, a safe cosy relationship—blossoming between them. Rhoda put the feeling into words, she said with a little sigh, " The honeymoon 'was good but this is much, much better."

CHAPTER FOUR

MISS FLOCKHART had awakened at the sound of her bedroom door closing very quietly. It was the manner of the closing that awakened her. Ordinary noises did not waken Miss Flockhart for she had shared a bedroom with two restless nephews for the past year. Her brother's house adjoined the Shaw Arms Hotel and her window looked out on to the yard and the bar. At first the noises had nearly driven her crazy but after a few weeks of broken rest she had become used to the noises, both inside and out, and had slept the sleep of the just.

The furtive closing of her bedroom door was a different sort of noise. Miss Flockhart awoke. The mists of sleep receded. There was a curious dream lingering in her subconscious mind. She felt as if there had been somebody in her room (a man, young and handsome, a sort of Fairy Prince) but that was rubbish of course. Nobody could possibly have been in her room. Before going to bed, Miss Flockhart had gone round the house most carefully, bolting every door and snibbing every window—every window except her own which she had left open a tiny crack, the tiniest crack imaginable. Oddly enough the window was now shut.

Supposing somebody was in the house, had managed to get in somewhere? Miss Flockhart sat up and listened intently. Somebody *was* in the house. There was no doubt about it. Who could it be? She got out of bed, opened the door and tiptoed on to the landing. The light was on in the hall and the front door was wide open. Miss Flockhart leaned over the banisters and saw . . . and saw a young and beautiful man stride into the house with a young and beautiful maiden in his arms . . . and she saw the kiss.

Something moved inside Miss Flockhart; it was as if her whole inside turned upside down for a moment and then righted itself. She had seen kisses on the screen and had watched them unmoved, but this was real. This was . . . there was no word for it. Her head swam. Her whole body tingled. She felt almost as if she were participating. It was not until the kiss was over that Miss Flockhart came to her senses with a long-drawn sigh and realising that she had seen what nobody had a right to see, scuttled back to bed.

It's THEM, thought Miss Flockhart, sitting upon the edge of the bed and trying to pull herself together. Well, of course it must be THEM. It was unthinkable that people with burglarious intentions should pause to kiss before opening the safe. Miss Flockhart considered the matter carefully; should she put on her dressing-gown and go down and welcome her new employers? Was it her duty to offer to make tea? She decided it was not. They did not want anybody. She would pretend she had not wakened. Miss Flockhart straightened her pillow and laid her head upon it, but there was an odd feeling of restlessness in her and it was some time before she was able to compose herself to sleep.

The morning was dark and rainy. Miss Flockhart had set her alarm at six-thirty for she had a lot to do. Although the house had seemed completely ready to James and Rhoda,

Miss Flockhart was not satisfied with it. In her opinion the furniture needed polishing and the china cupboard was improperly arranged. When the alarm went off Miss Flockhart awoke reluctantly for she had had a disturbed night and it was several moments before she came to her senses and remembered where she was. It was quite a while before she managed to sort out the real events of the night from the phantasmagoria of her dreams. In fact it was not until she had dressed and gone downstairs that she was sure she had seen Mr. and Mrs. Dering Johnstone arrive. The remains of their meal convinced her that she had and she took action accordingly.

Rhoda left James shaving and descended in some trepidation. Last night she had been able to take the whole thing lightly but this morning she felt differently about it. Rhoda had never possessed a cook of her very own before. She was not quite sure if it really was a cook—and, if a cook, how to address her —and it was so important, so vitally important to make a good first impression. She crept noiselessly to the kitchen door and peeped in. Her nose and eyes instantly informed her that her guess had been correct: the smell of frying bacon and of newly-baked scones and the sight of a comfortably plump figure with a white apron tied round its waist.

" Oh," said Rhoda. " Oh, what a gorgeous smell! "

Miss Flockhart turned and smiled shyly and Rhoda was surprised to see that her new retainer was quite good-looking. Rhoda had steeled herself to behold an absolute gargoyle. Admittedly her new retainer's face was round and somewhat puddingy but she had nice white teeth this morning and her eyes, beneath the slightly surprised eyebrows, were definitely good, large and well-shaped and softly brown.

" We came a day sooner," said Rhoda apologetically.

Miss Flockhart stared at Rhoda. She was absolutely dazzled by Rhoda's beauty, by her golden hair and her dark blue eyes and her perfect complexion.

" We didn't know there would be anybody in the house," added Rhoda.

"I came—yesterday," said Miss Flockhart in a faint voice.

"How lucky!" Rhoda exclaimed. She hesitated after the exclamation. What should she say next? There was so much to be said that it was difficult to know where to begin. Perhaps it was best to say nothing, to take everything for granted until she could feel her way. "How awfully lucky!" repeated Rhoda.

Miss Flockhart nodded.

"We flew to Renfrew," continued Rhoda. "It was a lovely day—blue sky and fleecy clouds—simply heavenly."

Miss Flockhart said nothing. She was dumb with enchantment. She seemed to see an aeroplane swooping amongst fleecy clouds with the sun shining upon its wings. That was how they had come. Not in a lumbering, noisy, dirty old train but in a silver chariot swooping amongst the clouds.

There was a short silence. Miss Flockhart pulled herself together with an effort. "I hope you like bacon, Mrs. Dering Johnstone," she said.

"I adore bacon," replied Rhoda.

"I didn't know, you see," Miss Flockhart explained. "I just risked it. Some ladies like fruit to their breakfasts and nothing else, but gentlemen usually like bacon. I made porridge too, and oven scones. I just—risked it."

"You were inspired," declared Rhoda with conviction.

Miss Flockhart did not quite understand the meaning of the word but she realised from the expression upon her new employer's face that she had done well to risk it. "Mr. Brown liked bacon," she said.

"Wise man," commented Rhoda.

"He used to say my oven scones were—were ambrosial."

"The food of the gods," nodded Rhoda.

"I was with Mr. Brown before," continued Miss Flockhart, who was beginning to find her tongue. "I was housekeeper at Tassieknowe for ten years and three months exactly . . . and I'd be there now if he hadn't died."

Rhoda made a little sound of sympathy.

" He was old, mind you," said Miss Flockhart. " He had asthma and the doctor had told me his heart was bad and he might go off any minute, but still it gave me an awful turn when I found him sitting in his chair with his spectacles on and the chess all arranged on the table. It seemed—it would have been more—more natural if he had been comfortably in bed."

" Oh, no! " cried Rhoda. " You mustn't think that. I mean if he liked chess——"

" He was crazy on it. He'd sit for hours playing away by himself, working out problems he called it."

" Well then, how *much* nicer for him to die happily like that instead of being ill and lying in bed and getting worse every day! "

Miss Flockhart had opened the oven door and was taking out her scones. She said a little unsteadily, " I'd have nursed him faithfully."

" Of course you would," agreed Rhoda. " And I quite see how awful it was for you to find him like that; but honestly it was the best way for him."

" Maybe, but it wasn't best for me. There was a lot of nasty talk in Drumburly. Folks said I should have had him in his bed and looked after him. They'd not say it to my face but I knew fine there was talk."

" How horrid of them ! How absolutely beastly! "

" It was that," agreed Miss Flockhart, warming to her new employer more and more.

" It must have upset you dreadfully," said Rhoda in sympathetic tones.

" Och well, there's always talk. I was a lot more upset with—with something else."

Rhoda immediately inquired what else had befallen.

" Do you think people can see what's happening here after they're dead?" asked Miss Flockhart, answering Rhoda's question with another.

" Yes," said Rhoda.

" I think so too," said Miss Flockhart sadly.

" Something happened? Something he wouldn't have liked? "

" Mr. Brown was scarcely cold in his grave before his house was pulled to pieces," said Miss Flockhart dramatically.

Rhoda gazed at her aghast.

" And he was that fond of Tassieknowe," continued Miss Flockhart, busying herself about the kitchen as she talked. " It seems that the wee hillock where the house is built used to be a Roman fort, and it was called after a Roman general— Tacitus his name was. I didn't pay much heed to what he said, poor old gentleman, but he used to talk about it, even on."

" Why did they pull it down? " Rhoda inquired.

" They didn't exactly pull it down," explained Miss Flockhart. " But they made an awful hash of it. He'd let it go a wee bit of course; he didn't like changes, poor old gentleman. He'd not have a tree cut down nor a bush cut back. It was the same indoors; he'd not have the rooms painted or papered. Well then, when he died the place was bought by a rich gentleman from London and he got on to it straight away and pulled the place to bits. I'll tell you what, I wouldn't have known it was Tassieknowe when I went up to have a look at it. Shaved and shorn it was," said Miss Flockhart with a little gulp. " Not a tree left, nor a bush, and the house gutted as if there'd been a fire."

" Goodness! " exclaimed Rhoda.

" There it was, sitting on the hill *naked,* and the place full of foreign workmen—from Liverpool. Drumburly folk were not good enough for Mr. Heddle to employ. Alec felt it a bit (Alec is my brother and he's the best painter in the district) but I just said to Alec he'd have got no good out of *that* job if he'd got two hundred pounds. It's gone," added Miss Flockhart. " Yon naked wee house on the bare hill is no more Tassieknowe than it's Holyrood Palace. And what's Mr. Brown feeling about it, that's what I say."

" He doesn't mind," declared Rhoda, who had followed the story with breathless attention.

" He'll mind if he can see it."

" No," said Rhoda earnestly. " No, he doesn't mind. I think people in the next world can see what's happening in this world but it doesn't grieve them. Honestly that's what I think. I'm not just saying it to comfort you. I've thought about it a lot. You see, after my mother died my brother did something—something very unkind. As a matter of fact he was engaged to a girl and then suddenly without any warning he broke it off and married somebody else. I wondered if Mother knew."

Miss Flockhart nodded gravely; the tray was ready to carry in, but she waited.

" And then I was *sure* she knew," declared Rhoda. " Mother knew and she was sorry but it didn't distress her as it would have distressed her when she was here. She understood *everything*," said Rhoda earnestly. " She understood the whole miserable tangle inside and out—and of course if you really understand a thing and see it in proper perspective it doesn't make you unhappy."

Miss Flockhart was not quite convinced.

" ' Tout comprendre, c'est tout pardonner,' " said Rhoda. " That means you can forgive anything if you know the truth, and if you understand and forgive people you feel much better. When I really understood about Derek and how it had happened I forgave him at once. It was being angry with Derek that made me miserable, you see."

James came down to breakfast whistling cheerfully. He had shaved with soft water, he had donned comfortable clothes; he had looked out of the window and seen the hills. The hills were not really a very cheerful sight this morning for they were garlanded with scarves of trailing mist and it was raining gently but inexorably as if it never meant to stop, but James didn't care.

" Gosh! " he exclaimed when he saw the breakfast table. " Gosh, so she *is* a cook! "

" Yes, isn't it marvellous! And she's terribly nice. I've been talking to her for ages."

" I suppose Mamie engaged her for us."

" I suppose so," agreed Rhoda.

" Didn't you ask? "

" No," said Rhoda. " No, as a matter of fact——"

" What's her name? " inquired James, as he helped himself to a large plateful of porridge. " Is she staying permanently? I suppose we've got to pay her the earth! "

" Er——" said Rhoda. " Um—— I don't know, really."

" You don't know? I thought you said you had a chat with her."

" We didn't talk about that," said Rhoda, giggling feebly.

" What did you talk about? " James wanted to know.

" Death, principally," replied Rhoda, shaking with internal laughter. " We talked about death and about whether people in the next world can see what's happening here."

" Oh, quite," said James, nodding.

" We did, really," Rhoda assured him. " I don't quite know how we got on to the subject—oh, yes, I do. It all began with Mr. Brown."

" Oh, naturally it would," agreed James. " It began with Mr. Brown."

" Do be sensible, James," Rhoda implored.

" Sensible! " cried James in mock dismay. " I like that! Sensible! I suddenly discover that I have married a lunatic and—and——"

They laughed uproariously. They positively rocked with laughter.

" Listen, James," said Rhoda at last, wiping her eyes with a wisp of cambric which she was pleased to call a handkerchief. " *Do* listen, it's really very interesting indeed. Do you know anything about a place called Tassieknowe? "

It appeared that James knew quite a lot. He had met the rich gentleman from London and had disliked him at first sight. (" He's a heavily built man with crinkly black hair and he walks

37

with a springy sort of step like a cat," was James's description of Mr. Heddle.) James had actually been to the newly-decorated Tassieknowe, had been a guest at a terrific party there. He was engaged in telling Rhoda about the orgy of food and drink and gaiety which had taken place at Tassieknowe when the door opened and Miss Flockhart appeared with a further supply of newly-baked scones and a dish of marmalade.

Rhoda made a face at James and said firmly, " Yes, the rain is badly needed so we·mustn't complain about it."

" It's exactly what's needed," agreed James. " Oh, good morning—er——"

" Miss Flockhart," said Miss Flockhart.

" Miss Flockhart, of course," said James smiling in a friendly manner. " I hope you're finding everything all right, Miss Flockhart? "

Miss Flockhart said everything was fine and went away, closing the door softly but firmly behind her.

James waited for the click and then leant forward. " Rhoda," he said in a whisper. " That's not her."

" Not her? "

" No, honestly. *That* woman is nice looking. She's got nice eyes for one thing. She's got nice hair. That's not the woman I saw in bed."

" Of course it is, you donkey! "

" It—is—not," declared James. " The woman I saw in bed was hideous. She was an absolute freak—no teeth, no hair! I told you——"

" Don't be silly," Rhoda adjured him. " Her hair was probably in curlers, her teeth were—were in a tumbler on her dressing-table, her nice brown eyes were shut. *Of course* the poor darling didn't look her best! "

CHAPTER FIVE

ON Sunday night James and Rhoda went over to Mureth by special invitation. Wanlock took them across the river in a farm cart. He was going to spend the evening with the Bells and was magnificently attired for the occasion.

" There's that pretty girl—Mrs. Bell's sister," whispered Rhoda to James.

" Daisy," agreed James, nodding. " Yes, I thought of that too." He laughed and added, " I see you're getting the Mureth outlook upon things in general."

" What do you mean, James? "

" A few weeks ago you wouldn't have been interested in Wanlock's love affairs, would you? In fact you wouldn't have thought of Wanlock as a human being at all. It's only country dwellers that take an interest in one another's affairs."

Rhoda saw that this was true, or at least only slightly exaggerated. She thought about it as they dismounted from the cart and walked up the path to Mureth House.

In comparison with little Boscath, Mureth House was a palace; it was a trifle shabby of course but shabby in a very pleasant way, for everything in the house had grown old together and mellowed into a harmonious whole. The hall was square, and large enough to give an impression of spacious ease; the oak table gleamed with many years of polishing, so did the grandfather's clock with its big moon-like face; the stairs swept up to a half-way landing which was lighted by a well-proportioned window with square panes of clear glass.

James and Rhoda walked in without ringing and James shed his coat, flung it upon an oak chest and, raising his arms above his head, exclaimed " Mureth! " in a tone of satisfaction and delight.

Rhoda smiled. She, too, was fond of Mureth. She was fond of the house for its own sake, for its absence of fripperies and for its beautifully proportioned rooms, but she was even more fond of it for its atmosphere of friendliness and kindness which emanated from the people who lived and moved and had their being within its walls. In Mureth House there was not only physical comfort but mental and spiritual comfort as well. You could be yourself here. You could say what you liked without the slightest fear of being misunderstood and you could do what you liked without the slightest fear of giving offence.

" Mamie! " bellowed Jock, dashing out of his library into the hall. " Mamie, they're here! "

Mamie came running down the stairs. "James! Rhoda! Darlings! " cried Mamie in excitement.

There were greetings and questions and a flood of talk and laughter. Rhoda began to explain why they had suddenly taken it into their heads to fly home and Mamie began to explain how she had managed to clean the house. James declared that they had enjoyed every moment of their honeymoon but there was no place like Mureth, and Jock kept on saying he was glad to see them back. In the midst of all the noise and chatter Lizzie suddenly appeared and, walking across the hall to the gong, she proceeded to beat it unmercifully.

" All right, all right! " bellowed Jock. " We're all here. There's no need to make that din."

" It's a welcome," declared James laughing. " That gong is the voice of Mureth. That gong is one of my earliest recollections. I remember being allowed to beat it when we used to come to Mureth for the Christmas holidays.

" I've made a soufflé," explained Lizzie. " You're to go and sit down before I bring it in."

" We're to have fatted calf," said Jock. " Mamie killed it this afternoon."

" And Jock has opened a bottle of champagne," added Mamie laughing.

They went into the dining-room and sat down. The curtains had not been drawn but it was beginning to get dark and the oak-panelled room was dim and shadowy, candles in silver candlesticks stood upon the polished mahogany table. There was a low silver bowl of crimson dahlias in the middle, their large velvety petals nestling amongst green leaves.

" This is grand," declared Jock as he unfolded his table-napkin. " This is what I like to see—just the four of us—and the best of it is we're going to see it often. You're looking fine, Rhoda. Marriage seems to agree with you. Maybe when you've been married a bit longer you'll be as pretty as Mamie."

" Don't be silly ! " cried Mamie. " You know perfectly well I never was half as beautiful as Rhoda even when I was young."

" That's a matter of opinion," said Jock. " Maybe James doesn't agree with me but we're all entitled to our own opinions."

They began to talk about the farms. James wanted to know all that had happened in his absence.

" Nothing much has happened," said Jock. " Except that we've had a lot of trouble with Tassieknowe. I knew from the start Heddle would be an unsatisfactory neighbour but it's worse than I expected by a long chalk."

" They've got a good shepherd, haven't they ? " James inquired.

" He's been sacked."

" What! " cried James. " That nice old Highlander ! "

Jock nodded. " Sutherland has been sacked. He was too scrupulous for Heddle, too high-principled—at least that's what they're saying—so he got thrown out. They've taken him on at Hawkbrae, that's the wee farm that marches with Boscath on the north, it's just across the river from Tassieknowe."

" He's there, is he ? He won't have much scope at Hawkbrae."

" And the shepherd's cottage is awfully isolated," put in

Mamie. "I feel sorry for Sutherland, he was at Tassieknowe for so many years. He and Mrs. Sutherland were sort of dug-in, they seemed part of Tassieknowe."

"I told him he'd be better to go right away," continued Jock. "I could have got him a good job over near Peebles, but he wanted to stay in the district for some reason or other so it was no use."

"We've heard a great deal about Tassieknowe," said Rhoda.

"From Miss Flockhart, of course," said Mamie. "I hope Miss Flockhart is a success."

"She's a marvel!" Rhoda cried. "She's a perfect darling and a first-class cook. It *was* clever of you to find her, Mamie."

Jock was not particularly interested in Miss Flockhart so the conversation divided in half and while the female portion discussed Miss Flockhart's virtues (and Mamie described how Miss Flockhart had literally been thrown into her arms) the male portion continued to bewail the shortcomings of Tassieknowe.

"We've had to mend some of their dykes ourselves," said Jock gravely. "It's the very devil—there's been a tup loose on the Tassieknowe hirsel since the end of September."

"Good heavens!" exclaimed James in horror-stricken tones.

"What?" asked Rhoda, tearing herself away from Mamie's story to hear what frightful catastrophe had befallen.

Jock repeated his piece of information.

"But what is a tup?" asked Rhoda who envisaged some species of wild beast loose upon the hillside. "Is it a sort of wolf?" she added.

"It's a ram," replied Jock smiling. "It'll not eat the ewes if that's what you're thinking, but it's nearly as bad. The tups are kept in a field near the farm most of the year and put out at the end of November; then we know the lambs will be arriving the end of April. No hill-farmer wants lambs arriving in February or March when the weather's too cold and there's maybe snow on the ground. Besides we want to know the pedigree of our lambs, we want the strain kept pure ... and dear knows what kind of queer beast this is! Reid has seen it and says it's a hairy-polled creature with a crooked horn."

" It's the limit! " cried James.

" Just about," agreed Jock. " Reid is furious. He's taking his gun with him when he goes round by Tassieknowe. He says it's rabbits he's after but I'm wondering. I wouldn't put it past him to shoot the brute and bury it in the moss."

" If it was on our ground——" began James.

" Whether it was or whether it was not, who's to know? Och well, it can't be helped but it's the devil and all to have a neglectful neighbour. You know, James," continued Jock. " You know I wanted to buy the place when old Brown died. I thought I'd get it at a reasonable figure because the house was in such a dilapidated condition that nobody else would want it. The state of the house didn't matter to me; it was the hirsel I wanted not the house."

" Yes, you told me," said James. " Heddle's agent turned up at the sale with orders to buy it at any price."

Jock nodded. " That was the way of it. I don't know when I've been so disappointed for I'd made up my mind to have Tassieknowe, and as a matter of fact old Brown wanted me to have it after he'd gone. He said as much one evening when he was here. You remember, Mamie? "

Mamie nodded. " Yes of course I remember. Mr. Brown said Mureth and Tassieknowe ought to be farmed together."

" He was right," declared Jock. " The two hirsels adjoin, they're complementary, and together they would make a fine bit of property."

" *That* belonged to Mr. Brown," said Mamie, pointing to an oak tallboy which stood in the corner of the dining-room. " We bought it at the sale and we bought a few other things as well. Of course the Heddles didn't keep anything belonging to the old man, they made a clean sweep."

" Are they really dreadful people? " asked Rhoda.

" They're pretty bad," replied Jock soberly. " They fill the house with their smart friends and turn night into day. Brown would have been shocked at the carryings on at Tassieknowe that's one thing certain. Brown was a real old type of Border Scot, an elder of the kirk and a sound farmer; he was a man of high principles, a wee bit narrow in some ways and maybe a wee bit prejudiced but thoroughly good at heart." He paused for a moment and then added with a grim smile, " I'll tell you something else but you'd best keep it to yourselves: Reid says they're eating their lambs."

" Not really ! " cried James incredulously.

" So Reid says—and Reid knows what he's talking about. Reid asked me if I wanted to do anything about it but I'm not keen to take up the job of common informer, or whatever it's called, so I told Reid to keep it dark."

Rhoda was looking puzzled.

" You see, Rhoda," said Jock with a humorous smile, " farmers are not allowed to kill a sheep—not even their own sheep—without a permit. I dare say it sounds a bit strange but that's the law of the land. But Tassieknowe is away up in the hills and who's to know if Mr. Heddle kills a lamb and has a nice saddle or a fine juicy gigot for his dinner ? "

" He's láying himself open to blackmail, isn't he ? " said James thoughtfully.

" Just that," agreed Jock. " You've hit the nail on the head. Sutherland wouldn't stand for it so he got the sack. The new shepherd does exactly what he likes and Heddle daren't say a word. That's the position—it's a mess and no mistake."

Jock having said the last word on the subject they turned to others more profitable. He asked how Boscath was shaping.

" Oh, I'm making a start," said James. " You're not to come until I tell you."

" Ha ! It's like that, is it ? "

" Just like that," nodded James.

" No help needed ? "

" Not at present," said James. " But if you could spare Daniel Reid I'd like the loan of him some time. I want to take him round the hill."

" I'll send him over one of these days," promised Jock.

CHAPTER SIX

IT was mild after a night's rain, mild and yet bracing, the sky was pale blue, the distances clear. It was, in fact, one of those early autumn mornings peculiar to Scotland, one of the delights of uncertain weather. The scent of the moist earth was intoxicating; there was a faint tang of pines in it and a faint musty smell of mushrooms. Some of the leaves had fallen from the hawthorn bushes, and lay all round them making a carpet of golden brown, and from this carpet arose the little stunted trees ablaze with scarlet berries.

James had breakfasted early and was walking down to the ford to meet Daniel Reid. He looked about him and sniffed the air and was very happy. There was something good and wholesome about this land, it was good and wholesome work to tend it. When he was in Malaya he had felt that the land was evil, that there was age-old evil in the very earth. It was foolishness, he supposed, because Malaya was as much God's earth as this was, but that was how he felt. The glaring sun, the swiftly growing jungle plants, the poisonous snakes were horrible to James but they did not frighten him; it was night in Malaya that was frightening. Others had felt the same unreasoning terror. Talking it over and trying to face this fear they had decided that the old spirits of the earth can be sensed more strongly in the dark hours than in the light . . . not ghosts but elemental spirits, inhuman and ruthless. There was cruelty in *this* land too but it was a straightforward cruelty, the cruelty of wind and rain and rock and torrent, the cruelty of blinding snow and blizzard, but thank God these could be faced with manliness, they were a challenge to courage.

James was not finding his new job easy. It was a job that took all his mind and strength and if he had had twice as much mind and strength it would have taken that as well. He had stayed at Mureth before his marriage and had learnt a good deal about farming; he had gone out upon the hills with Daniel Reid, the Mureth shepherd, and had absorbed a certain amount of information about sheep; he had learnt to milk cows and to clean out the byres; he had helped to drain a meadow and to build a dyke; he had worked in the hayfield, had shawed turnips and been instructed in the art of hedging and ditching. But James had had no responsibility at Mureth, he had done what he was told, that was all. Now he suddenly found himself saddled with the responsibility of managing a farm on his own.

Boscath Farm was much smaller than Mureth and there were fewer sheep upon the hirsel. James had two men to help him, a young shepherd called Roy and an orra-man called Wanlock (the duties of an orra-man are multifarious, he does anything that needs doing and makes no bones about it). These two men lived in a little cottage on the hill and Roy's mother kept house for them. Of course James could appeal to Mureth for advice and help if he needed it, but he knew that Jock wanted him to work Boscath himself, standing upon his own feet and learning by experience, and he was determined to do his best to justify Jock's confidence.

The farm needed a lot of attention for the grieve who had been at Boscath before had let the place go downhill pretty badly. Hedges and ditches, dykes and gates, were all in poor condition and must be attended to—in local parlance they needed sorting. James had not been born and brought up in Scotland but already he had adopted a good many expressions from his neighbours (had adopted them more or less unconsciously) and the verb " to sort " was one of the most useful additions to his vocabulary. To sort a gate is to mend it thoroughly, to put it into proper working order (as a matter of fact you can sort anything from a broken toy to a broken-down tractor, you can sort an untidy room or a misunderstanding between friends). A ditch which has become blocked needs right sorting and a leak in the roof of the byre should be sorted straight away. It is even possible to give a man a sorting, in other words to tell him what you think of his behaviour in plain unvarnished language and to set his feet in the path of duty. "I'll sort it" is a promise to put the thing right. "I'll sort him" is a threat with sinister implications.

James saw that his first job must be to sort the men who had become extremely slack and careless. He waited for a day or two, observing them carefully, and then he waded in and gave them the works. They were somewhat surprised, for they had heard a good deal about James from Mureth and had formed the opinion that he was pleasant and easy-going and would be an indulgent boss.

"We've got to get a move on," declared James, when he had told them exactly what he thought of them. "This place has got to be as good as Mureth. Go over to Mureth and have a look round, you won't see any blocked ditches there. If you don't want to help me to get this place into decent order I'll get somebody else to help me, that's all."

They were a little sulky at first but when James took off his jacket and got down to it himself they were shamed into following his example. Quite soon they began to take an interest in the work, and even a certain pride. James, working with them and watching the improvement he had wrought, decided that they weren't bad fellows—all they had needed was a right good sorting.

James was thinking about this as he waited at the ford for Daniel Reid. Presently he saw Dan coming down the slope. He waved to Dan and Dan waved back and shouted. It was amusing to see Dan's method of fording the river; he did not hesitate on the brink as so many people did, nor did he trouble to remove his boots and turn up his trousers as James would have done. He simply walked straight through it boots and all as if it were not there. The water was up to his knees in midstream because of the rain in the night, but he ploughed through it unconcerned and his faithful sheep-dog walloped through it beside him, covering him with spray.

" Goodness," said James as he wrung Dan's hand. " You're wet to the skin! "

" I'll soon dry, Mr. James," replied Dan.

They were glad to see each other for they had shared some curious experiences and had become fast friends. James admired Daniel Reid, he was as straight as a die and an expert at his job. Although he was small and ugly, with a weatherbeaten face and a large nose and bushy eyebrows, there was a quiet sort of dignity about him.

" I wanted you to have a look at the ewes," said James as they breasted the hill together. " They're quite healthy but they're light compared with the Mureth ewes and the wool seems poor."

" Inbred most likely," nodded Dan. " You should buy some good tups at the Lockerbie Sale."

" Yes," agreed James. " You'll have to advise me about that. Another thing I want is a sheep-dog."

Daniel smiled. " That's not so easy, Mr. James. Nobody would sell a good dog and nobody would buy a bad one."

" Where did you get Gyp? "

" I got her as a puppy. She's got Loos blood in her, and Loos was the cleverest creature that ever was. But you'd not want a puppy, it's a made dog you want."

" A dog just like Gyp."

" Is that so? " said Dan gravely. " What would you give me for Gyp? "

James laughed. He knew that Dan would not have sold Gyp for all the gold in Ophir.

They talked about other things after that, James inquired about the wild tup which was loose upon Tassieknowe hill but failed to draw Dan upon the subject.

" It never would have happened in Sutherland's time," declared Dan. " Yon new chap is useless. He neither knows his job nor cares about it."

" But what about the beast? Have you seen it lately? "

" I've not seen it for a wee while," replied Dan in non-committal tones.

James glanced at him and noticing a curiously grim smile upon his countenance forbore to question him further.

" And they're letting the place go to pot," continued Dan after a short silence. " There's a nice wee sheltered meadow near the river; Sutherland used it for sick sheep. Well, there's a couple of drains got clogged and the whole place is reverting to bog. I spoke to yon new chap about it and he just grinned and said he was not bothering. ' There's enough land without that for all the sheep we need,' he said. What d'you think of that, Mr. James? "

" Not much," said James. He could not help feeling slightly amused at the way Dan spoke of the new shepherd at Tassie-knowe. Apparently the man was so despicable that he had not even a name.

" It's deplorable," declared Dan, rolling out the word so that it seemed twice its usual length and conveyed more than twice its usual meaning.

As before, .when they had walked Mureth hills together, James found it took him all his time to keep up with his companion. Dan's legs were short and seemed shorter because he walked with them bent at the knee in a curious ape-like manner, but in spite of this he covered the ground at a steady pace which never varied; up hill or down dale was the same to Dan. Fortunately he stopped every now and then and sent Gyp careering off to round up a little group of ewes and bring them to him to be examined.

They went all round the hill, round the back of Winterfell and back over the saddle between Winterfell and Crowthorne—it was twenty miles or so—and all the time Dan talked about sheep and James made mental notes and asked questions. When at last they parted at the ford, and Dan splashed through the water and went home, James was so mentally and physically tired that he felt completely dazed. He sat down upon the bank

D

and rested for a bit and then crawled back to Boscath, leaning upon his crook like an old done man.

But I've learnt a lot, thought James. At least I suppose I have —when I can get it sorted out and digested.

CHAPTER SEVEN

BOSCATH Farm-house was small but Rhoda was pleased with it; the rooms had been painted and papered and her colour-scheme of dove grey and turquoise blue was a great success. It was restful; pictures looked well upon the walls and various pieces of furniture which she and James had acquired from their relations seemed to be settling down together uncommonly well.

The outside of the house was perfectly plain but its austerity harmonised with the landscape of rolling hills. There was no attempt at a garden round the house (the kitchen-garden lay in a sheltered hollow behind the farm); the soft green turf swept up to the very walls of Boscath so that the house looked as if it had grown out of the grass of the hillside like a mushroom. It was square, built of grey stone, but a little wing jutted out at right angles from the main building and in the sheltered corner there was a huge bush of old-fashioned white roses, tiny roses like white silk rosettes, which smelt as sweet as attar. Above the house was a little grove of rowans and beyond were the hills.

Rhoda had not been looking forward to housekeeping at Boscath; to begin with there was no electricity nor gas. To Rhoda this seemed odd to say the least of it, she expected the house to be wrapped in Stygian gloom save for a flickering oil-lamp which would reek of paraffin; but Miss Flockhart was used to lamps and had a way with them, she kept them clean and well-trimmed so that they neither smelt nor smoked and, far from being gloomy, the house was better lighted than many which boast electric current, for (as Miss Flockhart explained) paraffin was cheap and you could afford to keep a lamp burning in several places at once. There was none of that groping about for a switch nor moving from a brilliantly lighted room to a dark passage. The whole house glowed with a mellow warming radiance.

The absence of a telephone at Boscath was a much more serious inconvenience. When Rhoda first learnt of this extraordinary circumstance she had laughed and said, "How long will it take to put in?" But to put in a telephone at Boscath would have meant not merely a few weeks' delay and a few men climbing on to a telephone pole and a few wires festooned about the house. Putting in a telephone at Boscath would have necessitated nearly five miles of wire and sufficient poles to carry it from Drumburly Bridge. This was out of the question and it seemed equally out of the question to bring it across the river from Mureth.

"But there's a post every day," Rhoda was told when she complained about the lack of communications. A post there most certainly was and what they would have done without their pleasant, smiling little postie Rhoda could not imagine. He called at Boscath every morning delivering and collecting letters and parcels and, as he happened to be a second cousin of Miss Flockhart's brother's first wife, he was only too willing to do any small commissions in Drumburly or to take a message across the river to Mureth on his way home. At first Rhoda was slightly shocked at the idea of making His Majesty's Mail her private messenger, but Miss Flockhart had no qualms about it whatever, and after a few days it seemed perfectly natural to interview the postman in the kitchen (where he was usually having a cup of tea with his kinswoman) and to ask him to bring half a pound of carpet tacks or a reel of black cotton or a few boxes of matches when he came the next morning.

There was no difficulty at all about getting in stores (or at least Rhoda was put to no inconvenience in the matter), for Miss Flockhart was used to keeping house in the depths of the country and made her own arrangements. Vans from Drumburly with bread and meat and groceries were extremely reluctant to face the perils of the daft road but they visited Mureth regularly and Miss Flockhart arranged with Lizzie to take in supplies for Boscath and to send them across the river with anybody who happened to be available. The messenger was usually Lizzie's son who was readily available after school hours. It was nothing to Duggie to wade across the ford with bread or meat for Boscath and Miss Flockhart took care to reward him for his trouble with a large slice of home-baked cake or a slab of gingerbread.

Miss Flockhart did everything without the slightest fuss and in addition she anticipated Rhoda's wishes in a way that seemed magical. There is a kind of love—a selfless passion—which breeds this form of magic. Rhoda called her Flockie and Miss Flockhart liked it, as indeed she would have liked any name which Rhoda chose to bestow upon her. Mr. Brown had called her Miss Flockhart; he had treated her well but there had been no real cordiality between them, his attitude had been decorous in the extreme; her family called her Dorrie and treated her with affectionate contempt, but Mrs. James treated her as a human being and gave her friendship and sympathy. She had a brand new personality and a new name.

In some ways it was a pity that Flockie was so capable for it meant that Rhoda had very little to do. James was busy getting the farm into order and was out all day . . . the days were long and extraordinarily quiet. The only sounds that broke the stillness were the far-off bleat of a sheep, the twitter of a bird and the murmur of the river. The sound of the river was always there, sometimes one's ear grew tired of the sound and failed to register it . . . and then suddenly one would become aware of it again. It could almost have been the sea, in fact if one shut one's eyes it was easy to imagine waves breaking upon a beach; or it might have been the wind—the

west wind rustling through trees—or it could have been the
voice of London, far-off, continuous, murmurous as one hears
that busy voice in one of her quiet squares.

Rhoda was sometimes homesick for London and all that
London meant. She had had many friends in London and there
was scarcely an evening that she did not go out to some sort of
party, to a dinner or a dance or a play or perhaps just to spend
a couple of hours at a friend's house and have a chat. All that
was over now, as she had known it would be, and although
she was perfectly sensible about it she was missing it more than
she had expected.

In this new life Rhoda had time to think—or no, it was not
quite that, it was more that she had the inclination to think.
She had had leisure before but she had not used it for thought.
This place moved unhurriedly. People here moved more
slowly and did things more slowly—and perhaps more thoroughly. Rhoda had always been a dasher, she liked speed.
Her craving for speed of movement had been satisfied by the
acquisition of a motor bicycle which went like the wind under
her expert guidance, but " Blink " had been sold and her
father had given her a small car instead and in any case the daft
road was no speed track. Rhoda could not indulge her passion
for speed.

The house was so small and well arranged that Rhoda could
have managed it herself quite easily but James was determined
that she should have leisure for her painting. Rhoda had
remonstrated; she had told James that it must be one or the
other, marriage or painting, and she had chosen marriage, but
James would not listen; he would not believe her; he was not
going to allow Rhoda to become a household drudge. Rhoda
must paint and go on painting. When Rhoda had pointed out
that it was a waste of money to have a cook when she could
run the house herself James replied that he could afford it,
but that if it worried her she could make enough money by
her painting to cover the cook's wages. Rhoda had no answer
for that. Before her marriage she had begun to sell her pictures

—just a few of them here and there—and had made a good deal more than enough to cover a cook's wages!

The north bedroom at Boscath had been made into a comfortable, business-like studio; the window had been enlarged, the floor stained, the walls lined with shelves and cupboards. James had planned the whole thing and the alterations had been carried out secretly, as a surprise for Rhoda when they returned from their honeymoon. James had taken a great deal of trouble over the studio—and of course it was sweet of him—but so far Rhoda had not used it. Her paints and easels and palettes and canvases which had been sent from London had not been unpacked. Rhoda went and looked at them occasionally. I can't, she thought, I don't want to. I shall never paint again.

Mr. Flockhart had said that his sister enjoyed the pictures and would want to go out occasionally and this was natural and right; Rhoda was only too pleased to allow Flockie a day off to go to the pictures. Curiously enough Flockie seemed reluctant to go. "I'm not caring," she would say when Rhoda suggested she should have a day off, but when Mr. Flockhart's birthday came in sight and Flockie was invited to be present at the party she allowed herself to be persuaded to accept. She would have to stay the night in Drumburly and come back the next morning for there was no way of getting back to Boscath late at night. As the day drew near she had serious qualms about the project and if Rhoda had not been firm with her she would have given it up altogether.

The day came and Flockie departed unwillingly; Rhoda drove her to Drumburly and left her there.

It was rather odd to be without Flockie (Boscath felt even more quiet and lonely), but James came in for supper and they had it by the fire in the sitting-room and were reminded of their first night at home. It was not very long ago of course but to both of them it felt like months, to Rhoda because she had too little to do, and to James because he had too much. They washed up the dishes together and were very happy about

it, and after a little more chat by the fire they went upstairs
to bed.

As Rhoda drew aside the curtains she saw that the night was
stormy, a wind had got up—a gusty wind—blowing down the
valley and bearing with it a few sharp spatters of rain, clouds
were coming over the hills, over Winterfell and Crowthorne,
they were moving rapidly and the moon showed through the
rifts. At one moment the landscape was dark and the next it
was flooded with pale cold light. Rhoda shivered, there was
something a little eerie about the moon and the hills and the
flying tattered clouds.

She was still watching them when she saw Wanlock come up
the path, he waved to her and shouted.

" Is Mr. James in bed? " cried Wanlock. " The wee heifer
is calving. I've got Roy helping me but we could do with
Mr. James."

James had begun to undress but it did not take him long
to get ready and as he had helped Willy Bell on similar occasions
he knew what he was in for and put on his oldest clothes.

" You don't mind being left alone, do you? " he said as he
kissed Rhoda and rushed away.

Rhoda did not mind. Why should she? She was a sensible
person and a farmer's wife. She got into bed and lay there
looking out at the hills and the clouds and the sudden swift
glimpses of the moon. It was not a pleasant sight and she
realised that it would be better to draw the curtains and go to
sleep or to light the lamp which stood upon the bedside-table
and read a book, but although the sight was unpleasant it
fascinated her and she felt unable to rise and blot it out. Besides
even if it were blotted out it would still be there, thought
Rhoda uncomfortably.

She was alone in the house. She had never been alone in
a house before. No, never, thought Rhoda looking back down
the years. She had been alone in a flat in London but that
was different for there had been people all round, moving about
and breathing and there was the sound of people in the street.

Here there was nobody, nobody moving or breathing or making a sound. The only sound was the sound of the wind which had suddenly risen to gale force and was sweeping down the valley in squally gusts; it whistled in the chimneys for a few moments and was gone . . . then it came again, roistering round the little house, battering at the doors and windows like a wolf trying to get in. Sometimes it roared in fury, sometimes its voice dropped to a sibilant whisper which was even more disturbing to the nerves.

It was even more disturbing because during one of these partial lulls Rhoda could hear a door banging. It was the wind of course. It must be the wind. She listened intently and she heard the stairs creak. There was somebody coming upstairs, coming up quietly, furtively, one step at a time.

Rhoda's heart pounded, her throat was dry. For a moment she was paralysed with fear . . . and then she pulled herself together and rushed to the door and flung it open. There was nobody.

"You're a fool," said Rhoda as she got back into bed. "You're a perfect idiot to be frightened of the wind. You'll just have to get used to it, that's all."

There were all sorts of things that Rhoda had to get used to in her new life—not only the wind. She had known it would be different of course but she had not realised how utterly and completely different it would be. Rhoda felt that if she had been translated to Mars she would not have found life upon that planet more utterly and absolutely different from her previous life than this. Boscath was not a different part of the country, it was a different world.

If James could have spent more time at home the different world would have been a pleasant place, but James had so much to do that he went out early and returned home late. Rhoda visited Mureth frequently and Mamie came to see her (this helped to fill up the day), and then twenty-four hours of heavy rain turned the river into a raging flood and cut off communications between Mureth and Boscath . . . and life was suddenly impossible. Yes, it was impossible. Rhoda could not bear it; she would have to go. She would go home for a week or ten days. Flockie would look after James. Several times she made up her mind to speak to James about it, but when James came in the desire to go away from Boscath vanished and she said nothing. As a matter of fact Rhoda was rather ashamed of herself. She had never felt so unbalanced before—at one moment wanting this, at another moment that—she had prided herself upon knowing her own mind. Now apparently she did not know it. She was annoyed with herself for not being able to settle down, but being annoyed with herself only made things worse. Dozens of people had said to her, " You're going to live on a hill-farm in Scotland? How frightful! You'll never be able to bear it. You'll be cut off from everything—no theatres, no dances, no social life! " Of course Rhoda had realised all that, but it had not worried her for she would have James. She could be happy on a desert island with James. Well, here she was on a desert island and she was not happy. Her friends had been right.

CHAPTER EIGHT

ONE morning Rhoda had seen James off as usual and as usual had returned to the breakfast-table to finish her coffee. James had taken some sandwiches with him, so he would not be home until tea-time, if then. She had a whole day before her, a whole long empty day. She was sitting and thinking about it—and wondering if she would ever get used to it—when a tiny flower fell on to her plate.

This was no miracle of course, the explanation was simple, Rhoda had picked some sprays of *viburnum fragrans* in the kitchen garden. She had gone out yesterday morning to pick brussels sprouts and had been beguiled by the tiny pink flowers growing upon the black leafless twigs. She had brought them in and arranged them in a bowl and placed them in the middle of the table—there was no more to it than that. Rhoda was about to brush the flower from her plate when suddenly the perfection of it struck her . . . one tiny flower-head but quite perfect. It was so small and insignificant that she herself who had picked the sprays and arranged them (and incidentally prided herself somewhat upon her percipience) had not noticed the beauty of it. As all artists Rhoda looked for beauty but she had been bold in her painting, she had gone for effect, she had not thought of looking for beauty in so small and insignificant a thing; a thing which, to be properly appreciated, required the aid of a magnifying glass.

Of course Rhoda had certain duties to accomplish (she could not sit and look at a tiny flower-head all morning like an Indian Yogi) but, although she moved about and made the bed and talked to Flockie about food, the thought of the small insignificant thing with its perfection of beauty remained with her and gave her happiness. The floweret had dropped on to her plate. Look, it said. Here I am—and there are millions like me—and each one of us is perfect—perfectly beautiful. Here's your world. It's full of beauty. Be happy in it.

When Rhoda had finished discussing food with Flockie she went back to the dining-room and taking up the bowl of *viburnum fragrans* she carried it upstairs to the studio. Her fingers had begun to tingle.

Mamie had been asked to tea at Boscath; she arrived at the appointed hour but on hearing that Mrs. James had been shut up in the studio all day—except for a hurried and extremely perfunctory lunch—she refused to allow Flockie to disturb her.

" We mustn't *ever* disturb her when she's painting," explained Mamie in muted tones. " She's a wonderful painter, you know, and Mr. James is very, very anxious that she should not give it up."

"Of course," agreed Flockie. "I tell you what, Mrs. Johnstone, I'll make you a pot of tea and you can have it comfortably in the sitting-room. There's a nice fire there and a new Vo-jew for you to look at."

" What? Oh, yes, of course," said Mamie with a glance at the shiny copy of *Vogue* lying upon the table. " Yes, that sounds very nice but I'd rather come into the kitchen and have tea with you, Miss Flockhart."

" Just as you please," said Miss Flockhart inhospitably.

Mamie was not in the least put off by the luke-warm welcome; she had not expected shouts of delight. She was not even put off by the unsmiling countenance of her prospective hostess. Miss Flockhart might have a poker-face, schooled to show no pleasure at the prospect of entertaining Mrs. Johnstone to tea, but her expressive eyes gave her away.

The kitchen was cosy and spotlessly clean. Miss Flockhart placed a chair for her guest and laid the table and soon they were sitting down together eating ambrosial scones, drinking strong tea and talking their heads off. They were in complete accord. Mamie thought there was no couple in all the world as good and beautiful as her nephew and his wife. Miss Flockhart shared this view.

The subject lasted for some time and was succeeded by others. Miss Flockhart explained her arrangements about supplies for Boscath and Mamie approved of them.

" If only the river would behave itself! " said Mamie with a little frown.

" The river," nodded Miss Flockhart. " But we'll not starve with flour and eggs and milk and butter and tins to fall back on. What I always say is, God sends the weather and it's not for us to grumble. There were times at Tassieknowe when we were snowed up for weeks . . ." and she told Mamie all she had done and how she had warded off starvation.

Mamie could not help wishing that Lizzie were more like Miss Flockhart, not only in her attitude towards inclement weather but also in herself. Mamie was very fond of Lizzie and she was pretty certain that Lizzie was fond of her—but never in all the years that Lizzie had been at Mureth had she and

Mamie talked like this. They had run the house together, they had cleaned and baked and weathered all sorts of domestic storms, but they had never had a heart to heart talk. Lizzie was taciturn, she was inarticulate, her views on things in general were locked up in her own breast and although Mamie had searched for it she had never found the key.

Her first introduction to Lizzie had taken place at the schoolhouse in Drumburly where three bus-loads of women and children had arrived from Glasgow as evacuees. They had been distributed to the hospitable houses and farms in the district in a haphazard sort of manner; Lizzie had come to Mureth and, unlike the other women, she had stayed. What had been Lizzie's history before she came to Mureth? Mamie had tried to find out from Lizzie but without much success. All Mamie knew was that Lizzie's husband had been a sailor, and that Lizzie had lived in a flat in Clydebank—a flat that had been completely demolished by a bomb.

Lizzie had nobody belonging to her but her children, and for this reason alone one might have expected them to be precious to her, but Lizzie seemed to have little in common with her children. To begin with they were quite unlike her in appearance, dark-haired and dark-eyed and slender in build, and whereas Lizzie was rather a stupid woman the children were clever—or so it appeared from their school reports. Lizzie treated them in a detached sort of way as if they did not really belong to her at all and she often grumbled about them; about the way they wore out their clothes and the mess they made coming into her kitchen with dirty boots. She was especially impatient with Duggie who was now of an age to resent his mother's constant nagging. Mamie often felt sorry for Lizzie's children (she was fond of children and it was a great grief to her that she had none of her own); she had tried very hard to make friends with them but she had found it extremely difficult. It was difficult not only because the children were shy and refused to co-operate but also because Lizzie kept them in the background and indeed behaved as if she were slightly ashamed of them. Mamie had managed to win Greta's confidence with the present of a black doll, which she had made herself; and Greta no longer fled from her as if she had the plague. Duggie was a different proposition and so far Mamie had found no way of making contact with him.

The only echo from Lizzie's mysterious past was a certain Mrs. Crow, who had lived on the same stair and had been with Lizzie in the air-raid shelter when their homes were blown to pieces. Lizzie sometimes mentioned Mrs. Crow in connection with various recipes and household duties. " Mrs. Crow always put a wee pinch of salt in her puddings," Lizzie would say. " Mrs. Crow cleaned her windows with a wee drop of vinegar in the water." " Mrs. Crow always changed the beds on a Friday." Sometimes Mamie thought well of Mrs. Crow's ideas and sometimes not but it was useless to question her dicta. In Lizzie's opinion the woman was omniscient.

Mamie found this annoying. " Where is Mrs. Crow now? " inquired Mamie one day when her patience had become exhausted.

" How would I know? " replied Lizzie, answering question with question in her usual exasperating way.

" You were friends, weren't you? " pursued Mamie but Lizzie remained silent.

Having failed to elucidate the mystery Mamie decided that Mrs. Crow was a second Mrs. Harris, there was " no sich person," and gave up the struggle. Apart from the legendary figure of Mrs. Crow, Mamie knew of nobody and of nothing in Lizzie's previous existence; Lizzie and Duggie and Greta were a sort of flotsam, cast up by the storm of war.

How different was Miss Flockhart! How much more interesting! In ten minutes or a quarter of an hour Mamie had learnt more about Miss Flockhart than she had learnt about Lizzie in ten years. She had heard all about Miss Flockhart's relatives, about her sister-in-law, Janet, and the children and the far from satisfactory manner in which they were being brought up.

" Not like we were," declared Miss Flockhart sipping her tea in a genteel manner. " We were very strictly brought up. It was church twice on Sundays and there had to be some good reason if any of us wanted to get off—and I tell you what, Mrs. Johnstone, if we'd spoken to our father the way Tom and wee Andrew speak to theirs we'd have got our head and our hands to play with! "

Mamie nodded sympathetically. She was interested to observe that Miss Flockhart had caught the infectious gambit. " I tell you what " had sounded quite natural upon the lips of Mr. Flockhart but seemed out of place upon the lips of his sister.

" Now take Duggie," continued Miss Flockhart. " He's a nice boy, that. He knows the way to behave. He gets a bit of cake when he brings my messages and he never forgets to say thank you."

Mamie was glad to hear it. " Does he talk to you at all? " she inquired.

" Well, I wouldn't say *talk*," replied Miss Flockhart reflectively. " He's a silent kind of boy, you can never tell what he's thinking, but I'd rather have that than impudence any day of the week."

CHAPTER NINE

DOUGLAS FAIRBANKS SMITH—to give him the title which was written in the list of pupils at Drumburly School—was an enigma to most people with whom he came in contact. In appearance he was small and dark-haired with slender hands and feet. He had no friends at school, nor did he consort with the other children at the farm, his only companion and confidante was his sister, Greta. It was to Greta that he showed his first attempts at drawing and Greta admired them. Greta saved up her Saturday pennies and bought him a box of chalks and with these Duggie worked away industriously. He was happy when he was making pictures. When they were finished he was pleased with them, and Greta was pleased too. But when he started having drawing-lessons at school he discovered that his ideas were different from those of the drawing-master and this led to trouble. The drawing-master was there to teach drawing and was annoyed when Duggie argued with him and refused his advice.

Somehow the discovery that drawing was a lesson and must be done at certain hours and in a certain stereotyped manner took all the pleasure out of it and Duggie put his chalks away and made no more pictures. He missed the pastime of course and for a time he was at a loose end, bored and miserable and incidentally a great trial to his relatives and his friends . . . and then, quite suddenly, he discovered a new pastime and life was once more worth living.

Duggie was eleven years old when he discovered the joys of reading, before then he had imagined that reading was an exercise performed at school, you did as little of it as you could, it was dull and troublesome, but when he started reading for pleasure it became a positive mania. The library in Drumburly was open on two evenings a week and supplied books to suit all tastes. Duggie had no tastes nor anybody to advise him and, as a matter of fact, the reading bug soon got hold of him so firmly that it did not make much difference what he read. He would choose a book from the shelves at random and be off with it, hot-foot. In this way Duggie learnt a good many curious things about the Big Wide World beyond the encircling hills—or at least he learnt about a whole host of extraordinary people whose conditions of life were quite different from his own—and having no background, no standard of comparison, his mind became a very strange jumble.

The *Adventures of Dickson McCunn, Adam Bede, Eric or Little by Little*, these and many others, old and new, good, bad and indifferent were grist to Duggie's mill. He found a novel by Rhoda Broughton entitled *Not Wisely But Too Well* and read it all through. He read an abridged version of *Robinson Crusoe*, and *Under Two Flags*, and *Coral Island* with equal concentration. He read *Little Women* and *Wuthering Heights*. Cheyney he found difficult, for the people seemed to speak an unfamiliar language, but he struggled on manfully all the same.

Needless to say Duggie did not understand one half of what he read. He took his reading like a drug; he absorbed it as a drunkard absorbs whisky, and the everyday world became dream-like and unreal. Unfortunately he had little peace at home to pursue his passion, for if his mother found him reading she would rout him out and give him some sort of job to do. She would set him to peel potatoes or to scrub the wash-house floor, which in her opinion were more useful exercises than reading. This being so Duggie was forced to find a refuge and after some search he found an admirable one, it was a little cave high up in the rocks of the quarry from which Mureth House had been built. There was a rowan tree growing upon the ledge in front of the cave which screened it from view. Greta knew of the cave, of course, he had no secrets from her, and sometimes she would follow him to his lair and sit beside him nursing her black doll and thinking dreamily.

At first Duggie confined his reading to holidays and to week-ends when he was free from school, but soon he became dissatisfied with these poor snippets of time and began to play truant. The school bus which fetched the children from the valley stopped every morning at Mureth Farm and sometimes if he and Greta were ready early he found it possible to slip away and hide (Greta, who would do anything he wanted, would say he had a cold and was at home in bed). Then, when the bus had disappeared down the road, Duggie would be up and away to the hills and the quarry.

One day when Duggie was playing truant in this reprehensible manner he was discovered by Daniel Reid, or rather by Gyp the sheep-dog who was questing about in search of stray sheep. The dog barked and Daniel climbed up the face of the quarry and found him. Duggie would have escaped if he could but there was only the one way up to the cave so he was fairly trapped.

" I'm doing no harm," said Duggie defiantly.

" I never said you were," replied Daniel. " It's a nice wee cave. I knew it when I was a lad no older than yourself. Me and my brothers used to play smugglers in it. Why are you not at school, Duggie?"

Duggie's face took on a mulish expression, but he said no word.

" Umphm," said Daniel nodding. " So that's the way of it. You've learnt to read. Maybe you're too stupid to learn any more."

" I'm not stupid. Mr. Greig says I could be in a higher class if I worked harder."

" Then you're stupid, my lad," declared Daniel. " You're not making the most of your powers and your opportunities. That's stupid."

" But, Mr. Reid——"

" Now listen," said Daniel gravely. " Just you listen to me and I'll tell you something worth remembering. When we're young we make our beds and when we're older we have to lie on them. I'd make myself a comfortable bed if I were you —straight and tidy with the blankets well tucked in at the foot— then it'll not come adrift when you lie in it. If a bed's not properly made at the start the blankets'll maybe fall off in the night and you'll wake up shivering." He nodded to Duggie in a friendly manner and away he went with his dog bounding gracefully beside him. Duggie watched him until he disappeared.

Daniel Reid's homily had its effect upon Duggie but it is doubtful whether the effect would have been lasting if another interest had not come into Duggie's life.

It was a Saturday, a few days after his encounter with Daniel Reid, and Duggie had been commissioned to take two loaves of bread and a basket of groceries to Boscath; he went to the back door as usual but Flockie was out and Rhoda answered his knock. Rhoda had heard about Duggie from Flockie and was interested in him, she was even more interested when she saw him. Good bones interested Rhoda and this boy's face, though marred by a slightly sulky expression, was well constructed. It was not a child-like face, there were no half-formed contours, no chubbiness of boyhood in Duggie's face. His face would grow larger but it would not change for already it had taken on maturity. Models were scarce at Boscath and here was one to her hand, she took Duggie upstairs to the studio, gave him a large piece of cake to keep him quiet and proceeded to make a charcoal drawing of his head and shoulders. It did not take long for Rhoda was a quick worker and Duggie was a good model, he sat perfectly still eating the cake with obvious enjoyment and gazing out of the window. When she had finished Rhoda invited her sitter to come and look at his portrait.

"Jings, that's me!" exclaimed Duggie in amazement.

"Yes," agreed Rhoda. "Of course it's you. Who did you think it would be?"

"I thought it would just be a picture of me," explained Duggie.

Rhoda took the point. She had received more flowery compliments but few that had pleased her better.

"I used to draw pictures," added Duggie. He spoke regretfully for the sight of Mrs. James drawing and her evident pleasure in the work had roused nostalgic longings in his bosom.

"Did you?" said Rhoda, smiling. "Why did you stop?"

He could not find an answer to that. It was too complicated.

"I tell you what," said Rhoda. "I've got some things to do but you can sit here and draw a picture if you like." She gave him a large block of drawing paper and the charcoal pencil and went away to put on the potatoes for dinner.

There were several things to be done and it was some time before Rhoda went back to the studio but Duggie was still there working away industriously; sheets of paper covered with half-completed drawings were strewn upon the floor.

He looked up as she came in. "I can't do it," he said in exasperation. "I know fine how I want it but it'll not come right."

Rhoda took up the block, she was prepared to be encouraging and indulgent but the words died upon her lips. She gazed at the drawing in amazement. Duggie had been sitting opposite the open door of the studio which led on to the top landing and that was what he had drawn, or had tried to draw: the open door, the banister of the stairs and a shaft of sunlight shining through the skylight. It was an extraordinary subject to choose and miles beyond his powers, the perspective was wrong and (Duggie being unused to charcoal) the whole thing was a mess but Rhoda knew there was something out of the ordinary here, she recognised it instantly.

"Look!" she exclaimed, taking up the charcoal pencil. "Look! Use your eyes. You don't see it like that." She put in a few swift strokes as she spoke.

"That's it!" he cried eagerly, snatching the charcoal pencil from her hand. "That's what I meant—here—look—it's like this. The sunshine makes a shadow on the floor."

Rhoda began to laugh for she was excited and amused and Duggie laughed too. The laughter changed his face completely and filled it with light. It was suddenly the face of a young boy, impish and puck-like.

"Take another sheet," said Rhoda. "Now look, Duggie. Look first and then draw. Here's the doorway. You drew it straight because you knew it was straight; you didn't *look* at it properly."

He saw what she meant at once and taking the pencil began to draw again: the open door, the banister beyond. The thing took shape before her eyes, it was quite startling.

"Who taught you to draw?" she asked.

"Nobody. The man at school gave us oranges. Who wants to draw oranges!"

"But you have to learn."

"Not with him," said Duggie scornfully. "You said *look.*

67

He never said look. He was angry when I wouldn't do it his way. He'd never learn me to draw in a hundred years." He paused and raised his eyes to Rhoda's face . . . and his eyes reminded Rhoda of a spaniel who had been her dear companion when she was twelve years old. Yes, Bengie had looked at her just like that when he had wanted another biscuit.

" All right," said Rhoda with a sigh. " I'll teach you if you really want to learn and if you promise to work hard and do what I tell you, but I'm not going to waste my time on you unless you're really keen."

He nodded gravely.

" You can come twice a week when you bring the bread," said Rhoda. She smiled and added, " If you come with dirty hands you'll be thrown out."

" I'll wash them," Duggie said.

CHAPTER TEN

NOW that Rhoda had begun to paint she found it easy to continue, in fact she would have found it difficult to stop. She took her sketch book and went out and about the farm; there were plenty of subjects to keep her busy: men in action, shawing turnips or loading carts or ploughing; horses straining at their work or standing patiently awaiting the word of command; cows in the byre turning their big stupid heads and gazing reflectively. All these things and many more were grist to Rhoda's mill.

The clipping was over of course but one morning Rhoda found Roy in the stack-yard seated upon a low bench with a sheep held firmly between his knees, he was divesting it of its fleece in an expert manner. Roy looked up and smiled as she approached for " Mrs. James " was popular with her husband's employees. At first they had thought her stuck-up (principally on account of her speech which sounded affected to their un-accustomed ears), but very soon they had discovered their mistake. There was no nonsense about Mrs. James, she had no airs and graces.

" I thought they'd all been clipped! " exclaimed Rhoda in surprise.

" There's usually a few that gets left over," replied Roy seriously. " It's usually the old ones, too. This is an old ewe —a crone we'd call her. I saw two of them on the hill this morning and brought them in. Some folks think sheep are stupid beasts but I'm not so sure."

" How do you mean? "

" Och, I just mean they might not be wanting their coats off," said Roy with a sly grin.

" You mean they hid from you! " inquired Rhoda incredulously.

Roy shook his head doubtfully, he was not prepared to answer such a straightforward question in the affirmative, besides he was busy. The fleece was coming off nicely, half of it was already separated from its owner and fell back like the open flap of an overcoat; the inside was beautifully clean and white and soft, the outside shaggy and matted. Roy's shears flashed in the sunshine, one of his strong bare arms was folded tightly round the sheep's neck so that it was helpless in his grasp.

It is always a joy to see skilled hands at work, and Roy was an expert. He neither hastened nor hesitated but went ahead with practised confidence. To Rhoda the sight was beautiful, not only for its own sake but for its traditional associations. Clipping is an age-old skill, in some ways like the skill of the blacksmith, surviving into modern times from the dim misty past.

" Do you mind if I make a sketch of you? " asked Rhoda.

" Of me? " asked Roy in surprise. " You're not wanting to draw me in my oldest clothes? "

" Just as you are," she replied, smiling at the idea of Roy in his Sunday best, an idea which obviously was in Roy's mind as a suitable subject for her pencil. "You must go on with your work as if nothing was happening, it won't take many minutes."

Fortunately there was another ewe waiting to be clipped so Rhoda had time to get a hasty impression of the scene before Roy's task was finished and, perhaps because the scene had stirred her imagination, she managed to catch the inner significance of the picture before her eyes and to invest it with fire and movement. The young strong man with his head slightly inclined, intent upon his task, and the helpless sheep firmly imprisoned between his knees. Behind was the open door of the barn indicated with a few firm strokes of the pencil.

"Gosh, that's real good!" exclaimed Roy, looking at it in astonishment. "I suppose it would take a good few years to learn to draw like that."

Rhoda admitted that it had taken a number of years and went home to dinner feeling quite satisfied with her morning's work. She had had a feeling that marriage would interfere with her art, for art was an avocation which demanded a singleness of purpose, but she had discovered that on the contrary marriage had given her a new confidence.

Rhoda was her own most severe critic (sometimes she was satisfied with her work and at other times not) and it was fortunate that she was able to judge her own work for no other critic was available. James, Mamie and Flockie all took a tremendous interest in Rhoda's pictures but an interest which was entirely free from discrimination. They admired everything whole-heartedly and admired everything for all the wrong reasons; so, if by any chance they admired one thing more extravagantly than another, its creator was immediately assailed by a conviction that it must be bad. For instance when Rhoda showed Mamie the study of a tree (of which she herself was rather proud) Mamie exclaimed, "Oh, Rhoda, how lovely! Anybody would know it was the old elm down by the river. I don't know how you can get it to look so *like*!" and Rhoda had to resist a sudden impulse to hit Mamie on the head (dear Mamie, it was a terribly wicked impulse!), because of course Mamie should have appreciated the composition of the study and commended the quality of the paint and admired the effect of the afternoon sunlight falling through the foliage and making pools of gorgeous colour on the ground.

One afternoon Rhoda settled herself upon her doorstep with easel and palette and paints and began to paint the view which lay before her: the sweeping line of hills, the winding river, the little patches of wood and faded heather. Rhoda was not particularly interested in landscape but this picture was a labour of love. It was intended for her father's birthday and would go to him with the title " View from Boscath Door-Step." She and James had invited Admiral Ware to come to them for Christmas, they realised it would be very lonely for him all alone at Ashbridge but Admiral Ware seemed a little unwilling to come. He liked his home, he enjoyed shooting and he was in a deep rut. The view from Boscath doorstep was a bait.

Rhoda could see the ford from where she was sitting and presently she noticed somebody crossing, wading through the water with bare legs and skirts kilted above the knee. Mamie often visited Boscath in this manner but this was not Mamie. The figure disappeared for a few minutes behind a hillock and then reappeared, coming up the path towards the house. It was a slender girl with dark hair, clad in well-worn tweeds. She had resumed her shoes and stockings and was walking with a firm light step.

" Hallo! " cried Rhoda in a friendly manner and laying down her brush she rose to meet her visitor.

" But you're busy," said the girl as they shook hands. " I won't bother you. It's frightfully annoying to be interrupted. I just came to call. I'm Doctor Forrester's sister."

" I'm very pleased to see you, ' Doctor Forrester's sister,' " said Rhoda smiling.

The girl smiled in return. She had a charming smile which lighted up her face like sunshine. She had lovely teeth and hazel eyes, flecked with brown. Not exactly pretty, thought Rhoda, but definitely attractive.

"But that's what I am," declared the girl. "Everybody in Drumburly calls me 'Doctor Forrester's sister.' I have no identity of my own at all."

Rhoda nodded thoughtfully. "I'm James Dering Johnstone's wife or, sometimes, Mamie Johnstone's niece by marriage. How long does it take to establish an identity of one's own?"

"It won't take you long," replied the girl with conviction. Rhoda was too lovely, too alive, too full of personality to remain a nonentity.

They went into the sitting-room together and almost immediately Flockie appeared with tea for, although it was not yet four o'clock, country hospitality demanded that visitors should be fed.

Rhoda was a social creature, she was fond of her fellow human beings and every time she met somebody new she expected him—or her—to be a delightful surprise. Of course she was sometimes disappointed but not as often as one might imagine. People were apt to be at their best with her. This girl, arriving unexpectedly out of the blue, was going to be one of the delightful surprises. Rhoda felt sure of it.

"And you," said Rhoda, continuing the conversation which she found interesting in more ways than one. "You won't remain Doctor Forrester's sister for ever, will you?"

"We've been here for five months and there isn't a creature in the place who calls me Nan."

"I shall call you Nan," declared Rhoda. "It suits you down to the ground, but as a matter of fact I didn't mean that, exactly, I meant that some day——"

"Oh, I shall never marry," Nan said. She hesitated for a moment and then added, "It sounds silly, I know, but there was somebody—we weren't really engaged but—and then he just—just changed his mind. So you see!"

Rhoda saw. She was surprised, because Nan was a dear. Nan was not startlingly attractive at first glance but definitely attractive at second glance and Rhoda felt pretty certain that she would become more and more engaging as one grew to know her better. Rhoda would not have been astonished if no man had looked twice at Nan, but here was a man who, apparently, had looked at Nan quite often and then gone away.

" It's amazing," said Rhoda frankly.

" Oh, I don't know," replied her visitor. " It's over, anyhow. It just means that I shall go on being ' Doctor Forrester's sister ' as long as Adam needs me. I keep house for him, you know."

" The man must be a perfect fool! " Rhoda exclaimed. She did not mean Adam Forrester of course, fortunately his sister realised that.

Nan smiled, rather sadly, and replied, " No, he isn't a fool by any means. He's terribly clever. But don't let's talk about it any more."

In one stride they had crossed the boundary of acquaintance-ship and become friends. It was Rhoda's way to cut out unnecessary formalities but this *rapprochement* had been accom-plished more rapidly than usual; perhaps a trifle too rapidly to be absolutely safe. Rhoda knew she had received a confidence which was given to few, one which in calmer moments might be regretted. It would be a pity if Nan, looking back upon the conversation, felt uncomfortable about it. The only thing to do was to give largely in return.

Having decided upon this course Rhoda proceeded upon it forthwith and before they had finished tea and done justice to Flockie's baking they knew a good deal about one another. Nan heard how Rhoda had very nearly lost James by her own stupidity; how she had refused him because of her painting and then regretted it and how Mamie had written warning her that if she wanted to marry James she had better do something about it quickly because he was being pursued up hill and down dale by another girl.

" Who? " inquired Nan, her eyes wide with horror.

" Holly Douglas," replied Rhoda. " Perhaps you know her.

She's Lady Shaw's niece. She's very pretty and terribly attractive. I don't *like* her, of course," declared Rhoda frankly. "Apart from James and everything, Holly isn't the sort of person I like, but I can see how absolutely staggering she is. James says he never intended to marry Holly but I don't quite believe him. I think he was swithering a bit, poor darling."

"I've seen her. She isn't nearly as beautiful as you."

Rhoda was pleased. She had no use at all for compliments as such, but this was no compliment, it was a statement of absolute conviction. Who could fail to be pleased?

Nan was interested in houses for she and her brother had bought a little house in Drumburly and had spent a good deal of time and trouble and rather more money than they could afford upon its embellishment, so when Rhoda asked if she would like to see over the house she accepted with alacrity. They went into every room and Nan admired everything intelligently, she was able to give her hostess advice upon several knotty problems. The studio was the last room to be displayed. Nan walked in and looked round. Her eye fell upon a charcoal drawing which was standing upon an easel.

"Duggie!" exclaimed Nan in astonishment.

"Yes, do you know Duggie?"

"It's wonderful," declared Nan, gazing at it. "Yes, I know Duggie; but this! You've found something that I didn't know Duggie had. I mean," said Nan, struggling to express herself. "I mean—oh, I can't explain!"

"Try to explain," said Rhoda, perching herself upon the table and looking at her new friend with a good deal of interest.

"I've seen Duggie at school," Nan told her.

"At school?"

"Yes. You see Adam and I are rather short of money so I've got a part-time job at Drumburly School. I teach some of the smaller children and I've been helping with the Christmas concert. The children are going to act some scenes from *The Merchant of Venice*—perhaps you knew. Duggie is to be Shylock and I've been coaching him a bit and making a long black gown for him to wear and trying to make some sort of wig."

" So you're the lady, are you? "

" The lady? "

" Duggie told me," explained Rhoda. " You aren't ' Doctor Forrester's sister ' to him. You're ' the lady that's making my wig.' Nice for you, isn't it? But this isn't getting us any nearer the mystery."

" It is, really," Nan told her. " The Duggie I know is quite different from your Duggie. He's a problem-child. Apparently his mother has no control over him, he runs wild and does what he likes and only attends school when he feels that way inclined."

" Nan! "

" Oh, I'm exaggerating a little," admitted Nan, smiling. " But it's no exaggeration to say that Duggie-at-school is a headache. Nobody understands him. He has ability but he doesn't use it and nothing will make him use it. Duggie's school-face is blank or else sulky—or sometimes vague. Wait! " cried Nan eagerly. " Wait, it's coming. You've found Duggie's soul."

" What am I to do with it? " said Rhoda, half laughing.

" That's your look-out," returned Nan.

Rhoda had laughed a little at Nan's assertion but she did not forget it and after Nan had gone she went and looked at her charcoal drawing of Duggie and wondered about him. Nobody understood him at school and it was pretty certain that he was not understood by his family. If Rhoda were the only person who understood him (who had found his soul as Nan had put it) she was burdened with a responsibility. It was a trifle alarming. It was alarming because Duggie was worth understanding, because he had outstanding potentialities for good—or for evil. She had promised to teach Duggie how to draw but drawing was not everything. Could she accept the burden of teaching him how to live?

It had been agreed that Duggie was to come twice a week for his drawing-lessons but gradually he got into the way of coming more often, of coming whenever he could. Sometimes the studio was empty but that did not matter, Flockie had instructions to let him in and not to bother about him. The studio was a refuge to Duggie; when he opened the door and went in he felt a surge of happiness and peace. He liked the smell of paint; he liked the mess—which was not really a mess at all but a sort of ordered chaos.

Rhoda made a bond with Duggie (he knew all about bonds, of course) there were certain things he must do and others that he must not and in return she showed him everything he wanted to see and answered all his questions. She gave him subjects to draw and criticised his efforts unmercifully; she allowed him to watch while she mixed her colours, cleaned her brushes and stretched her canvases. Presently Duggie took over some of the necessary duties of the studio and Rhoda found that he could be trusted to perform them conscientiously. One day she happened to remark that she must clean the windows and the next day Duggie arrived with a chamois leather and cleaned them. As a rule Rhoda preferred to be alone when she was painting but the presence of Duggie did not disturb her. He would sit in his own corner at a solid little table and draw for hours without making a sound and sometimes she forgot all about him.

Duggie liked to be forgotten. He liked to watch Mrs. James at work, silent and absorbed. He liked it when Mr. James came in from the farm and they talked to each other as if he were not there. At first he could not understand what they were saying for they talked quite differently from the way in which they spoke to him. They talked more quickly and the talk went backwards and forwards as if they were throwing a ball. Duggie was bewildered at first, he was completely left behind. They laughed and he had no idea what amused them. But, being a sedulous little ape, he set his mind to it and soon he began to follow. He saw that they left things out; there was a lot left unsaid (things that they both understood without speech) and he saw that quite often they said the exact opposite of what they meant, not to mislead one another but just for fun. For instance one afternoon when Duggie and Mrs. James had been working away silently and companionably for some time, the door opened and Mr. James appeared.

" Are you busy? " he asked.

" Very busy. Go away, horrid man! " said Mrs. James in a cross voice.

Of course Duggie expected Mr. James to retreat in disorder but not a bit of it. Mr. James laughed and came in and, sitting down in the old basket-chair which stood beside the fire proceeded to light his pipe, and Mrs. James abandoned her painting and sat upon the hearth-rug with her hands round her knees and said, " Go ahead, tell me all about it. Did you buy some lovely, great, big Cheviot tups? "

How interesting it was, thought Duggie. Mr. and Mrs. James were far more interesting than people in books. Some day he would talk like that; quickly, missing things out, saying things he didn't mean and throwing the ball of talk backwards and forwards.

CHAPTER ELEVEN

QUITE a number of people in the district called upon Rhoda; they called either because they were fond of Mamie or because they were inquisitive. Mrs. Ogylvie Smith called for the first reason, Miss Heddle for the second. Both these ladies braved the daft road in large cars with disapproving chauffeurs, both found their quarry had gone out for a walk and both left cards. Lady Shaw of Drumburly Tower and Mrs. Duncan of Crossraggle wrote to Rhoda and explained that they would have liked to call but they were very busy and the road was so bad. They hoped Rhoda would excuse calling and come to see them instead. Rhoda wrote back politely. She was glad all these people wanted to know her for, as has been said before, she was socially inclined. She would have to return the calls but there was no desperate hurry about it. In the meantime she was seeing a good deal of the Forresters, they were young and interesting and fortunately James liked them as much as she did. Sometimes the Forresters came to Sunday lunch at Boscath, bicycling over the daft road, and sometimes Rhoda dropped in to see Nan at tea-time or if she happened to be shopping in Drumburly on a Saturday morning, and sometimes—but not too often—she took Nan a rabbit or a fowl or vegetables from Boscath garden.

It was not mere chance which had brought Adam Forrester to Drumburly to be assistant to old Doctor Black. Adam had been in a big hospital on the outskirts of London and Nan had been assistant matron at a school nearby. They were both unhappy and lonely and they often talked of going back to Scotland and of making a home together. Henry Ogylvie Smith was the physician in charge at the hospital and one day he happened to mention that the doctor at Drumburly was getting old and was looking for an assistant. The salary was small but it would be enough for Adam and Nan to live on quietly and carefully. They could be together. They could have a home. Adam and Nan had never had a home before, their father had been in the Indian Army and their mother had died when Nan was born, so they had been handed round amongst their relations as if they had been parcels and somewhat inconvenient parcels at that. They had never had anybody except each other and they had never had enough of each other's company.

There was a little money which Adam had inherited from an old aunt, it was enough to buy a house in Drumburly High Street and to furnish it. Most people in their position have some little pieces of furniture, handed down from parents or other relatives, but Adam and Nan had not so much as a clock or a chair or a book-case. Everything had to be bought and only the barest necessities were within their means.

The house was tiny, it was a sort of doll's-house. There was a green gate with a brass plate upon it which informed the world that Adam Forrester, M.B., Ch.B. lived here. Three strides from the gate brought you to the door with a fanlight above it. The hall was scarcely more than a passage but the two front rooms were of reasonable size, on the left was the living-room where the doctor and his sister took their ease, on the right was the consulting-room where the doctor saw his patients. The kitchen was at the back and in addition there was a room which should have been the dining-room but as Adam and Nan had no dining-room furniture they had their meals in the kitchen and Adam took the room as his. Here was his bed, a couple of chairs, a small dressing-table and a fitted cupboard in the wall. He had hung up some pictures which he valued for their artistic merit and some college groups which he valued for sentimental reasons. The floor was of stained oak so a couple of rugs was all that was needed to complete the furnishing scheme. The room had french windows opening on to the garden, which was enclosed by a beech hedge. Beyond the hedge was a lane following the bank of the river. The garden itself was very small indeed, it consisted of a plot of grass and a herbaceous border but Adam enjoyed the garden —it was his very own and he had never owned a piece of ground before—quite often he woke early and went out and listened to the voice of the river and the singing of the birds; sometimes, returning from a sick-room in the middle of the night or at dawn, he would linger in the garden and find peace before he went back to bed.

Upstairs in the little house there were two small bedrooms and a bathroom. Nan had chosen the front bedroom which looked on to the street and as she lay in bed she could hear people passing quietly upon their lawful business (there was very little unlawful business in Drumburly). She could hear footsteps coming in the distance, passing the gate and going away. She could hear snatches of conversation, odd bits of talk which seemed strangely meaningless without their context. Sometimes the footsteps stopped at the gate and came up the path . . . which meant that poor Adam would have to get up and go out.

Adam and Nan had been nomads and now they had a home. They talked interminably, for they had mutual tastes and had had divergent experiences; both of them were intelligent, broadminded and humorous. The relationship between a brother and sister is peculiar in the sense that it is unique for it is the only one in which the two sexes can meet as equals on a purely personal basis. No brother thinks of his sister as a woman and few sisters can see their brothers as men. For this reason there can be real friendship between them. Nan took her friendship with Adam as a natural thing but Adam often thought about it. He knew that in some ways Nan was a better person than he was, she was a stronger character. Adam admired the way she stood up to trouble when trouble came her way. He had courage, he hoped, but he lacked the quality of fortitude, of sticking it out, which was a part of Nan's make-up. Adam looked into the future and saw them growing old together. Nan would never marry because of that wretched love affair and he would never marry because no woman could suit him as well as Nan.

One evening James and Rhoda came to supper. They had been invited to come early and go to the Pictures afterwards with their host and hostess, it had seemed an excellent plan. Nan had provided a very good supper and Adam produced a bottle of hock which had been given him by a grateful patient and which he had been saving for just such an occasion. The four young people were on intimate terms by this time and were very happy together.

"Must we go to the Pictures?" said Adam suddenly. "Isn't it rather a waste when we've got agreeable guests?"

"But that was the whole idea!" objected Nan who liked to see a plan carried through to its proper conclusion.

" We'll be late," declared Adam. " The picture will have started and we shall never find who's who or what's what."

Nan chuckled. " Adam never knows who's who or what's what."

" I'll sit beside him," offered Rhoda. " I'll hold his hand and tell him all about the story as it goes along. It will be lovely for Adam and awfully interesting for people sitting near us. There's nothing so delightful as to hear the story of a film being unfolded by another member of the audience."

" But look here! " cried James. " Who's going to hold my hand and tell me the story? "

" Nan, of course," said Rhoda.

Eventually however nobody held anybody's hand because by the time they had finished discussing the matter it was far too late to go and Nan accused Adam of deliberately prolonging the discussion to gain his ends. It was all great fun. They washed up the dishes together and settled down round the fire.

Duggie would have enjoyed himself thoroughly if he could have been there for the ball went backwards and forwards merrily as they talked of this and that and capped one another's stories. Rhoda told the story of how she and James had arrived at Boscath without any key and of James's discovery of the Sleeping Beauty. Adam and Nan together told of their arrival at Drumburly and of their struggles to collect some furniture and to make the house fit to live in.

" I'd never carpentered before," said Adam ruefully. " We bought a cupboard for five bob at a sale. It was in ruins of course and the idea was that I should take it to pieces and put it together again. It was Nan's idea, really. I was a bit doubtful about it from the start."

" You never saw such a mess as he made of it," said Nan chuckling. " The cupboard was for my room and I couldn't keep anything in it because the door wouldn't open or, if by sheer brute strength I managed to force it open, it wouldn't shut. We had to get Angus Lowther in the end."

" He sorted it, I suppose," put in Rhoda.

" He sorted it in about twenty minutes," nodded Adam. " I tell you I never felt such a fool in my life but he was awfully decent about it and when he was going away he said, ' Aye, I can mend your cupboard easy enough but it's beyond me to mend your leg.' It wasn't until after he'd gone that I saw the point," said Adam smiling broadly.

" You know," said Rhoda thoughtfully. " It shows a depth of perception and a délicacy of feeling . . ."

" It shows kindness," declared Nan.

" People here are quite different from southerners," said James. " They're different physically as well as mentally. I suppose it's the shape of their heads——"

" Goodness! " cried Nan. " If you start Adam on that! "

Adam was not to be put off by his sister's interruption, he leant forward eagerly. " There isn't much in phrenology," he declared. " It's a crude way of measuring intellectual capacity. We did some very simple psycho-analysis at the hospital and found it a help in the treatment of patients—and, as a matter of fact, I'm doing a little here in Drumburly School. Mr. Greig is quite keen on it."

" You ask them questions, don't you? " said Rhoda.

" But how does that work? " inquired James. " I mean one person might happen to know the answer but that wouldn't necessarily mean he was brighter than a person who didn't."

" You're confusing intellect and knowledge," Adam explained. " The questions are designed to measure intellectual capacity and not to measure knowledge at all. They're standardised so that you measure by what a child should be able to answer at a certain age. A boy of twelve years old might be only eight years old in mental capacity."

" What good does it do? " asked James.

" It helps tremendously with backward children. Backwardness at school may not be a sign of intellectual inferiority; it may be from some other cause, it may be due to environment or to some complex which can be removed. Take Duggie for instance, Duggie was very difficult at school—not exactly backward but inattentive—but I discovered that his intellectual capacity was above normal."

" Well above normal! " exclaimed Rhoda impulsively.

" What was the matter? " asked James.

" His environment," replied Adam. " He was unhappy at home. His mother was impatient with him, he was frustrated and misunderstood. Nothing Duggie could do was right—so he left off trying. Now that Rhoda has taken him in hand he's a different creature."

Rhoda was delighted though not really surprised for she had noticed a difference in her protégé. " It isn't my doing—not really," Rhoda said. " It's because he has found himself."

" You helped him to find himself," declared Nan.

" Well, that's how it works" said Adam who was anxious to continue talking about his theories. " And, of course, the method is the same when you're dealing with older people. Quite a lot of grown-up people are facing the world with a twelve-year-old standard of intelligence."

" I wonder what mine is," said Rhoda, smiling. " But we haven't time to go into that to-night."

" It's quite early——" began Adam.

But James stood up. " There's the daft road between us and home," said James. " I think we'd better get a move on."

CHAPTER TWELVE

ONE morning Mrs. Ogylvie Smith rang up Mamie and invited her to tea and asked her to bring Rhoda with her. She explained that she had called on Rhoda but had not seen her and added that it would be much more sensible if Rhoda could come to tea instead of returning the call in a formal manner. She added that her son Henry would be at home so there would be somebody young for Rhoda to talk to and this would be all the more agreeable because she and Mamie could have a good chat. Mrs. Ogylvie Smith loved to get hold of Mamie and talk about old times and about people who had lived in the district long ago for Mamie was sympathetic and adaptable. Sometimes Mrs. Ogylvie Smith forgot that Mamie was twenty odd years younger than herself and talked to her as if she were a contemporary. Mamie accepted the invitation and sent a message to Boscath and at three o'clock Rhoda came over to Mureth and the two set out for Blackthorn House in Mamie's car.

" You had better tell me about them," said Rhoda. " It's better to know about people beforehand in case one says the wrong thing. Have they any skeletons in their cupboard? "

" No," replied Mamie, smiling. " No, I don't think they have a single bone in their cupboard. Mrs. Ogylvie Smith is Spanish, she was very beautiful when she was young. She used to go to dinner-parties wearing a mantilla of black lace. Some people thought it a pose but I'm sure it wasn't. I think it seemed natural to her; certainly it was very becoming. Of course she's lived here for years and years, ever since she was married, but she still speaks with a slight accent especially when she gets excited or very interested in what she's saying. The odd thing is she really speaks better English than we do. I mean she seems to be able to find the right word." Mamie sighed and added, " I never can. I mean even if I know the right word to use I can't use it."

" Why? " asked Rhoda.

" It seems so stuck up to use long words," explained Mamie. Rhoda smiled. She said, " Well, go on about them."

" Mr. Ogylvie Smith is quite old, well over seventy, I should think. They've always lived at Blackthorn House ever since I can remember. They're devoted to one another and they have one son who's a doctor and very clever indeed. He's staying with them so you'll see him."

" Married? " asked Rhoda.

" No, not yet. The Ogylvie Smiths are rather sad about it,

they would love grandchildren. They really are ideal grand-parents, if you know what I mean?"

Rhoda nodded. "Is it a farm?" she asked.

"No, not a farm. It's a lovely house. It was built by Mr. Ogylvie Smith's grandfather. There's a beautiful garden."

Mamie was looking forward to the tea-party; it would be very pleasant to introduce Rhoda to her old friends, Rhoda was something to be proud of. To-day Rhoda was wearing a velvet-corduroy coat and skirt of soft dove-grey and the scarf which she had twisted round her neck matched her eyes exactly. She had brought a small hat with her and offered to put it on, if Mamie thought it more *convenable,* but Mamie assured her there was no need . . . and indeed Rhoda's hair was so glorious, so golden and wavy and full of life that it would have been positively sinful to cover it.

"Well, that's all right," said Rhoda, throwing the hat on to the back seat. "I hate hats, really, but I didn't want to disgrace you by appearing improperly turned out. Is it a big party or just ourselves?"

"The Shaws might be there. Perhaps Holly Douglas. You won't mind meeting Holly, will you?"

"On the contrary," said Rhoda, smiling. She could well afford to smile at the prospect of an encounter with her unsuc-cessful rival. "I shall be very pleased to meet Holly, she may not be quite so pleased to meet me, of course."

But neither Lady Shaw nor her niece had been asked, it was quite an informal party, and after greeting her guests Mrs. Ogylvie Smith took Mamie by the hand and settling her firmly upon a large sofa sat down beside her for the promised talk. Rhoda was amused at this obvious manœuvre. She looked at the young doctor who was standing beside her near the fire-place and saw that he also was amused.

"Quite blatant," he said nodding. "Mother loves to get Mamie to herself and discuss ancient feuds and scandals."

Mamie had not said much about Henry Ogylvie Smith but something in her voice had prepared Rhoda to like him and she was not disappointed. He was tall and dark and slender; there was a slight foreign air about him, not so much in his appearance as in his bearing, and, although he was like his mother he was extremely virile, there was nothing effeminate about him as there so often is in men who resemble their mothers. He had an interesting face, it was sad in repose but it lighted up when he smiled. Rhoda had a vague feeling that she had seen him before . . . or that she had seen somebody like him.

" Have we met before? " Rhoda asked doubtfully.

" No," he replied. " Quite definitely, never."

" You seem very sure."

" I am absolutely certain." The way he said it, smiling as he uttered the words, was a compliment, implying that he would not have forgotten.

" Oh, well," said Rhoda. " I just thought I might have seen you somewhere. I don't mean we knew each other but just that we might have met casually at a party." She hesitated for a moment and then, feeling she had been gauche, she added, " I was living in London for some years before I married James."

" Rather a change coming to live at Boscath! "

" Yes, it is; but I'm beginning to get used to the different speed."

He laughed. " The speed is certainly very different. What were you doing in London? "

" Painting," she replied.

" A painter! " he exclaimed, looking at her with interest. " That's rather—exciting. Yes, definitely exciting. I hope you haven't stopped painting and taken to cooking instead. If I hadn't been a doctor I should have liked to be a painter. It's a silly thing to say, isn't it? "

" Why is it silly? "

" Second choice," he explained. " If I had really had it in me it would have come before anything else."

This was true, but Rhoda had done much the same thing.

She had put James first; she had quite deliberately chosen marriage and given painting second place. She explained this to Henry Ogylvie Smith.

" But it isn't the same," he said. " I was never anything but an amateur—a mere dabbler—and I gather you're a Real Painter, with capital letters."

" I suppose I am, really. I can't help seeing things in terms of paint. For instance the first thing I thought when I saw you was how I would paint you if I got the chance."

" Me? " he exclaimed in surprise.

" Yes, you," smiled Rhoda.

Mr. Ogylvie Smith had been listening. He said suddenly, " I wish you would, Mrs. Dering Johnstone. Why don't you? It would be delightful to have a picture of Henry."

" I shall only be here for a few days," said Henry quickly.

Rhoda said nothing. She had spoken lightly but now, quite suddenly, she wanted to paint this man. She saw exactly how she would do it: a dark background, his head turned a little as if he were listening and that curious light in his face. Rhoda clasped her hands and looked down at them . . . it was silly to mind so much.

" Please do," said Mr. Ogylvie Smith. " I'm sure Henry could find the time. My wife and I—it would give us a great deal of pleasure, even if it were only a sketch."

" I should like to," Rhoda said uncomfortably. " But perhaps—perhaps it would bore your son."

No more was said about the matter; in fact the young doctor changed the subject so abruptly that it was obvious he had no wish to be immortalised. He spoke of the Shaws and asked Rhoda if she had met Holly Douglas. Rhoda mentioned the Forresters, for she was aware that he was a friend of Adam's.

" Is Adam liking the work? " asked Doctor Ogylvie Smith. " I feel a bit responsible because it was I who spoke of him to Doctor Black."

" I'm sure he likes it. And their little house is charming."

" All the same I feel he's buried here. He was with me as

assistant at a hospital just out of London so I know him pretty well. I left the hospital soon after Adam. I wanted a change."

His face was suddenly strained and tired as if the recollection was painful.

" You weren't happy there," said Rhoda impulsively.

He evaded the question. " A change is good for everybody," he replied. " You can stay too long in the same place. I'm in Glasgow now, and I find my new work absorbing. I took my medical degrees at Glasgow University so I know a good many people there ... and another advantage of being in Glasgow is that I can come home occasionally for week-ends. The parents aren't getting any younger, and I'm the only child. I felt I ought to be nearer home. The parents haven't seen much of me for the last few years."

Mrs. Ogylvie Smith, who had approached while her son was talking, overheard what he had said.

" Indeed we have not! " she exclaimed, putting her hand through his arm. " What is the use of having a son at all? First he must go to school, then to a university and then, no sooner had Henry become a doctor than war was declared, and he joined the Navy. Off he went to the Mediterranean Fleet and we saw nothing of him for years! Then when the war was over and we hoped he might come to be near us, again we were disappointed. There was this grand appointment at the hospital where they worked him to skin and bone and he could not obtain leave of absence even for a few short days to visit his mother. The only way I could see Henry was to become very ill—and one cannot have a serious illness more than twice a year."

Henry smiled down at her. " Yes, your son has been a poor bargain," he said.

" When did I say so! " she cried. " My son is the best in the world. All that I complain of is that I cannot see enough of him. But come and have tea. We are having it in the dining-room to-day instead of comfortably here before the fire, because Thomson thinks that is the right thing when we have guests and I am too frightened to tell him otherwise."

Everybody laughed and the party moved into the dining-room.

" Come beside me, Rhoda," said Mrs. Ogylvie Smith as she took her seat at the head of the table. " You will not mind if I call you Rhoda? I am old enough to be your grandmother, my dear."

" Of course you must call me Rhoda! " Rhoda exclaimed.

" And we shall be friends? "

Rhoda nodded. " I should like that very much indeed."

" But first I must warn you that we are very wicked people, here at Blackthorn House," said Mrs. Ogylvie Smith in solemn tones. " It is only fair to warn you at the beginning how wicked we are. I am not good, like Lady Shaw, who tells everybody how to behave properly and who goes about and opens bazaars all over the county. I do nothing at all except stay at home and look after my husband—and alas, he is wicked too, for he has no farm and does no work whatever except to grow flowers and vegetables in the garden. He inherited Blackthorn House from his father and his grandfather. You see how wicked we are! "

" Anybody can see you're a wicked old lady," said Henry, laughing.

" But Rhoda does not mind," his mother pointed out. " She is smiling at me quite kindly, so *that* will be all right, and now she can never turn round and say how terribly wicked we are because I have told her about it first."

Rhoda smiled and promised that she would not forget. She had been trying to get a word in edgeways for some minutes and now seemed a good opportunity for Mrs. Ogylvie Smith was silently intent upon the business of pouring out tea.

" I'm sorry I was out when you called," said Rhoda.

" It was a thousand pities," agreed her hostess. " Tell me, does Mamie like sugar in her tea? "

" A little sugar. Perhaps you'll come again and have tea with me. We could arrange a day so that I wouldn't be out. Do come, I should love to have you. Come soon."

" No, dear Rhoda, not soon," replied Mrs. Ogylvie Smith regretfully. " It is impossible for me to come until Blaikie has forgotten your road, and unfortunately he has a very good memory. I should like to come, above everything, not only because already we are good friends, you and I, but also because you have Dorrie Flockhart as your cook. She is the best baker in the district and I am a greedy old lady as well as being a wicked one, but Blaikie will not bring me in the car (I know it, so it is useless to ask him and would only make him cross) and I cannot walk so far."

Henry chuckled. He said, " Let me tell you, Mrs. Dering Johnstone, Mother's longest walk consists of going round the garden and that's only on particularly fine days."

" It is what I said, Henry," said Mrs. Ogylvie Smith reproach-fully. " I said I could not walk so far and it is true." Having disposed of her son's interruption she turned back to Rhoda and continued : " You must not think too badly of Blaikie, he is an estimable man; his wife is an invalid and he looks after her most kindly and carefully but he has very strong prejudices and soon there will not be a house in the district which I shall be permitted to visit. He will not take me again to Boscath because he has too much regard for his springs—which inciden-tally are not his springs at all, but mine—and he will not take me to Tassieknowe any more because he was not invited by Mr. Heddle's butler to come in and have a cup of tea. Drum-burly Tower is another house to which I may not go, for the last time we were there Sir Andrew's shooting dog was naughty against the wheel."

There were shouts of laughter, amongst which could be heard Mamie's voice asking anxiously if Mrs. Ogylvie Smith were still allowed to come to Mureth.

" Oh, yes, dear Mamie," replied her friend. " Mureth is perfect. Blaikie and I are agreed upon that. We will come to Mureth as soon and as often as you are pleased to invite us."

CHAPTER THIRTEEN

MISS HEDDLE had called upon Rhoda and it was necessary for Rhoda to return the call.

" I shall have to go," she said to James.

" Yes, of course you must," replied James. " As a matter of
fact I think you'd be interested in the set up."

Rhoda decided to go that very afternoon and as it was a
particularly beautiful day she made up her mind to walk. She
could walk up the left bank of the river and cross higher up at
Tassieknowe. Flockie, who was interested in the expedition,
assured her that the river was much smaller at Tassieknowe and
she would be able to cross without much difficulty.

It was now the end of November and there was a nip of frost
in the air. The sky was pale blue, the hills were reddish brown
with withered bracken and there were patches of dark brown
heather and greenish-yellow grass. There was a sprinkling of
snow on the higher tops and the early afternoon sunshine
glistened upon them, making them sparkle like crystal. Under-
foot the ground was hard, for there had been frost in the night,
but in sheltered spots where the sun had shone warmly the
" bone " (as James put it) had melted into bog. Rhoda walked
along, inhaling the keen dry air, she felt extraordinarily fit, a
sense of well-being filled her whole body, and her heart sang.
She could smile at her doubts now; how foolish she had been
to entertain them for a moment! James was dearer than ever
but she had got used to being without his company during the
day. Gradually she had filled the empty space with other
things: with her painting; with friends; with long conversa-
tions with Flockie whose gentleness and simplicity were very
endearing and last but not least with Duggie. The responsi-

bility of Duggie had been thrust upon her, so to speak, and at first she had been afraid that it would be a nuisance but Duggie was never a nuisance. She enjoyed teaching Duggie, it was a worth-while job because she was perfectly certain that some day her young pupil would do marvellous things. Having studied for years in an art school Rhoda was competent to judge ability and had complete confidence in her judgment.

Rhoda had intended to make painting her career for she had outstanding talent. She had said to Mamie once that she was a good painter and could be very good if she continued to make painting her career (if anything this was an understatement, and Rhoda knew it) but, now that she had married James, he was her first consideration and painting was second. Sometimes she wondered if she had done right (her master at the Art School did not think so). Was it right when you had been dowered with an artistic talent to bury it in a napkin? She had never for one moment regretted her decision to marry James for she loved him with all her heart, she had just wondered sometimes if she had done right. The question was one of principle, it had nagged at her. Duggie was the answer. Duggie was going to be a great painter, far better than she could ever have been, and she had been given the privilege of helping him. This comforted her; it satisfied her completely. She was justified.

The path wound along the bank of the river and, here and there, ascended the shoulder of a hill. It was used occasionally by carts and the deep ruts left by their wheels were full of crackly ice as thin as cardboard. Little burns came tumbling down the hillside and the spray from their tiny waterfalls had fashioned glittering icicles amongst the rocks.

Rounding a bend of the path Rhoda suddenly found herself looking across a deep cleft in the hillside. It was an unexpected sight—as if the hill had been split open by a giant's axe—the sides of the chasm were steep, almost perpendicular black rock dripping with water. The path snaked down into this curious cleft and at the foot of it two burns met in a turbulent whirlpool before hurling themselves into the river.

Rhoda descended into the chasm looking about her with interest. A heavy plank had been laid across the larger burn as a bridge, it was dark and slippery with frozen spray; she crossed it cautiously. She was now on a tongue of land above the meeting place of the streams, standing upon a smooth stretch of emerald green turf. The black beetling cliffs were wet and slimy; ferns and small twisted rowan trees grew in the crevices . . . it was cold and dank here for the sun scarcely ever penetrated into the chasm and the noise of rushing water echoed backwards and forwards filling the ears with a medley of roaring sound.

Rhoda stood there for a few moments. She was amazed at the place. Although the cleft was not large there was something vaguely alarming about it—something uncanny. She had a feeling that it was a bad place . . . perhaps it had a dark history attached to it. She did not dally long, but pulled herself together and, leaping across the second burn which was deep and narrow, climbed the scree of loose stones on the other side.

It was a relief to find herself out upon the bare hillside with the pale golden sunshine all round her and the hills in their tawny coats stretching from her feet to the pale blue sky.

In front of Rhoda was a high stone dyke, marking the boundary of Boscath hirsel (beyond was the hirsel of Hawkbrae). There was a gate in the dyke and a tall spare man with a brown craggy face and very blue eyes was leaning upon the gate. As Rhoda approached he opened the gate for her and took off his cap.

These actions were accomplished with such a dignified air that Rhoda wondered who he was.

" You'll be Mistress Dering Johnstone," he said with a smile and a flash of white teeth. " I have been hearing about you. It is a fine day for a walk."

Rhoda was always ready to be friendly; she admitted she was Mrs. Dering Johnstone and asked who he was.

" Sutherland is my name," he replied. " I was the shepherd at Tassieknowe when Mr. Brown was alive."

" Of course, I've heard about you! " exclaimed Rhoda and she held out her hand.

They shook hands gravely; Rhoda's small hand disappeared into the enormous brown hand of her new acquaintance. It was gripped firmly and released. There was something very satisfactory about the hand-shake. They talked for a few minutes about the weather and about Sutherland's dog which had sat down and was waiting patiently for his master to finish his conversation.

" That's a horrible place," said Rhoda, pointing to the chasm in the hill from which she had just emerged. " Is there some story about it? "

" They call it The De'il's Cleugh," replied Sutherland gravely. " It has a bad reputation and there are few people who would care to visit it in the dark. There is a story that a Covenanter lived there in a cave in the Killing Times and he would sing psalms at night to keep his spirits up."

Rhoda shuddered. " He must have been a brave man," she declared.

" The Covenanters were brave men," agreed Sutherland. " They were fanatics—and fanatics are usually brave. It is said that his spirit haunts the place and you can hear the sound of psalms coming from the cleugh on still nights; but I have been round this way at night and I have never heard anything . . . except the falling water and maybe the screech of an owl."

" You think it may be haunted? " Rhoda asked him.

" Why not? It is a queer place and there are queer things in the world, Mrs. Dering Johnstone."

Rhoda was silent for a few moments. Then she said, " You don't belong to this part of Scotland, Mr. Sutherland."

" I come from Helmsdale," he replied. " Maybe you are thinking I look different and talk different from the people here. We folk from the north-east are big and bony for there is Norse blood in our veins."

" The Vikings! " exclaimed Rhoda.

He nodded, smiling. " They would come across the sea and

raid our lands, but sometimes if their ship was wrecked they
would settle down amongst us and marry and become good
farmers. Sometimes I have thought that I have done the same
thing in a peaceful way, for I came to this part of the country
twenty-five years ago and settled here."

" And became a good farmer," added Rhoda nodding.

He laughed. " Well, maybe," he said. " I married a local
girl and we settled down very happily, that certainly is true."

" I'm sorry you had to leave Tassieknowe."

" It was a grief to us," Sutherland admitted. " When you
have been a long time in one place it is as if you belonged
there . . . but it could not be helped. Mr. Heddle is not a
good man to serve."

Rhoda was impressed with the dignified, temperate way he
spoke. If Sutherland had raged and stormed against Mr. Heddle
it would have impressed Rhoda much less forcibly than the
quiet condemnation he had uttered. Mr. Heddle was not a
good man to serve, so Sutherland had refused to serve him.

" Do you live near here? " she asked.

He turned and pointed.

Rhoda saw a tiny cottage high up in the hills with a few
stunted trees huddled about it. She had never imagined anybody
could live in such an isolated spot. Compared with Sutherland's
new home Boscath was in the midst of civilisation.

" It must be lonely! " she exclaimed.

" Loneliness is inside a person," replied Sutherland. " It is
possible to be lonely in a big city. If a person is contented and
has enough work to do he will not feel lonely amongst the hills
. . . but it is a wee bit out of the way and would not do for a
man with young children who were attending school. All the
same it is a solid little house and comfortable. If you are going
in that direction Mistress Sutherland would be pleased to give
you a cup of tea."

Rhoda thanked him and explained why she was unable to
accept the invitation.

" Maybe another day," said Sutherland nodding. " Any day

95

that you are walking in this direction you have only to chap on the door."

Rhoda promised to come, and fully intended to keep her word for she was tremendously interested in Sutherland and felt she would like to meet his wife. She said good-bye to him and walked on. When she looked back she saw him mounting the hill with long loose strides . . . to Rhoda he looked more than life size. She would have liked to paint him.

Rhoda's meeting with Sutherland had given her food for thought, not only because the man himself was worth thinking about but also because of his isolated life—which he had assured her was not lonely. The little cottage amongst the hills drew her eyes. She imagined the building of it. It had been built by men as a shelter for man—a primitive reason for building. A man must live here to look after sheep so a house had been built for him—and because it was necessary it was eminently suitable to its surroundings. It was really a part of Nature . . . but indeed all the houses in this sparsely peopled land seemed actually a part of Nature. There was nothing artificial about them. They were built of the stone of the hills in which they were set and so were in harmony with the nooks which sheltered them. There was no nonsense about them; they were built strong and without the slightest attempt at adornment and the tempests which raged about their snugly-fitting roofs were powerless to destroy them.

Rhoda was getting to know this land and to make friends with it. In certain lights it was sad and lonely and cold but when the sun shone suddenly from behind a cloud the whole landscape smiled. She had seen the same thing happen in the faces of her new neighbours: austere they were (eminently paintable with those interesting bones which seemed so close to the surface), but often sad and cold. Then would come the smile of friendship . . . the sun broke through the clouds and their whole aspect changed and was brightened with its kindly rays.

CHAPTER FOURTEEN

SO thinking and musing as she walked along Rhoda came to the top of a rise and looking down saw Tassieknowe. There it stood. It was Jock's Naboth's vineyard. It was Flockie's grief. The river made a bend round the hillock upon which it was built and beyond the hillock the hills rose steeply. Never having seen it before Rhoda could not compare the present aspect of Tassieknowe with its aspect in the lifetime of Mr. Brown and as a matter of fact she was agreeably surprised by its appearance. The house was rectangular and solidly constructed, there was nothing beautiful about it but it pleased her eye for proportion. It was bare, of course—Flockie had called it naked—but for a thing to look naked it must first be clothed, so it did not look naked to Rhoda. She noticed, too, that it would not look bare for ever. Mr. Heddle had planted a few trees here and there upon the knoll and at one side of the house a rockery was in process of construction.

Rhoda was a little early so she sat down upon a rock and looked at the place. Somebody had said the house was built upon the site of a Roman Camp—perhaps Flockie had told her—it was easy to believe. If Rhoda had been a general she would have chosen that knoll for her fortress. The bend of the river would defend it upon two sides and the view up and down the valley was uninterrupted. The idea was fascinating. This place had once been a station upon a Roman road, it had once been full of Roman soldiers. Battles had been fought round its walls; small savage men had swarmed across the river and flung themselves fiercely upon their hated invaders; and the Legions of Rome clad in glittering armour had stood firm behind their walls and thrown them back.

Rhoda was a trifle hazy about the history of the Roman occupation of Southern Scotland but what she did not know she could make up for quite easily by imagination. She could almost see it happening as if in a vision, and it was all the more easy to visualise because there could not have been many changes here. Perhaps in those far-off days there were more trees—dark forests where wild beasts roamed—and most certainly there was more boggy ground but apart from that the surroundings of Tassieknowe were the same as they had been long ago: the same hills, brown and tan and green and golden-yellow, the same rocks and silver river, the same far-off pale-blue sky.

It was too cold to sit for long so after a few minutes she got up and went down to the river. She expected to be able to cross the river dry-shod, scrambling from rock to rock and she walked up and down looking for a suitable crossing place. Presently she found one, two boulders in mid-stream made a couple of reasonably easy stepping-stones; she crossed carefully, balancing herself upon them, and walked up the hill.

The new owners of Tassieknowe were fond of bright-blue paint, that was evident, for the doors and windows and rones and waste-pipes all bore evidence of what to Rhoda was an unfortunate predilection. Apart from this there was nothing very staggering about the outside of the house, the inside was a different matter. Rhoda who had walked over the hills and scrambled across a river was not in the right mood to appreciate the *décor* of Tassieknowe. The bright-blue, fitted carpets, the white walls with gilt mirrors and the light wood furniture of ultra-modern design looked artificial and garish. What were these things doing in an old-fashioned farm-house? James had said she would be "interested in the set up." It was interesting, certainly.

Miss Heddle was at home; Rhoda was conducted up the stairs and ushered into a room which she guessed must be Miss Heddle's private sanctum. It was decorated in the same style as the rest of the house but with some slight differences. The plain white walls were hung with photographs and some extremely feeble water-colour sketches, the chairs had cushions in them. There was a straggly plant, of a species unknown to Rhoda, on a book-case in the corner, and, by the fire, a dog's basket with a pink rug in it. Tea was laid on a low table and Rhoda was glad to note that there was plenty to eat; her walk had given her an appetite.

Miss Heddle did not appear for a few minutes and Rhoda, left to herself, sat upon the arm of a chair and looked about her; she formed the opinion that the excrescences on the modern austerity of the room were expressions of Miss Heddle's personality. If so it meant that the modern austerity expressed Mr. Heddle's and it also meant that Mr. Heddle was the dominant partner. Miss Heddle was merely camping in the apartment set aside for her use, camping in much the same manner as one camps in a hotel bedroom.

It was extraordinarily quiet. There was not a sound to be heard, not even the murmur of the river. There seemed to be no birds in the vicinity, perhaps because the trees had been cut down. There were no noises inside the house either, the thick, blue, fitted carpets deadened every sound; the clock upon the mantelpiece was an electric one and completely silent. It was almost, thought Rhoda, as if one had suddenly become deaf . . . but she had no time for further reflection for the door opened and her hostess came in.

Rhoda had seen Miss Heddle in church so she knew her by sight; she was tall and thin with black hair, turning white, her eyes were dark brown and her complexion sallow. She was beautifully dressed and it was obvious that she frequented an expensive dressmaker. This afternoon she was wearing a dark-red woollen frock trimmed with fur and although it suited her it gave her a slightly exotic appearance. Rhoda became uncomfortably conscious of her own thick tweeds and muddy shoes and stockings.

" I *am* sorry I wasn't ready," said Miss Heddle cordially.

" The fact is I didn't hear your car. It's funny because I usually hear cars coming up the drive."

" I walked," said Rhoda, shaking hands and smiling.

" You *walked*! " exclaimed Miss Heddle in amazement. " You walked from *Boscath*! "

" It isn't very far and it was such a beautiful afternoon."

" It's miles and miles! Why, it took me nearly three-quarters of an hour in the car. We had to go through Drumburly and over a bridge and after that miles and miles along a cart-road."

" It isn't so far if you walk," replied Rhoda.

" It isn't so far if you walk? " echoed Miss Heddle incredulously. " But it must be exactly the same distance, and of course it would take *much* longer."

Rhoda explained, or tried to explain, the topography of the country but she soon realised she might have saved herself the trouble for Miss Heddle was incapable of taking it in. With chalks and a blackboard it might have been possible to make Miss Heddle understand but without these to help her she was powerless.

" If you had only told me you were coming I would have sent Mason to fetch you," declared Miss Heddle. She said it several times and continued to say it even when Rhoda assured her that the walk had been agreeable in the extreme.

" I never walk," said Miss Heddle. " Nestor likes walking but I never walk at all. You must be absolutely exhausted; I'm sure it's bad for you. Mason will take you home."

They sat down to tea.

" Isn't the house pretty? " said Miss Heddle. " Dear Nestor planned it, of course. You haven't met Nestor, have you? He's *very* clever. Do you have many guests? "

" No," replied Rhoda. " We haven't had any yet. We've just been married."

" We have a *great* many guests; they're Nestor's friends of course. They like coming here for ten days or a fortnight because it's *new*. Nobody has ever seen anything like this before—or at least none of Nestor's friends have. It's *new*, you see. People get tired of ordinary things, of living in London and going to parties or going to Italy or the Riviera or yachting so they like to come here. It's quite, quite *different*. You must feed them well, but I see to that. I give them good plain food —and that's different too. We can get plenty of *lamb* of course and plenty of eggs and cream, which makes it easy."

" Yes," agreed Rhoda. Her hostess's conversation was a little muddled but it was very revealing. Rhoda could imagine Nestor's friends from London, jaded with parties, arriving at Tassieknowe and saying how *new* and *different* it was. She could imagine it all the more easily because she had met people just like Nestor's friends who did nothing but chase pleasure from morning to night without ever catching up with it.

" Do you like living here?" asked Miss Heddle.

" Yes," said Rhoda. She was about to say why she liked it and then she saw that Miss Heddle was not listening . . . or at least was not listening to her. Miss Heddle was listening to something else.

" What is it?" asked Rhoda.

" Oh, nothing," Miss Heddle said casually. " It was just poor Mr. Brown coughing, that's all."

" Mr. Brown!"

" He lives here, you know," nodded Miss Heddle. " *Do* have another of these little cakes. I'm sure you must be hungry after your walk."

" Mr. Brown lives here?" inquired Rhoda, taking one of the little cakes without noticing what she was doing.

" Yes," said Miss Heddle. " I haven't seen him of course, but I often hear him coughing. Poor man, he has a dreadful cough."

" You haven't seen him?"

" No," said Miss Heddle. " I shouldn't *like* to see him. *That* would frighten me. You can't be frightened of a cough, can you? Listen . . ."

Rhoda listened. It was very quiet indeed.

" You can hear him, can't you?" Miss Heddle said. Her

dark eyes were fixed upon Rhoda with a curiously compelling gaze. " You can hear him, can't you? "

" I'm—not sure," said Rhoda uncomfortably, nor was she. Perhaps there had been some slight sound.

" Some people can't hear him," admitted Miss Heddle. " Nestor always says he can't hear him but I think Nestor *does* hear him sometimes."

There was a short silence while Miss Heddle gave her guest another cup of tea.

" You see," said Miss Heddle in confidential tones. " You see it's *quite* simple, really. It's just that Mr. Brown hasn't gone away. I think he's waiting for *us* to go away—that's what I think. Nestor doesn't understand; Nestor thinks money can buy anything; he thinks he bought Tassieknowe, and of course I thought so too, *at the time*."

Rhoda gazed at her without speaking.

" You understand, don't you, Mrs. Dering Johnstone? " said Miss Heddle, smiling confidently.

" But Mr. Heddle did buy Tassieknowe."

" Oh, well," said Miss Heddle. " I suppose he did, *in a way*, but there are some things you can't buy for money, you have to be given them. You know what I mean, don't you? "

" Yes," said Rhoda faintly. The woman was mad, of course, and yet . . . and yet there was a sort of sense in her words . . . and she didn't look mad. Miss Heddle's manner and demeanour were perfectly calm and collected. She looked perfectly sane.

" For instance," continued Miss Heddle with the air of a schoolmistress explaining a mathematical problem to a child. " For instance when my dressmaker retired she sold her business and Madame Delavine bought it. Madame Delavine bought the shop and all the fittings and paid a *lot* of money for them, but the goodwill of the business was *given* to her. It's *such* a pity Nestor wasn't given the goodwill of Tassieknowe, isn't it? " added Miss Heddle with a sigh.

" Yes."

" I knew you'd understand."

The strange thing was that Rhoda *did* understand. The matter had been explained to her with absolute lucidity, and she understood it perfectly, but it was crazy all the same. She's like the Red Queen, thought Rhoda. She really is. The Red Queen talked arrant nonsense with just that common-sensical air.

CHAPTER FIFTEEN

RHODA was so busy identifying her hostess with the Red Queen (and incidentally herself with Alice) that she lost the thread of the conversation and did not realise that the subject had been changed.

" You will, won't you? " Miss Heddle was saying in earnest tones.

" I—er—— " said Rhoda doubtfully, for who would care to make a pact with the Red Queen before knowing exactly the terms of it?

" Just a sketch," Miss Heddle implored. " He wouldn't *sit,* of course; you wouldn't expect him to, would you? But it would be so nice to have a picture of dear Nestor—*so* much nicer than a photograph."

" It would be difficult without sittings," said Rhoda, picking up the thread.

" Oh, I *know,* but of course I would pay you more."

" It isn't that. It's just that I couldn't do a sketch without sittings—and I haven't seen Mr. Heddle."

" *There!* " said Miss Heddle, taking a large glossy photograph off the wall and putting it into Rhoda's reluctant hands. " There, that's dear Nestor. He's *very* handsome, isn't he? Of course a photograph doesn't do him justice, because it's really his colouring that's so unusual . . . Oh! " exclaimed Miss Heddle, struck all of a sudden by a brilliant idea. " Oh, I *know* what to do! You can take the photograph home with you and make a sketch of Nestor, and then you would just have to see him and colour it."

"That isn't the way I work," said Rhoda with remarkable restraint.

"But if I pay you," urged Miss Heddle. "I would pay you *twice* as much as you get for *ordinary* portraits and I'm sure you could do it *beautifully*!"

Rhoda had begun to wonder why she was not angry with the woman. She was not in the least angry. It's because she's the Red Queen, thought Rhoda, looking at her.

"You will, won't you, Mrs. Dering Johnstone," said the Red Queen. "I'll take it out of the frame and wrap it up in paper for you——"

"No, Miss Heddle," said Rhoda firmly.

"I'm sure you could. It's often done," declared Miss Heddle. "I remember when my eldest brother was killed at Mons—in the first war, you know—my parents had a *beautiful* painting of him done from a photograph."

"But Mr. Heddle hasn't been killed," Rhoda pointed out. "Mr. Heddle can easily give me some sittings if he wants me to do a sketch of him. I should want at least three sittings, perhaps more." She handed back the photograph as she spoke.

Whether or not Miss Heddle would have accepted this as the final word upon the subject is open to doubt, for at that moment the door opened and the original of the large glossy photograph walked in. He was large and glossy with black wavy hair and dark brown eyes. James's description of Mr. Heddle had done him less than justice for he was very good-looking indeed. Rhoda, thinking of the proposed sketch and seeing him in terms of paint, decided that if she had her way she would paint Mr. Heddle in oils, wearing oriental garments, with jewelled bracelets upon his arms and a golden fillet encircling his head . . . but it was very unlikely that she could have her way.

Miss Heddle was so startled at the sudden entrance of her

brother, just when they had been talking about him, that she forgot to make the proper introductions.

" Oh, Nestor, I thought you were out—I mean I didn't know you had come in," babbled Miss Heddle nervously.

" How do you do ? " said Mr. Heddle, shaking hands with Rhoda.

" She walked over," continued Miss Heddle. " I could have sent Mason easily, but I didn't know. It's *miles* beyond Drumburly—across the hills."

Mr. Heddle did not look at his sister. He was looking at Rhoda and smiling. " You ought to be hungry," he said. " I hope my sister has given you a good tea."

" We *must* send her home in the car," said Miss Heddle anxiously.

Mr. Heddle shook his head. " We won't talk of sending her home—why should we anticipate sorrow ? It isn't every day we have the privilege of entertaining an angel unawares."

Rhoda was used to admiration; she had found that men of Mr. Heddle's age (which she guessed to be about forty-five) were often the worst and went down like ninepins on beholding her. As a rule it amused her, but Mr. Heddle's admiration did not amuse her at all. Mr. Heddle was so overpowering, he seemed to fill the room. There was a sort of elemental magnetism in his personality, as if he were not quite civilised. You could imagine him doing—anything—really, thought Rhoda uncomfortably.

" If I'm home by six o'clock——" she began, and somehow she felt a trifle breathless as if the air in the room had become close and hot and vitiated.

" Nonsense ! " exclaimed Mr. Heddle. " We aren't going to let you go without any dinner. That would be very inhospitable when you've come so far. We can ring up your home—Anna will ring up and say we're keeping you to dinner."

" It's very kind of you," Rhoda said. " But I'm afraid I can't stay. My husband is expecting me. I don't think Miss Heddle told you—I'm Mrs. Dering Johnstone."

She saw his face change. "Oh, from Boscath!" he said. "My sister said you'd come from beyond Drumburly."

"It *is* beyond Drumburly," put in Miss Heddle. "I know it is, because when Mason took me in the car we had to go *through* Drumburly."

"Because that's the nearest bridge," said her brother shortly.

Miss Heddle was quelled. She still did not understand, but it never occurred to her to question Nestor's dictum. She poured out a cup of tea and handed it to him and offered him scones and jam.

Sitting on a sofa near the table Nestor proceeded to have his tea. There was a sulky expression upon his face and it was obvious that he had lost interest in the golden-haired angel.

"I've seen you in church," said Miss Heddle to Rhoda, speaking in a low voice in deference to her brother's presence. "That's why I called on you—because I was sure we should have a *lot* in common. I mean I knew you came from London. Of course Nestor hasn't seen you before and he didn't know who you were. Nestor never goes to church but he doesn't mind me going and he *always* lets me have the car."

Rhoda felt an almost uncontrollable urge to say, "How kind of him!" but managed to refrain.

"I *like* going to church," continued Miss Heddle. "I find it so *peaceful*. Of course it's a very ugly little church and the organ isn't very good, but——"

"You take it as a sedative," said her brother.

"As a sedative?"

"Yes, you sit and listen to an old dotard who tells you that you'll go to heaven when you die. That comforts you, doesn't it?"

Rhoda was seldom shocked but this shocked her. It was not only the words but the casual scornful tone in which they were uttered and, perhaps most of all, the unkindness that shocked her. Rhoda had lived in London on her own and, mixing with all sorts and conditions of people, had heard a good many arguments for and against the existence of an after life; but although the arguments had been closely reasoned and occasionally had led to fierce altercations this cold-hearted bitterness was a thousand times worse.

"That comforts you, doesn't it, Anna?" repeated Mr. Heddle, insisting upon an answer to his question.

"Yes—it does—really," said Miss Heddle in a low voice.

"Why shouldn't it?" demanded Rhoda truculently.

"Because it's false comfort," replied Mr. Heddle, turning and looking at Rhoda with a baleful eye. "And because people like Anna who comfort themselves with false hopes are cowards at heart. They can't face up to this life so they bolster themselves up with the idea that there will be a better one. I suppose you believe in a Heaven, Above the Bright Blue Sky?"

"Yes," replied Rhoda with spirit.

"Have you never looked through a telescope?" asked Mr. Heddle in a patient voice, such as one might use to a moron. "At night a telescope reveals stars which are so far off that the light from them takes millions of years to reach this earth. Where is your Heaven?"

"It's somewhere," Rhoda said. "I'm quite sure of that in spite of your telescope. When I was a child I didn't know where Australia was. Now I know where it is. Some day, when I've grown up a bit more, I shall know where Heaven is."

"It's incredible!" exclaimed Mr. Heddle, with a laugh. He rose as he spoke and left the room.

"Dear Nestor didn't *mean* to be rude," said Miss Heddle nervously. "He didn't *mean* to be unkind. He's so clever, you know—lots of clever people don't believe in Heaven—and he's apt to get a little cross when people contradict him. It isn't your fault of course. *You* couldn't know, could you? I ought to have *warned* you that Nestor doesn't like people to contradict him."

"It wouldn't have made any difference if you had," said Rhoda frankly.

Miss Heddle did not understand this. Rhoda's meaning was lost upon her; she continued to assure Rhoda that Nestor did not mean to be rude or unkind, but he was so clever, and of course, Rhoda was not to blame because she had not been warned in advance that Nestor could not brook contradiction.

Rhoda ceased to listen. She sat back in her chair and lighted a cigarette. Her hostess had not offered her this solace but she felt she had earned it. As a matter of fact Rhoda was rather surprised at herself.

Presently, when sufficient time had elapsed to make her departure seem a natural impulse and not the result of her host's rudeness Rhoda got up from her chair and said she must go. Miss Heddle made no attempt to detain her but rang the bell and ordered the car to take her home.

CHAPTER SIXTEEN

THE idea of painting a portrait of Henry Ogylvie Smith had appealed to Rhoda greatly, but she had realised that the idea of sitting for his portrait did not appeal to him, so she had dismissed the matter from her mind. She was all the more pleased when she received a letter from him asking if she had really meant what she said and if so when it would suit her to begin. " The parents would like it," he wrote, " and the fact is I should like to give them pleasure; they have not had much pleasure out of their only son. Perhaps it could be ready for Christmas, but if not it does not matter. I shall not tell them anything about it, so that it will be a surprise. As Boscath is not on the telephone I shall walk over on Wednesday afternoon but please do not stay at home on my account, just leave a message for me."

The letter arrived at breakfast-time on Wednesday morning and she showed it to James.

" Did you mean it? " asked James without enthusiasm.

" Yes, of course. I always mean what I say. I wonder if

he could stay for a sitting this afternoon. I shall have everything ready in case."

" I thought you were going to tea with Nan."

" Nan! " said Rhoda vaguely. " Oh, yes, but Nan won't mind. I want to paint him. I wanted to paint him the moment I saw him."

Already Rhoda had begun to compose her picture; she had imagined his head against a dark oak panel, where could she get one? When breakfast was over she went upstairs and began to make her preparations.

Henry arrived about two o'clock; he had walked across the hills with a sandwich in his pocket and had lunched on the way, but he was quite pleased to drink a cup of coffee with his hostess and to eat one of Flockie's scones. When he had finished, Rhoda took him up to the studio. By this time she was absolutely determined to paint him in oils and over-ruled all Henry's objections.

" It won't take long, honestly," declared Rhoda. " Once I've made a start I can do quite a' lot without you. Just come when you can; any time will suit me."

In face of this enthusiasm what could Henry say? He took the chair she had arranged for him as meekly as a lamb.

Henry had expected to feel embarrassed (to sit there like a stuffed owl while a young and extremely good-looking woman gazed at one's face was bound to be embarrassing), but he soon discovered his mistake. Rhoda was so businesslike, she gave him his pose in much the same crisp but encouraging manner as he himself assumed when he was about to give a patient an injection and although she gazed at his face it was in such a purely impersonal way that he felt no discomfort.

Rhoda hung a picture on the wall and invited her sitter to look at it. For this purpose she had chosen a reproduction of Don Quixote de la Mancha. It seemed to Rhoda that there was something of Don Quixote in Henry's personality. Perhaps it was merely that they were compatriots—Henry being

Spanish on his mother's side—or perhaps it was something else. Rhoda was not sure, she had a feeling she would know more about Henry Ogylvie Smith when she had painted him.

" Shall I smile? " inquired Henry, his eyes firmly upon the picture.

" Good Heavens, no! " exclaimed Rhoda. " You aren't having your photograph taken. Don't think of your face at all and don't stare at poor Don Quixote as if he were a gorgon. Just talk and try to forget what I'm doing."

Thus adjured Henry relaxed his features and began to look more natural; they chatted about this and that and time passed very pleasantly indeed. Rhoda had just called a halt and given permission to her sitter to abandon his pose and smoke a cigarette when the door opened and Duggie appeared.

Duggie was looking and feeling unusually trim and jaunty for he had just had a birthday and was clad from top to toe in new clothes. The brown tweed jacket and shorts and the dark green pullover with the polo collar had been presents from " Mrs. James." Mrs. Johnstone had knitted him some brown stockings to match and he had managed to wheedle his mother into buying him a pair of brown brogues. He intended to keep this magnificent outfit for his visits to Boscath; it was much too good for school.

" It's a half-holiday," said Duggie, hesitating at the door. ". I just thought—but if you're busy——"

" It's all right, come in," said Rhoda.

He came in and held out his hands.

" Very nice and clean," nodded Rhoda, taking one of the slender brown hands and examining it closely. " You see," she added, turning to 'Henry. " You see Duggie and I have made a bond."

" Like Shylock," Duggie explained.

"Just like Shylock. But our bond is a bit more complicated and has a much wider scope. One of the principal clauses in the bond concerns Duggie's hands. If he appears in the studio with dirty hands he gets thrown out."

" That's so," agreed Duggie. " I wash them. Miss Flockhart lets me wash them in the kitchen sink."

" Nice hands, aren't they? " continued Rhoda, spreading out the long thin fingers for Henry to admire.

" Well worth taking care of," agreed Henry.

" They're useful, too. They clean my paint brushes and tidy up the studio. That isn't in the bond."

" I like doing it," said the boy quickly. He hesitated and then said, " Can I show him some of your drawings, Mrs. James? I think he'd like to see them. Can I show him the one of Roy clipping the ewe? "

Rhoda was not particularly anxious for her work to be displayed but she could not refuse without appearing churlish. As a matter of fact she was so surprised at Duggie's request that she could find no words of refusal. She had never seen Duggie behave like this; usually when strangers were present Duggie retired into his shell—even with James he was shy. Perhaps his new clothes had given him confidence. He certainly looked very nice in his new clothes!

Duggie had taken the folder off the shelf and was standing beside Henry showing him the drawings. " This is Miss Flockie," he said. " Maybe you've not seen her. It's just exactly like her ... and here's Roy clipping. Isn't it splendid? "

" It is splendid," agreed Henry, taking it and looking at it with interest.

" It was a wonderful subject," Rhoda said.

" Yes," said Henry, nodding. " And you've got so much movement there. I don't know enough about drawing to say the right things but I know when I see something really fine. It gives one a feeling of satisfaction. I can't describe it in any other way."

Rhoda thought he had described it very well. She decided that she liked Henry Ogylvie Smith immensely. He was natural and kind, and he was coming through a somewhat trying experience with flying colours, and Rhoda was pleased to see that he was admiring the drawings which she knew to be good and saying less about the others.

"That's enough, Duggie," said Rhoda who had begun to feel she could bear the ordeal no longer. "You can put the drawings away. Doctor Ogylvie Smith has seen enough of them."

Henry looked at her and smiled. "He hasn't," said Henry, "but he realises that this isn't much fun for the artist. Put them away, Duggie. Perhaps we may look at them some other time."

Duggie put them away. He looked surprised and a little crestfallen and it was obvious that he did not understand.

"Tell me about this bond," continued Henry. "I'm interested in this bond of yours. Am I allowed to ask what other clauses it contains?"

"Duggie will tell you," said Rhoda.

Duggie smiled a little doubtfully.

"Come on," said Henry encouragingly. "What's in the bond?"

"Well," said Duggie. "There's a lot of things besides clean hands. I've to talk properly and never to say ' Jings! ' I've to breathe through my nose and I've not to read any books without showing them to Mrs. James first."

"You see?" said Rhoda solemnly.

Henry nodded, equally grave.

"My commitments are easier. I teach Duggie the rudiments of art. I tear up his drawings into little bits and throw them into the waste-paper basket."

"You kept the one of you," said Duggie, grinning so widely that his mouth seemed to stretch from ear to ear.

"So I did! I must have been too busy to tear it up. Shall we show it to Doctor Ogylvie Smith?" Rhoda got up as she spoke and, taking a folder from the shelf, opened it and found the sketch. She handed it to Henry and Henry took it with an indulgent smile.

Suddenly the smile vanished. "Hallo!" exclaimed Henry

in amazement. He looked up and met Rhoda's forbidding stare.

" Hum," said Henry. " Yes, it's—it's Mrs. James's back. She was painting when you did this sketch of her."

Duggie nodded. " She didn't know I was doing it. That made it easier . . . besides nobody could do her face."

" Nobody could do her face? " asked Henry in surprise.

" It's too beautiful," said Duggie simply.

Rhoda had the grace to blush.

" I believe you're right," said Henry in a thoughtful tone. " If Michael Angelo were alive——"

" Have you got a new book from the library, Duggie? " inquired Rhoda.

Duggie had. He took a small red book from his pocket and handed it to her.

" *Tristram Shandy!* You *do* go in for variety, don't you? It was *Black Beauty* last week. I don't know much about *Tristram Shandy* but I have a feeling he's rather strong meat for the young."

" It's full of little stars," Duggie pointed out. " I wondered what they meant."

" I can tell you that," said Henry. " They mean somebody has been through Mr. Sterne's book with a blue pencil and taken out all the interesting bits."

" Why? " exclaimed Duggie in surprise.

His elders did not reply to this not unnatural question.

" In that case I suppose he may read it? " asked Rhoda.

" If he can," nodded Henry. " But if Duggie can read it I'll take off my hat to him."

Duggie was now a little doubtful as to whether he wanted to read it. He took it in his hands and flipped the pages over. " I go by the name," he explained. " It sounded nice—*Tristram Shandy*—I thought maybe it was a pony, or a dog."

" I'm afraid you'll be disappointed," Henry told him.

The interval was over. Duggie settled himself at his table and Rhoda went on with her work. Henry, having nothing to do except gaze at Don Quixote had ample time for thought. He thought about Duggie. Who was Duggie? Where did he come from? He was a queer object to fall from the skies in this outlandish place. Henry knew the district and therefore was aware that there were no houses within miles from which Duggie could have come. The obvious conclusion was that Duggie was the son of a shepherd, or a ploughman, but Henry was sure he was not. Henry was interested in the boy, he had an unusual face, full of bright intelligence, and his manner was good, neither too forward nor awkward and shy . . . and that sketch of Rhoda! (Henry was calling her Rhoda by this time if not to her face most certainly in his mind.) That sketch of Rhoda's back as she sat at her easel painting! It was amazing. Not only was it unmistakably Rhoda's back, but it was drawn with firm strokes and an economy of line which showed that the young artist had considered his subject before he started and had known exactly what he intended to do; most curious of all it was drawn with an individual touch, the touch which makes a signature unnecessary. Henry had a feeling that if he saw another drawing of Duggie's he would know who had drawn it.

This conviction brought Henry back to where he had started. Who was Duggie? A genius in the making? Lucky for him he had fallen into the right hands! Henry was a doctor and therefore an expert in human relationships and it seemed to him there was something really beautiful in the relationship between Rhoda Dering Johnstone and her *protégé*. They understood one another perfectly. They trusted one another. They were useful to one another. That was the ideal relationship of one human being to another human being . . . usefulness . . . to take and give service.

"That's enough for to-day," said Rhoda at last. "I'm tired and you're tired—at least you ought to be."

Henry had not realised he was tired but he found he was. He rose and stretched himself. "I suppose I mustn't see it," he said.

"You may if you like. It's a bit of a mess, of course."

He went over and looked at what she had done. It was a bit of a mess, as she had said, but Henry knew enough about painting to realise that neither he nor Rhoda had been wasting time.

"It's marvellous!" he exclaimed. "I'd give anything to be able to do that!"

"Your skill as a physician?" asked Rhoda, smiling at him. "No, Henry, you wouldn't."

He smiled thoughtfully in return. "I see what you mean," he said, "and, of course, you're right: I wouldn't. Each to his own trade."

CHAPTER SEVENTEEN

CHRISTMAS was approaching rapidly and so was the Christmas Entertainment at Drumburly School. Rhoda had looked for signs of nervous apprehension in Duggie, who was taking the part of Shylock in *The Merchant of Venice*, but Duggie seemed calm and confident.

"It was a job learning the words but I know them now," was all that Duggie would say upon the subject.

Rhoda had promised to go and to tell the truth she was looking forward to the entertainment with pleasure. This fact, when she realised it, surprised her a good deal. When she had lived in London she had often gone to an entertainment with less pleasurable anticipation. She could not help smiling to think what some of her friends would say if they could know her feelings: the sophisticated Charmian, or Buttons with his velvet jacket and long hair! How they would laugh if they knew she was setting forth to see *The Merchant of Venice* acted in a school gymnasium by village children and expecting to enjoy herself enormously!

Mamie was going, and of course Lizzie, for she was in the proud position of parent to Shylock. Mrs. Couper's Alice was playing Nerissa, so naturally Mrs. Couper would be there too.

" You'll get a good laugh anyhow," promised James as he saw Rhoda off in the little car which had replaced Blink.

" But I mustn't laugh," objected Rhoda. " That would be frightful. I think on the whole it would be better not to sit beside Mamie."

" Think of something sad," said James, smiling. He stood back and waved as she drove off.

The gymnasium was a large hall with a stage at one end; it was beautifully decorated with flags and greenery. Rhoda was early but already the seats were more than half-full and more people were streaming in every moment. As she looked round the hall it seemed to her that everybody in Drumburly had come to the entertainment, it was a social occasion of the first magnitude, and she had made a sartorial error to come in a plain coat and skirt with a plain felt hat; she should have put on her smartest garments. *Here* was Lady Shaw in a black cloth coat and a hat with feathers, *there* was the butcher's wife in a hat that looked like a flower garden; Mrs. Ogylvie Smith was dressed up to the nines as also was Miss Heddle. Rhoda saw Mrs. Flockhart (Flockie's sister-in-law) and Mrs. Couper and Lizzie . . . and there were quite a number of men as well, including Adam Forrester. In fact practically every person in Drumburly that Rhoda knew was here and, of course, very many more that she had never seen in her life.

Mamie had kept the seat beside her for Rhoda. " I had the greatest trouble to keep it for you," she said. " Several people came and sat down beside me but I was quite firm with them about it."

Naturally Rhoda had to take the seat. " But we mustn't laugh," she said.

" Laugh? " Mamie exclaimed. " It isn't funny. It's the one about that horrid old man who wants his pound of flesh."

" Yes," agreed Rhoda. Already she could feel bubbles of laughter rising inside her. This is going to be awful, she thought.

" I hope Alice will be all right," continued Mamie in anxious tones. " Mrs. Couper says Alice knows it thoroughly but of course she's very shy and she's rather apt to cry for no reason 'at all. If she forgets what she has to say and bursts into tears it will be dreadful."

" Yes," agreed Rhoda. She realised that the honour of Mureth was at stake, and she could not help wondering whether it would be a worse disgrace to Mureth if she were to burst out laughing or Alice were to burst into tears.

The entertainment opened with Christmas hymns in which the whole school took part. They were fine-looking children with rosy faces and well-brushed hair and there were so many of them that they were packed like sardines upon the little stage, but in spite of this they sang exceedingly well and with tremendous vigour.

When this part of the programme was over Mr. Greig, the headmaster, came forward and announced that " Scenes from *The Merchant of Venice* " would now follow. He explained that as it would have been somewhat ambitious to present the play in its entirety he had chosen those portions which would best display the remarkable talents of his pupils. He, himself, would fill the gaps between the scenes with explanations of what was happening, so that members of the audience who were unacquainted with this magnificent example of the work of the Bard of Avon would find no difficulty in following the story.

Everybody clapped enthusiastically.

Mr. Greig bowed and waited for silence before announcing that the first scene to be presented was a room in Portia's mansion. He then stepped back and catching his heel in the edge of the carpet which was part of the furnishing of Portia's boudoir, he stumbled and almost fell. Fortunately, however, he was an agile man and with a bound which would have done credit to an acrobat he managed to save himself and avert catastrophe.

The curtain descended and all the lights went out.

"It's a good thing he didn't fall," whispered a woman who was sitting behind Rhoda.

Her companion agreed. "My heart was in my mouth," she added solemnly.

Several minutes passed, minutes of darkness and silence, and then without any warning the curtain rose and disclosed the back view of a young man in plus-fours and a pink shirt with braces over his shoulders. He was standing in the middle of the stage holding a flower-pot in his arms. For a moment he seemed unaware of his predicament and then something seemed to warn him that he was the cynosure of several hundred eyes.

He looked round. "Jings!" he exclaimed and dived for the wings, flower-pot and all.

"That's Tommy Brown," whispered Mamie. "He's *such* a nice boy. I expect he's been helping them to arrange the scenery."

After the departure of Tommy Brown the stage was vacant for quite a long time and Rhoda had a feeling that the contretemps had upset the actors and that they were being soothed and encouraged and reassured—but perhaps she was wrong, for the actors, when at last they made their appearance, seemed undismayed.

Portia bounded on to the stage followed by the cringing Nerissa. "By my troth, Nerissa, my little body is aweary of this grreat wurrld," announced Portia in loud and cheerful tones. The play was on.

It was a very interesting performance, so Rhoda thought, and as she watched the well-known story unfold she wondered what Mr. William Shakespeare would have thought if he were a member of the audience. Would he have been annoyed at the liberties which had been taken with his work by Mr. Greig? Mr. Greig had taken a good many liberties; for not only had he left out scenes and strung the remainder together with explanations which sounded a little like a running commentary on a football match, but he had tampered with the script as well, cutting down any particularly long and difficult speeches and inserting lines of his own devising in their place. It was quite cleverly done, however; the story hung together and was intelligible, so perhaps Mr. Shakespeare would not have taken exception to the presentation.

The dresses and the scenery were amazing and except for the somewhat unfortunate start there were no long pauses nor curtain troubles. The acting was uneven; some of the children were exceedingly good and obviously enjoying themselves thoroughly, others were inconceivably bad and seemed to be suffering severely, but even the worst was word-perfect and required no prompting. Portia, a healthy young woman with quantities of curly auburn hair, rollicked through her part with tremendous gusto and swept the stolid Bassanio off his feet. Nerissa, who in private life was Alice Couper, trotted round after her mistress like Mary's little lamb and neither forgot her lines nor burst into floods of tears. Jessica was delightful, she was natural and unaffected and had a pretty voice . . . but the honours of the evening were undoubtedly Shylock's. The bent figure in the shabby black gown and the snow white wig was an extraordinarily convincing personality. Duggie did not shout like the other children, his voice was low but clearly audible and he played his part in an unusually sympathetic way. Here was no cringing coward or ranting villain but a dignified and pathetic old man, a man with mistaken ideals but justified in his own eyes for his vindictiveness.

Parts of the play were excruciatingly funny and Rhoda had difficulty in stifling her amusement, but now and again there was a magical feeling in the air and for a few moments you were lifted out of your surroundings and transported to medieval Venice by the master's hand. You were lifted and transported and then suddenly you came down with a thump and found yourself sitting in a crowded hall watching a group of children wading doggedly through a play whose inner meaning they could never understand. There was magic in the scene between Lorenzo and Jessica; they were so young, so grave, they were really beautiful. Sitting upon the traditional bank they made shy love to one another with the moonlight shining upon them. Will would have liked this, thought Rhoda, as she listened to the flow of lovely words . . .

And then suddenly the magic spell was broken and here was Portia again, as full of bounce as a tennis ball and evidently no whit fatigued by her efforts at the trial.

" That light we see is burning in my hall.

" How far that little candle throws his beams!

" So shines a good deed in a naughty wurrld," declared Portia archly.

" When the moon shone we did not see the candle," bleated her little lamb. The inane remark sounded more inane than ever.

CHAPTER EIGHTEEN

THE play was over, speeches and applause had followed and players and audience had joined in the singing of " God Save the King." Mamie and Rhoda were making their way slowly towards the door surrounded by the polite and unhurrying crowd. It was plain from the conversation which was going on all round them that the play had made a great impression upon the Drumburlians.

" It was real exciting," one woman declared. " When I heard it was to be Shakespeare this year I was in two minds about coming, but I'm glad I came."

" Aye, it was as good as the Pictures," agreed her companion.

" Ishbel made the whole thing," said another. " She's got wonderful spirit. I liked yon bit in the trial when she started sorting the Jew."

" Did you like that bit?" inquired another voice in surprise. " I didn't, then. I was vexed for the wee Jew, they were all up against him."

By this time Mamie and Rhoda had emerged into the passage and here they encountered Mrs. Ogylvie Smith.

" My dear!" she exclaimed, seizing Mamie's arm. " Was it not a gorgeous performance? For me, I would rather see those children than a circus and I look forward to Mr. Greig's entertainment from one year to the next. Now *you* know everyone, Mamie, so you must tell me who they are. First of all the zestful Portia who would have made a so much better Carmen, who is she?"

Hemmed into a draughty corner of the passage by the slowly moving crowd the two ladies discussed *The Merchant of Venice* —and Rhoda listened. She was surprised to discover that they both knew a great deal more about the play than herself. Mamie's somewhat fatuous remark at the beginning of the performance had led Rhoda to believe that she knew very little about it, but now it appeared that she knew it well. Most people, Rhoda had found, pretended to more knowledge than they possessed; not so Mamie. Perhaps this was due to the same strange feeling of diffidence which prevented her from using the right word even when it presented itself to her mind.

The conversation was prolonged. Most of the audience had gone and a chill wind blew in at the open door and whistled round their ankles, but neither of Rhoda's companions seemed to notice the draught, they were too interested in what they were saying.

Mrs. Ogylvie Smith let fall the information that she had seen Ellen Terry in the role of Portia when she was a child and had been bitterly disappointed because Portia was not young and beautiful and romantic as Portia should be.

" I for one would almost rather see it played with zest and

gaiety as it was to-day," added the extraordinary woman. "You know, my dear Mamie, it is the mediocre that I find *ennuyant*. The good and the bad entertain me vastly."

"You must have enjoyed yourself this afternoon," Mamie declared.

"And this is the woman who pretends to be stupid!" exclaimed Mrs. Ogylvie Smith, turning to Rhoda as she spoke. "There was good and bad to-day but no mediocre at all so I enjoyed myself . . . but now I am not enjoying myself; if we stand here much longer I shall turn into an icicle. We will go and have tea at the Shaw Arms. I am to meet Henry there and he will want to know all about it. You will come, Mamie, and perhaps your daughter-in-law as well?"

Mamie accepted the invitation and they went out to find their cars.

"Did you hear what she said?" whispered Mamie to Rhoda. "Of course it was just a slip of the tongue. She knows you aren't, really. I hope you don't mind."

"It seemed quite natural to me," Rhoda assured her.

"Oh, well," said Mamie somewhat incoherently. "I'm glad you don't mind. Of course it's lovely for me to—to think people think like that, and if she hadn't been thinking like that it wouldn't have slipped out, would it? But Caroline might be hurt if she knew—I mean she's James's mother, isn't she—so perhaps I ought to—to say something—or do you think that would make too much of it?"

"I should leave it," replied Rhoda, smiling at her earnestness. "Caroline will never know and nobody will be a penny the worse."

The Shaw Arms Hotel was run by Mrs. Simpson; she had been there for years and knew Mamie well so she welcomed the three ladies with delight and set a table for them before a roaring fire.

"This is very pleasant," declared Mrs. Ogylvie Smith, throwing off her furs. "We shall be comfortable now and the good Mrs. Simpson will give us of her best . . . and here is Henry to make our party complete! Henry, my dear, you have missed something worth seeing."

" I couldn't get away from Glasgow any sooner," said Henry as he smiled at Mamie and Rhoda and kissed his mother affectionately. " You must tell me about it instead. Did you all disgrace yourselves by laughing at the wrong moment? "

" There were moments when it was difficult not to," Rhoda admitted. " But there were moments of magic as well."

" How did our friend Duggie sustain the part of Shylock? "

" You know that boy! " exclaimed Mrs. Ogylvie Smith. " He did not *sustain* the part of Shylock, he *was* Shylock. He made us weep for Shylock and his sins. So dignified, he was, standing with his hands folded inside his sleeves and saying, ' Nay, take my life and all; pardon not that. You take my house when you do take the prop that doth sustain my house; you take my life when you do take the means whereby I live! ' "

There was a short silence.

" Yes, he understood what he was saying," said Mamie thoughtfully.

" It's strange, isn't it? " said Henry. " Strange that a child can understand that feeling—the feeling that life is useless without the prop that doth sustain the house. How does Duggie know what it feels like to be bereft suddenly of all that makes life worth while? "

It was obvious from the way he spoke that Henry knew what it felt like.

" Duggie can't know," said Mamie.

" He could not have said it so beautifully if he had not experienced it," objected Mrs. Ogylvie Smith.

" People can, you know," said her son, stirring his tea thoughtfully. " Certain people have the gift of understanding an emotion they haven't experienced. The gift is compounded of sympathy and imagination and a dash of something very mysterious which some people call genius."

" He is a genius, this Duggie? "

Henry looked across the table at Rhoda, waiting for her to reply.

" I don't like the term," said Rhoda frankly. " It's too loosely used nowadays when everybody who has the smallest talent or is out of the ordinary in any way is immediately hailed as a genius; but when you come down to brass tacks what are you to call the Mysterious Something? Duggie has it, I'm sure of that. It shows itself in his painting."

" Yes," said Henry. " I'm sure of it, too."

" We have heard a great deal about this Duggie, but still we do not know who he is," complained Mrs. Ogylvie Smith.

" You're the only person who doesn't know, Mother," returned Henry with a smile. " This Duggie is the son of Mamie's cook, he is also the devoted *chela* of Rhoda. He draws her back view when she isn't looking because he says her face is too beautiful. Nobody could do it, he says."

" He has discernment," nodded Mrs. Ogylvie Smith. " I think I should like to meet this son of Mamie's cook."

" It's strange," said Henry reflectively. " I always have a feeling that Duggie is *like* somebody, but I can't think who it is."

" You do not know? " asked Mrs. Ogylvie Smith in surprised accents. " I can tell you that quite easily. The moment I saw Shylock I realised that he was like me."

Her three companions laughed.

" You are very rude indeed," said Mrs. Ogylvie Smith when she could make herself heard. " I cannot imagine why people should laugh when I speak no more than the truth. When I said I could not walk as far as Boscath, Henry laughed, and now when I say I am like Shylock you are all very much amused. But I am kind enough to make allowances, for none of you has seen me when I have just washed my hair—naturally I do not appear in public in that condition—but I can assure you that when I have washed my hair and it hangs about my face, shaggy and white, I bear a very strong resemblance to Shylock."

Her companions laughed again and laughed so heartily that she was obliged to laugh with them.

Mrs. Ogylvie Smith was in tremendous form and it was with regret that at last Mamie rose and broke up the party.

" I really must go," she said. " Jock will think I'm lost."

" That will be good for Jock," said Mrs. Ogylvie Smith cheerfully. " It is good for husbands to feel anxiety about their wives; not too often but just occasionally. Do not forget that little piece of wisdom, dear Rhoda," she added as she kissed her young friend good-bye.

CHAPTER NINETEEN

IT was not often that Adam Forrester got a whole free day, for Doctor Black suffered from rheumatism and was unfit for much work, but two days before Christmas he suddenly decided that his assistant had earned a holiday and chased him out of the surgery forthwith.

" Away with you," said Doctor Black. " You work too hard. You're making an idler of me."

Adam and Nan decided to visit Boscath. They could send no message of course, but the terms of their friendship with the Dering Johnstones made this unnecessary. Adam fetched the car while Nan completed her household duties in a perfunctory manner and they set off without more ado. The ground was hard with frost and slippery in parts but this inconvenience was off-set by the fact that the boggy part of the road was frozen. Adam negotiated it carefully and despite some slides and slithers they arrived safely at Boscath Farm.

James was just coming home to lunch, he waved wildly and hastened his steps; Rhoda, hearing the car, ran out to greet the unexpected guests and assure them of their welcome.

" You know," said Rhoda as they sat down to lunch. " I've

just discovered an *advantage* in having no telephone. If we were on the telephone you'd have rung up and said, May we come? and it wouldn't have been nearly such a lovely surprise."

They discussed various matters at lunch, amongst them *The Merchant of Venice*. Adam and Nan had both been present at the entertainment (Nan behind the scenes helping to dress the actors), so there was quite a lot to be said about it.

" The wig was most effective," declared Rhoda.

" That wig! " cried Nan, laughing. " What an awful job it was! I tried all sorts of ways of doing it and eventually I got a piece of canvas and made it to fit Duggie's head and then covered it with white fluffy wool—the kind you use for babies' jackets—pulling it through and leaving the ends hanging. It really is a work of art, though I sez it as shouldn't! You must get Duggie to show it to you."

" He's got it, has he? " said Rhoda.

" Oh, yes, he's got it," Nan replied. " Mr. Greig wanted to keep it in his chest of theatrical properties in case they should want it next year (his ambitions are soaring and he contemplates a production of *King Lear* by William Shakespeare and Thomas Greig), but Duggie absolutely refused to part with the wig and I'm afraid I backed him up."

" You coached him, didn't you? " said Rhoda.

" A little," replied Nan. " He didn't need much coaching. As a matter of fact there was a good deal of unpleasantness over Duggie's rendering of Shylock. Mr. Greig wanted it played quite differently and if there had been anybody else in the school who could have learnt the lines Duggie would have got thrown out on his ear. Fortunately there was nobody else, so the producer had to put up with Duggie and make the best of it."

" I wish I'd seen it," James said. " I shall make a point of seeing Lear. That ought to be even funnier."

After lunch the party divided and the two young men set off for a walk over the hill. James wanted to have a look at his sheep and Adam had evinced a desire to accompany him.

The day was grey and bleak, the glass had fallen and a thin chill breeze rustled through the heather, but in spite of the cold and the overcast skies Adam was enjoying the walk.

"This is your work," he said, and something in his voice told James that Adam felt slightly envious.

"Yes," agreed James. "It's grand country, isn't it? Sometimes it's bleak and hard and cold—like to-day, for instance—but working for it is a man's job. You're working for it, too, in your different way."

"I know," agreed Adam. "I feel the same about it, but sometimes I wish . . ."

"What do you wish?" asked James.

"Impossibilities," smiled Adam. "You can't have everything, can you?"

James felt that he had everything (sometimes he felt quite frightened when he thought of his good fortune and of all the blessings which had been heaped on his head), but his happiness had not blunted his sensitive feelings and after a moment's thought he said tentatively, "I dare say you'd like somebody of your own ilk to talk to."

"Yes," replied Adam, looking at his friend in surprise. "Yes, how did you know? When I was in the hospital there was far too much 'shop'; we talked about our cases interminably and I must say one got very tired of it, but of course if one were worried about a case it was a relief to discuss it and perhaps get someone else to give an opinion. Here, it's the other extreme. There isn't a creature who knows the first thing about medicine (except of course Doctor Black who, to be perfectly honest, is a little behind the times). Here, there is literally nobody to talk to about one's cases: interesting cases, worrying cases or cases that don't yield to treatment. If only there were somebody who understood, or knew the difference between a tibia and a fibula!" Adam laughed and added, "But don't listen to me, James. I'm an ungrateful pig. I've got Nan and I've got a home and I've got work which I love and which brings us enough to eat."

They had reached the dyke by this time. James sat down in its shelter and filled his pipe. He understood exactly what Adam's feelings were and felt inclined to say, " Why not try me? "—and this, not only for Adam's sake, but because he liked Adam immensely—but as he did not know the difference between a tibia and a fibula perhaps it would not be much good. He said reflectively, " I felt the same at first after leaving the army, you know. I was often bored stiff with the mess and all the ' shop ' but afterwards I missed it. I missed the companionship and the free and easy talk and, of course, I see it would be worse for you because you doctors are more specialised."

Adam sat down beside him and they looked at the view spread before them: the hills, the river, the little clusters of trees, and for a few minutes there was silence.

" Don't get it wrong," said Adam after a bit. " Don't think I'm regretting the fact that I chucked the post in London and came to Drumburly. I've never regretted it for a moment. The fact is I'm a Scot and, anywhere else on the face of the globe, I'm an exile. Sometimes when I was in London, surrounded by piles of bricks and mortar, I used to feel quite sick with longing to see a hill . . . a nice bald-faced, lowland hill with sheep upon it. I'd think of little bits of country that I knew: of a grey road zigzagging up the side of a brae or a burn running in links through a green moss with wild flowers growing beside it. I'd see a huddle of hills with a gap between them and, through the gap, another hill, far off and blue with distance. I'd smell the sharp tang of bog-myrtle or a whiff of peat smoke . . . and all this in a London street! " He smiled apologetically and added, " I'd rather be a pauper here than a Dives in any other place."

" It seems to me you're a poet, whatever else you are," said James.

Meanwhile Rhoda and Nan were having quite a different sort of talk, they settled themselves beside the fire and congratulated themselves on the fact that they need not go out in the cold. Rhoda produced a basket of darning and Nan insisted on helping with the task of mending the holes in James's socks. They worked away together in complete harmony.

" I suppose you're going to the party at Drumburly Tower? " asked Nan.

Rhoda nodded. " It will be fun, won't it? I haven't danced for ages, in fact I believe I've forgotten how. We're going to spend the night, or what remains of the night at Mureth." She pulled out another sock and displayed an enormous hole in the heel. " Look at that! " she exclaimed. " It's because he walks such miles, poor darling! And I've been so busy lately that I've let them pile up. When I'm really excited about my work I simply can't stop and mend socks and stockings."

" A new picture? " Nan asked.

" Yes, and it's going to be good," said Rhoda happily.

" Tell me about it. Is it a portrait or what? "

" It's a portrait."

" Somebody I know? "

" Yes, I think so," said Rhoda mysteriously. It was natural to assume that Nan had met her brother's friend.

Of course Nan wanted to see the portrait and as Rhoda was quite willing to show it to her they put the mending aside and went up to the studio together.

" There it is," said Rhoda. " It isn't finished of course, because he had to go back to Glasgow; but I've managed to do a good deal without him. One more sitting should finish it. You know him, don't you? "

She stopped, waiting for Nan's comment, but Nan was completely silent, staring at the portrait in a dazed sort of way. All the colour had drained out of her face leaving it haggard and wan. She put out her hand, groping for support.

" Nan! " cried Rhoda in alarm and she put her arm round her friend's waist and guided her to a chair.

" It's all right," said Nan shakily. " Don't worry—I shall be all right in a minute. It was just—just seeing him suddenly. I didn't know—you never said."

" I'm terribly sorry. It was idiotic of me," Rhoda declared.

" It's all right," repeated Nan. " I don't know why I was so silly. It's all over long ago. It's just—he's the man—the man I told you about."

Rhoda knew this already. She had known the moment she had seen Nan's stricken face. It was Henry who had been " not really engaged " to Nan and then had changed his mind . . . but she could hardly believe it! Henry was not like that.

" I'm sorry," Rhoda repeated. " I might have guessed."

" How could you possibly? " said Nan. " It was my fault for telling you a little bit and then stopping. I'd like to tell you it all if it wouldn't bore you."

" Of course you must tell me, but let's go downstairs to the fire."

Nan had recovered now. She went and looked at the portrait again before following Rhoda out of the studio. " I didn't tell you how good I thought it was," said Nan. " But perhaps that wasn't necessary. Do people often pass out on being shown one of your pictures? "

" Oh, frequently," declared Rhoda, taking her arm and dragging her away. " As a matter of fact one of my pictures had to be removed from the walls of Burlington House, because——"

" Rhoda! "

" Not everybody was affected, of course," continued Rhoda, with complete gravity as she piloted her friend downstairs. " Only very sensitive people were affected (as you know many people have skins like rhinoceri), but a few were so deeply moved that an extraordinary meeting of the committee was convened. A deputation, headed by Sir Alfred Munnings, called upon me and asked permission to remove the picture. Of course I was obliged to consent and the picture was taken from the walls and replaced by a reproduction of Landseer's ' Stag at Bay ' which, although affecting to members of the Society for the Prevention of Cruelty to Animals, was less painful to other members of the public."

By this time Nan was giggling helplessly and allowed herself to be led into the sitting-room and placed in a chair by the fire and, as Flockie had prepared tea in their absence, her restoration was completed by a cup of that cheering beverage and an ambrosial oven scone.

" I'd like to tell you," said Nan after a little. " You know most of it already of course and you've probably guessed a good deal. You know that he was in charge of the hospital in London and Adam was one of his assistants. Everybody in the hospital admired him; he really is brilliant. He was known as ' H.O.' Everybody called him H.O., some to his face and others behind his back."

" Rather neat! I always liked H.O. in the Would-be-Good Stories," said Rhoda nodding.

" Adam had to live in the hospital and I had to live in the school where I was assistant matron, so we didn't see very much of each other but we always met on Sundays. Adam used to talk a lot about H.O., how marvellous he was and what a brilliant diagnostician he was. Adam always used to say what wonderful hands he had. As a matter of fact I got quite tired of listening to Adam singing his praises and was quite prepared to dislike the paragon. But I didn't dislike him." She sighed and then continued: " One Sunday Adam and I had arranged to go for an expedition to Virginia Water. It was one of our favourite expeditions and I was rather annoyed when Adam rang up and said H.O. was coming with us. Well, he came and—and I liked him. After that he often came with us and we went to all sorts of places, the three of us together, and we had all sorts of funny little adventures. We talked a lot. He felt he could be natural with us and I think it was a relief to him, he had to be very proper and sedate in the hospital. He asked us to call him Henry and we did when we were alone with him or at least I always did (Adam found it difficult for he had always called him H.O.). He talked about his home at Drumburly and about the hills and the river and how beautiful they were.

" Adam and I love the country too. We had always said that some day we would go back to Scotland and make a home together, it was a sort of dream. We used to say, ' When we have out little house we'll have a green gate,' and Henry used to laugh at us. Then one day he heard from his mother that Doctor Black at Drumburly was looking for an assistant and he said to Adam, ' There's your chance, Adam. What about it? ' He said it in fun but Adam jumped at it. Adam was madly keen. This was what he had always talked of, hoped for, prayed for. I must give up my post at the school and come and keep house for him. We should have a home—a real home at last. If it hadn't been for Henry I would have been wildly happy because I had always wanted a home and wanted it just as much as Adam."

" But there *was* Henry," nodded Rhoda understandingly.

" Yes, and I could see he was far from keen on the idea. He had said it in fun and now he wished he hadn't. For one thing he didn't want to lose Adam, and for another thing . . . there was me. One Sunday Adam had to be in hospital so Henry and I went to Kew together and walked round the gardens. It was a cold, horrible day, but it didn't seem to matter. It was that day I knew for certain—or thought I knew— that Henry wanted to marry me. He didn't say anything definite, because every now and then it rained and we had to shelter in the hothouses which were packed with other people sheltering from the rain . . . and coming home in the bus it was crowded too."

Nan stopped and made a little helpless gesture with her hands. " I didn't know what to do," she said. " I couldn't say anything to Adam and yet I felt I ought to. How could Adam go to Drumburly alone? Goodness, how I worried! It just shows how silly it is—to worry," added Nan in a shaky voice. " As it was I needn't have worried."

Rhoda leant forward and patted her knee.

" That's all, really," said Nan. " At least it's nearly all. While I was still wondering what I should do Henry went away for a long week-end and when he came back he was quite different. He made it obvious that he had changed his mind. He had seen Doctor Black and spoken to him about Adam, and if Adam really wanted the post it was his. There was a house too, Henry said, a tiny house in the High Street which he thought would be the very thing for Adam and me ... and then he laughed and added that unfortunately the gate was brown but a pot of paint would soon put that right."

" Nan! " exclaimed Rhoda.

" It's all right," Nan said. " Don't worry. I suppose I was silly. Probably I imagined the whole thing. At any rate it's all over now and I'm quite happy with Adam ... very happy with Adam," added Nan emphatically.

CHAPTER TWENTY

THE sheep-farmer is always busy, first with one thing and then with another. Roy was doing well now and taking an interest in his work but he could not be expected to do all the work himself and James took it in turn with him to walk round the hills. The tups which James had bought at the Lockerbie Sales had been running with the ewes since the end of November and while they were out on the hills they had to be watched and herded and kept from straying. The ewes were divided into groups (to every forty or fifty ewes there was a tup) and this meant that James or Roy must walk round the hirsel at least once a day to make sure that all was well.

It was impossible to do this kind of work without a dog and Dan had managed to get one for them; he was a shaggy friendly creature who answered to the name of Shad. Shad was no beauty, and he was not as good a sheep-dog as Gyp, but he was improving and James was quite pleased with him.

Sometimes Rhoda went up the hill with James and they

took their lunch and had it together in the shelter of a boulder. Then James would go on, round the great bulk of Crowthorne Hill and Winterfell and Rhoda would amuse herself sketching until he picked her up on his way home. Rhoda enjoyed these outings, she enjoyed walking over the hill in James's company.

" I'm going round the hill to-day," said James one morning at breakfast. " It's too cold for you, I'm afraid. You can't sit and sketch, you'd be frozen."

" I'll come part of the way and then come back," replied Rhoda who was unwilling to forgo her walk.

They set out together with Shad bounding along beside them. It was certainly very cold but there was not a breath of wind; the sky above the hill-tops was pale and misty. There had been frost in the night and the film of it was silver-grey upon the withered heather and the rushes, and upon every blade of grass. The pools in the river were smoking delicately in the morning sun. James and Rhoda took the track to the hills, walking shoulder to shoulder. The sun was in their eyes as they went, it had risen from behind Crowthorne Hill like an orange ball but gradually it gained in power and the mists that swathed its rising were disappearing, evaporating in its rays.

" It *is* lovely," Rhoda said, with a sigh. " The funny thing about this place is that although it's freezing it doesn't make one cold. It's quite different from a town. In London when it's cold and frosty the chill goes right through to one's marrow. I'm almost too hot."

" Dry hill air and no wind."

" Yes, I suppose that's the answer."

They walked on and presently came to a stone dyke with a gate in it. James had had the gate mended; he opened it for Rhoda to go through and, as he did so, looked at it with pride.

" Yes, it's right sorted," said Rhoda, laughing at him.

James laughed too, and then suddenly was grave. " Rhoda," he said. " It's all right now, isn't it?"

" All right? "

" Don't pretend," James said. " I've known all along it was a risk but I just had to take it. At first I thought it wasn't going to work out, but now I think it is."

" Goodness! I had no idea you had noticed! "

" You had no idea I had noticed! " echoed James. " That's dashed funny! That's the funniest thing I've heard for a long time. You had no idea I noticed that you were homesick and miserable and couldn't paint! "

" You never said anything."

" I'm not a *complete* fool," declared James.

" No," agreed Rhoda, looking at him in affectionate surprise. " No, you certainly are not."

" Oh, well," said James deprecatingly. " If you love someone frightfully much that helps you to understand them . . . and of course I knew it was a risk. It's such an entirely different life—but it's going to be all right, isn't it? "

" Right as rain," Rhoda told him. " Though why rain should be right I can't imagine. It *was* a bit lonely at first, and the days seemed awfully long and empty, but now my life is filling up nicely, thank you."

" Good," said James nodding.

" Yes, I'm getting quite used to it. I've even got used to being without a telephone. Believe it or not that was one of the most difficult things to get used to. *How* many times did I leap from my chair with the intention of ringing up Mamie and asking her to come over, or ringing up the grocer for biscuits or the greengrocer for lemons only to sink back— frustrated! "

She spoke lightly but James knew it was true. He knew that quite often it is the small things which are most difficult to bear.

" I wish——" began James.

" Don't wish," laughed Rhoda. " It's all right. The wild bird is tamed. The bird knows she's lucky and she's as happy as a lark."

"All the same I *do* wish we were not quite so isolated. I can't help wondering what I should do if you were ill."

"Ill! I'm never ill ... but if the unlikely happened you could pop over to Mureth and ring up Adam."

"Yes I could," agreed James. Unless the river was in flood."

"James, don't be silly," Rhoda adjured him. "What did people do before telephones were invented? If the worst came to the worst you could take the car and go and fetch Adam, couldn't you? But the whole thing is simply absurd because I never felt better in my life."

"That's all right, then," said James· but he said it without enthusiasm for the fact was he had been worrying a good deal, and was still worrying, not only about the river but about the road.

One of the chief hazards of the daft road was a piece of boggy ground where it descended into a small valley between two hills. Jock Johnstone had poured many a cart-load of road metal into its maw, but any improvement was merely temporary. The recent rains had loosened some ground on the side of the hill and this had occasioned a small landslide which was gradually converting the piece of boggy ground into a veritable bog. James had been to look at the place several times and had consulted Roy and Wanlock as to whether anything could be done, if not to improve the conditions at least to prevent them from worsening, but the men had worked upon the road before and were thoroughly disgruntled with it.

"The only thing to do with the daft road is to remake the whole thing," Wanlock had said. Roy had nodded and agreed.

The road was still passable to motor traffic if one were extremely careful but soon it would not be, for the bog was increasing in area with every storm of rain. Soon the only means of communication with the outside world, in the event of the river rising, would be by means of the Land Rover which could climb the shoulder of the hill and make a wide détour across the moor. James had bought the Land Rover quite recently and was finding it exceedingly useful on the farm; in fact he had begun to wonder how he had managed to run the farm without it, but of course if the Land Rover were used for other purposes it would not be available for work at Boscath— even a Land Rover could not be in two places at once.

"Goodness, James, what a long face for a lovely day!" Rhoda exclaimed.

"I know," said James, trying to smile. "I'm just wondering what's going to happen when the daft road disappears into the bog. We'll be more isolated than ever. You won't be able to use the car at all."

"I still have the use of my legs," said Rhoda, smiling. "And I've got you, which is all that really matters. Listen, James, —you once quoted poetry to me—it was Browning, wasn't it? and now I'm going to retaliate with Tennyson." She stood a little above him on the hill, with the morning sunshine making a halo of her golden hair, and began a trifle shyly:

> "*And on her lover's arm she leant*
> *And round her waist she felt it fold,*
> *And far across the hills they went*
> *In that new life which is the old:*
> "*Across the hills and far away*
> *Beyond their utmost purple rim*
> *And deep into the dying day*
> *The happy princess followed him.*"

There was silence when she had finished. James could not speak. He put his arm round her waist and tightened it and they walked on together.

CHAPTER TWENTY-ONE

THE Shaws of Drumburly Tower often entertained people to lunch or tea but Sir Andrew and Lady Shaw were both indefatigable in social duties and were too busy to be bothered with parties of which the object was pleasure and pleasure alone.

For once, however, they had broken their rule and having decided to give a dinner and a dance it was natural that a brilliant organiser (as her ladyship undoubtedly was) should spare no trouble nor pains to make the affair a success. Sir Andrew took little interest in the arrangements. He stipulated that his study be locked and that he should keep the key and having received a promise that this should be so he dismissed the affair from his mind. Fortunately Lady Shaw had other helpers: her niece, Holly Douglas, for whom the party was being given; her son, Ian, who was reading for a degree in Agriculture at Edinburgh University; and her daughter, Eleanor, who was just fifteen and was home for the holidays after her first term at boarding-school.

The old Tower of Drumburly was a square peel-tower with walls five feet thick and although it still stood solidly upon the hill above the town it was not used by its owners as a residence. Near the old tower was a large comfortable house which had been built at the beginning of the nineteenth century by Sir Andrew's great-grandfather. It was here that the Shaws lived and, considering the austerity of the times, they lived in reasonable comfort.

Lady Shaw would have liked to give a party in the grand manner and ask all her guests to dinner and to dance but this was impossible, not only because she could not obtain sufficient food for over a hundred people, but also because she had not sufficient staff to serve them. It was a little difficult to decide which of her friends should be asked to dinner and which merely to dance, but the difficulty had to be solved and after some careful thought the invitations were written. Amongst the favoured few were the Johnstones of Mureth and their nephew and his wife; the young couple because they were so newly married (and brides are always fêted), the older couple for the simple reason that Lady Shaw was extremely fond of Mamie Johnstone. Lady Shaw had always liked Mamie and liked her all the more because upon one never-to-be-forgotten occasion Mamie had spoken her mind without fear or favour and given her ladyship a serious shock. The Ogylvie Smiths were invited too—chiefly on Henry's account—and these guests, together with friends of the young Shaws who were staying in the house, made up the dinner-party.

The Mureth car was the first to arrive and, as it drove up to the steps, the big door of Drumburly House was flung open and Sir Andrew appeared outlined against the brilliant light of the hall. He had taken no part in the preparations but he enjoyed making a gesture and had decided to welcome his guests with old-fashioned hospitality at the threshold of his house. The Ogylvie Smiths were close behind, they had come in Henry's car (whether this was because Blaikie had refused to bring them in the Daimler or for some other reason they alone knew). They all crowded up the steps and into the hall together, talking and laughing and exchanging greetings with their host.

"We have not met before," said Sir Andrew as he shook hands with the bride. "I have heard a great deal about you, Mrs. Dering Johnstone, and I have been looking forward to meeting you, not only because we are to be neighbours and good ones I hope, but also because I am told you are interested in pictures."

Rhoda murmured something suitable in reply.

"My Raeburn," said Sir Andrew, waving his hand towards a picture which hung above the big fire-place in the hall. "A portrait of my great-aunt, Mary Shaw, painted by the master in the year eighteen twelve when he was at his zenith."

Rhoda looked at the picture with interest and was about to say something about it but Mrs. Ogylvie Smith was before her.

"How fortunate you are to be the possessor of such a treasure, Sir Andrew!" she exclaimed. "Not only so valuable but so interesting as a family relic. She must have been a very beautiful woman, your great-aunt."

"She had the family features," agreed Sir Andrew. He stuck a monocle in his eye and regarded the picture complacently.

No more was said for by this time Lady Shaw had appeared and the three ladies who had just arrived were herded upstairs to remove their wraps and to powder their noses.

Rhoda was wearing her wedding-dress; it was a picture frock of soft, cream satin and Honiton lace.

"But how beautiful!" cried Mrs. Ogylvie Smith, looking at her in admiration. "And how right to wear no jewels—no jewels at all!"

"You're beautiful yourself," replied Rhoda, kissing her admirer lightly on the cheek; and this was by no means an empty compliment.

"Tush!" exclaimed the lady, laughing. "It is my mantilla you admire, and my diamonds and the red rose in my corsage. You need no jewels, Rhoda, and no colour in your gown to make your eyes more brilliant."

"When you have finished admiring each other——" began Mamie.

"Ah, here is one who is jealous!" cried Mrs. Ogylvie Smith. "Look, Rhoda, nobody has kissed dear Mamie and told her how beautiful she is! But Mamie is always beautiful, the soul shines through her face, and whether she is attired for gardening in her butcher's apron and a ragged skirt—as I have often seen her—or dressed for a ball at Drumburly House makes no matter," and so saying she slipped her hand through Mamie's arm and they all went downstairs to join the rest of the party.

The long dinner-table was glittering with silver and glass. It was decorated with sprays of holly, the dark green leaves and scarlet berries lightly powdered with crystal flakes to resemble snow. Rhoda found herself sitting at her host's right hand, an honour which was her due as a bride but one which she would have forgone very willingly. On her other side was a somewhat uninteresting young man, a friend of Ian Shaw's, and beyond him was Eleanor.

Rhoda had heard about Eleanor from James and was aware that Eleanor had rather a poor time of it and was seldom allowed to take part in festivities . . . but here she was to-night, looking very happy indeed. James had said she was like a fairy and Rhoda decided that the description was apt. She had fair straight hair, so fair that it was almost silver, and her large grey eyes and slender neck gave her an other-worldly look. Rhoda smiled at her and Eleanor smiled in return, it was a shy and rather appealing smile as if the child were anxious for Rhoda to like her. She's a darling, Rhoda thought. I must talk to her later. There was certainly no chance of talking to her at present for Sir Andrew was a demanding man and required the full attention of his dinner-partner. Presently however he ceased talking and putting his monocle carefully into his eye he leant forward and transfixed his daughter with a piercing stare.

" Eleanor," said Sir Andrew in strident tones. " What have you done to your mouth? "

He spoke so loudly that everybody stopped talking and, as was perfectly natural, gazed at Eleanor in alarm.

" It looks to me," continued Sir Andrew. " It looks to me as if you had *painted* your mouth with some sort of red material."

" Lip-stick, that's all," said Eleanor in a very small shaky voice. She looked down at her plate as she spoke and her fair silky hair fell forward like wings, hiding her cheeks.

" Lip-stick! " said Sir Andrew in disgusted accents. " Lip-stick! A girl of your age! Where did you get the stuff? "

Eleanor did not reply.

" Where did you get the stuff? " he repeated loudly.

" Really, Uncle Andrew! " exclaimed Holly who was sitting at the other side of the table. " What a fuss to make about nothing. I did Eleanor's mouth if you must know. Of course she's too young to use lip-stick regularly, but I thought it wouldn't matter for a party."

" I object to it strongly," declared Sir Andrew. " Kindly wash your mouth thoroughly after dinner, Eleanor."

" Perhaps you would like me to wash mine, too? " inquired Holly meekly.

Everybody laughed, a trifle uncomfortably, and began to talk again. The incident was over. The subject was closed. Sir Andrew, for once, was speechless.

Rhoda discovered herself shaking all over; her thoughts a turmoil of anger and pity and amazement. She was furious with Sir Andrew (literally furious, for if there was one thing she abhorred it was a bully), she pitied Eleanor from the bottom of her heart and she was amazed at Holly's courage. Yes, Holly had come out of it very well, thought Rhoda, glancing at that extremely attractive and soignée young woman with feelings very different from any she had entertained before.

Thinking thus, Rhoda lost track of her host's conversation —it was a bad habit of hers—but fortunately it did not matter very much for when at last she felt able to listen she discovered that he was reminiscing complacently about his experiences in the First World War in which, according to himself, he had taken a not inglorious part.

" But of course there were amusing incidents as well," Sir Andrew was saying. " Incidents which, though not amusing at the time, are amusing in retrospect. I remember one in particular, we had been through hell—yes, literally through hell," declared Sir Andrew, " and we had been sent back to a rest camp to recover from our experience. One morning we were told that a General was coming to inspect us, a very important personage and well known throughout the army as

a martinet. The guns were camouflaged of course, so there was
little to be done in the way of spit and polish but we did what
we could to smarten ourselves up for the occasion and I must
say that considering what we had come through so recently
the turn out was very creditable indeed. The General arrived
with military punctuality and we young officers were presented
to him. Then it was time for the inspection. He looked at the
turn-out in a cursory manner and without remark, and then
he went forward to one of the guns and signed to the crew to
open the limber." Sir Andrew paused dramatically. "What
do you think he found?"

"A pair of old socks," said Rhoda without a moment's
hesitation.

Sir Andrew gazed at her in amazement. "How did you
know?"

"It's always old socks," explained Rhoda in matter-of-fact
tones. "Gunners go all over the world (here, there and every-
where, ' Ubique ' and all that) and wherever they go the same
thing happens. It happens at Malta and on Salisbury Plain, it
used to happen at Lucknow: the same old thing; spit and
polish, inspecting General, old socks! I should think he must
be getting awfully tired of it. Why don't they put something
different in the limber for him to find?" Rhoda raised her
extremely beautiful blue eyes to Sir Andrew's face with an
expression of innocent inquiry. She was punishing him, but
of course he would not realise that. Would he be angry, she
wondered.

"My dear young lady, they don't *put* them there——" he
began.

It was almost too good to be true. Rhoda had the greatest
difficulty to maintain her gravity, but somehow or other she
managed it. "Somebody must put them there," she pointed
out. "Of course I don't know what ought to be in a limber
(I'm not even very sure what a limber is), but if the right things
were put there, just for a change, it would give the General
such a nice surprise . . . or perhaps it wouldn't," she added

thoughtfully. "Perhaps he likes to have something to grouse about."

"Er—um——" began Sir Andrew. He was assailed by the suspicion that the dear young lady was pulling his leg.

"Or if not the right thing at least something *different*," suggested Rhoda. "Supposing he opened the limber and found—and found a lemon?"

Sir Andrew was sure now. She was pulling his leg, but she was so young and pretty that he could not feel as angry with her as she deserved. He was annoyed of course, but not really angry. "You're very clever, Mrs. Dering Johnstone," he said.

Rhoda smiled. "It was naughty of me, wasn't it? It's nice of you not to be cross. There's another thing I'm going to be rather naughty about and I hope you won't be cross with me about that, either."

He looked at her in surprise.

"Later," said Rhoda, rising in obedience to a signal from her hostess. "It's a secret."

CHAPTER TWENTY-TWO

JAMES had had rather a miserable time of it at dinner, he had been sitting between two girls neither of whom he had seen before and, although this fact in itself need not have made him miserable, the facts that they knew one another intimately, had not seen one another for some time and were both crazy about hockey made James's position uncomfortable in the extreme. Reasonable conversation was out of the question, all James could do was to sit back as far as possible—consistent with the consumption of turkey and plum pudding and other seasonable delicacies provided by Lady Shaw—and allow the sweet young things to converse across his chest. He had heard Sir Andrew's devastating remarks, everybody at the table had heard them, and he had felt extremely sorry for Eleanor; he had also felt extremely anxious about his wife. Knowing his wife, and being aware of her usual fierce reaction to anything approaching cruelty to the weak, James half expected to see her rise from her chair and hit Sir Andrew upon the head or to take some other means of showing displeasure. In some ways James would not have minded for Sir Andrew deserved punishment (James himself would have given a lot to hit Sir Andrew on the head), but in other ways it would have been regrettable. The affair might have had serious repercussions and at the very least would have been an unconventional beginning to his wife's collocation in the county.

Thank goodness the incident had passed without the half-expected assault taking place! But still James was not entirely comfortable about his wife; her eyes were unusually brilliant and her cheeks were unusually pink and although he could not hear what she was saying to Sir Andrew it was obvious that she was saying a good deal. This in itself was alarming, for whenever James had tried to converse with Sir Andrew he had found little opportunity to get a word in. Sir Andrew talked and other people listened, that was the usual form, and if people showed any disinclination to attend to what he was saying he raised his voice until they were obliged to attend. James drew a breath of pure relief when the signal for the departure of the ladies brought the conversation to an end and removed his wife from danger.

The gentlemen did not linger over their wine for Lady Shaw had told them not to; they finished it up quickly and emerged into the hall.

James had thought it might be a trifle embarrassing to meet Holly (he had not seen her to speak to since his marriage) but it was not embarrassing at all. They met face to face in the door-way of the drawing-room which had been emptied of all its unnecessary furniture and prepared for dancing.

" Hallo, James! " said Holly, smiling at him in the friendliest way imaginable.

" Hallo, Holly! " said James. He smiled back and added, " I see you haven't washed your mouth."

" The kid hasn't either," replied Holly, laughing. " As a matter of fact I advised her to, in case she got sent to bed, but she's full of spunk."

James nodded. He knew this was true.

" You know, James, I like the kid," said Holly as if this were a matter for surprise. " Anybody else would have been crushed into imbecility long ago, but you can't crush Eleanor—or at least Uncle Andrew can't. It was a pretty exhibition wasn't it? We have them daily, of course, but it must be a bit staggering for people who aren't used to them."

" Yes," agreed James whole-heartedly.

They chatted a little and, while they chatted, more guests arrived and the big room with its shining polished floor began to fill up rapidly.

" Look here, Holly, can I have a dance? " asked James.

" You can have this if you like," replied Holly. " They're going to begin in a minute; there's Uncle Andrew speaking to the band."

Having pledged himself to open the ball with Holly, he asked for some other dances as well and was given two, later on in the evening. This was good, thought James, as he wrote them down on his programme. It meant that Holly bore him no grudge and was willing to let bygones be bygones.

By this time the Forresters had arrived. James, looking round, found Adam at his elbow and as he happened to know that Adam and Holly had never been introduced to one another he proceeded to introduce them.

" This is Adam Forrester," said James in cheerful tones. " I don't think you've met him, Holly. He's the fellow to send for when you've got a pain in your tummy. Adam, this is Miss Douglas."

" I never have a pain in my tummy," declared Holly, laughing gaily.

It was now Adam's turn to speak but he said nothing and

James, looking at him in surprise, saw him standing perfectly still with his eyes fixed upon Holly in a vague stare. James felt quite embarrassed for his friend, he had had no idea that Adam was shy, but shy he was—indeed he seemed to have lost all sense of social expediency. Why couldn't the fellow say something? Why didn't he ask Holly for a dance? Holly would think it so odd . . . standing there like a stuffed owl with that silly expression on his face!

But apparently Holly did not think it odd. Holly laid her hand on Adam's arm. "Let's dance, shall we?" she said confidingly.

They moved away together and James was left. It was his turn to look like a stuffed owl.

"That's how it's done," said Rhoda's voice in his ear.

"What?" asked James in bewilderment. "I mean—I mean she said she would dance this with me. I mean——"

"But then she thought she would rather dance with Adam," explained Rhoda. "That's all there is to it, you poor sap! You've seen a very neat piece of work and you'll see some more before the evening's over. She'll dance twice round the room with him and then lead him to the conservatory and tell him all her troubles."

James laughed.

"It's true," said Rhoda gravely. "And it isn't a laughing matter at all. He's too nice. I wish somebody would be taken ill quickly."

"I'll go after them——" began James in reluctant tones.

"Goodness, no! If she wants Adam, nothing you can do will stop her. You can dance this with me if you like, darling."

"Haven't you got a partner?" he asked in surprise.

"Adam," replied Rhoda succinctly.

They danced together which was extremely pleasant, in fact so very enjoyable that James quite forgave Holly for her defection. After that he danced with Eleanor and that was pleasant too for Eleanor was as light as a feather and an exceedingly good dancer.

James wanted to talk to Eleanor so they found a convenient sitting-out corner and settled themselves comfortably.

" How do you like school? " inquired James.

There are various ways of asking this question (which is so often put to the young), it may be merely a conversational gambit of course; in this case it was not. Having been instrumental in persuading Eleanor's parents to send her to school, James was anxious to hear the result of the experiment.

" I like it in some ways," replied Eleanor. " It's rather difficult, really. I'm too good at some things and frightfully backward in others. I'm not like other girls," added Eleanor with a sigh.

James had known this before; he had hoped that school would help her to become more like other girls, to conform to the pattern as it were. He had thought Eleanor would be happier with girls of her own age; it was lonely for her at home. It was touch and go, decided James looking at her affectionately. She would either conform to the pattern or else retire into her shell and remain there for the rest of her life.

" Some of the girls seem to like me," continued Eleanor thoughtfully. " But of course I can't ask anyone to come and stay."

She raised her beautiful grey eyes and looked at James to see if he understood, and of course he understood perfectly.

James had only half believed Rhoda's prophecy about Adam and Holly but before long he realised it was true; he saw them dancing together, and once when he was passing through the conservatory with Cathie Duncan he saw them sitting together upon a small sofa absorbed in earnest conversation. If he had wanted further confirmation he received it from Holly's own lips when he went to claim her for the seventh dance which she had promised him.

" James," said Holly in cajoling accents. " James, *do* you mind frightfully if I dance this with Adam? I know it's awful of me, but you don't mind do you? You're such an understanding person, James."

What could he say except that he understood?

Meanwhile Rhoda had been enjoying herself tremendously. She was the success of the evening. Everybody wanted to dance with her and if there had been twice as many dances on the programme there still would not have been enough to satisfy the demands of her admirers. She had kept several dances for James of course and she offered him those she had kept for Adam, for she was aware that Adam would be otherwise engaged, but unfortunately they were not the same numbers as those that James had booked with Holly so nothing could be done about it.

One of the few male guests who did not ask Rhoda to dance was Mr. Heddle. He and his sister had arrived late; Nestor looking larger and more glossy than ever in his beautifully fitting tails, Anna thin and elegant in a black dinner-gown and glittering with diamonds. Mr. Heddle bowed to Rhoda in a slightly exaggerated fashion and turned away (it was obvious that he had not yet forgiven her for contradicting him), but Miss Heddle smiled at Rhoda and complimented her upon her appearance.

"Your wedding-dress," said Miss Heddle nodding. " I always say there's nothing so becoming to a young girl as satin and lace—and nothing so becoming to a man as tails," she added with a glance at dear Nestor.

Sir Andrew had booked a dance with Rhoda but when the time came he asked if they would mind sitting out instead. He had not forgotten her enigmatic statement as she had risen from the dinner-table, " It's a secret," she had said. Sir Andrew had been a bit of a lad in his day—or at least he thought he had—and even now (though elderly and desiccated) he was moved by a pleasurable excitement at the idea of sharing a secret with a beautiful woman.

Rhoda was quite willing to sit out with Sir Andrew and allowed him to lead her to his study, the key of which was safely in his pocket. She sat down upon the comfortable sofa with a sigh of relief for the truth was she felt a trifle jaded.

Time was when Rhoda could dance all night without turning a hair but owing to her sojourn at Boscath she was out of training.

There was a bottle of champagne upon the table, flanked by a tray of glasses (Sir Andrew had put them there himself for just such an occasion) and the first thing he did upon entering the room was to open the bottle in an exceedingly expert manner.

"That isn't the first bottle of bubbly you've opened," said his guest admiringly. "I *do* like the pop."

Sir Andrew agreed that the pop was a pleasant sound. "Now, young lady," said Sir Andrew, when they were comfortably settled. "What is this secret?"

"Oh, dear," said Rhoda. "I thought that was coming. It isn't at all a nice secret, Sir Andrew."

He looked at her in surprise.

"I'm afraid you'll be annoyed," added Rhoda.

It was obvious that young Mrs. Dering Johnstone had changed her mind and intended to keep the secret to herself, but Sir Andrew was an inquisitive man; he pressed her for it.

"All right, then," said Rhoda with a sigh; she was extremely comfortable and most unwilling to disturb the harmony of the tête-à-tête. "All right, then, I'll tell you: it's about the picture in your hall."

"My Raeburn?"

"Yes, but it isn't a Raeburn."

"It isn't a Raeburn! Of course it's a Raeburn! I can assure you of that," declared its owner with conviction. "I have letters proving its authenticity. The picture was painted by Raeburn as I told you. It is of my great-aunt, Mary Shaw. There is no doubt about it whatever." He stopped and looked at Rhoda but she said nothing. "And anyway," he added, "you didn't examine the picture closely. How could you possibly tell?"

"How can you tell the difference between a Derby winner and a plater?" Rhoda inquired.

" This is crazy! " Sir Andrew declared. " Dozens of people have seen the picture and admired it."

Rhoda believed him; she had discovered long ago that the world was full of people who were practically blind. " I should say it was a copy," she told him. " The picture is painted in the Raeburn manner, in the low tone one associates with him. The lights are massed together and the shadows used to heighten them. These effects are characteristic of Raeburn's work. It is the actual technique that is poor; the decision and power are lacking."

Sir Andrew had listened to this recital with dawning horror. " I don't believe it! " he exclaimed.

" No," said Rhoda. " I didn't think you would. Of course it doesn't matter to me whether you believe it or not. I thought it was kinder to warn you because some day you might show it to someone who would know. You would look rather a fool, wouldn't you? " added Rhoda frankly.

Sir Andrew gazed at her incredulously. " My great aunt——" he began.

" I know," agreed Rhoda. " Your great aunt, Mary Shaw, had her portrait painted by Raeburn; you've told me so twice and I'm sure it's perfectly true. All I say is Raeburn did not paint the portrait in your hall."

" How could that be? "

" I've been wondering too," Rhoda admitted. " Perhaps one of your forebears had a copy made and sold the original. It has been done before. But if you don't believe me why not get somebody else to look at the picture? "

Sir Andrew got up and walked to the window and back. " I shall," he said. " Yes, I shall get a man down from Edinburgh. This is frightful. This is a terrible blow. I still can't believe that you're right."

" I'm sorry," said his guest repentantly. " I just had to tell you. It would have been much easier to say nothing at all." She rose as she spoke and Sir Andrew opened the door for her without a word. The cosy talk to which he had been looking forward had not been as enjoyable as he had hoped.

As they came out of the study they met Henry Ogylvie Smith who had been looking for Rhoda. This was the dance which she had promised him and it was nearly over, in fact the music stopped as they were walking through the hall.

" I'm terribly sorry," said Rhoda as they found seats in an angle below the stairs. " I was talking to Sir Andrew about something rather important and I couldn't get away."

Henry was very understanding about it. He knew Sir Andrew and therefore was aware that the elderly baronet was as difficult to get away from as the Ancient Mariner. " What about the picture? " he asked. " I've told the parents that Santa Claus has been held up and their present is unavoidably delayed. I've roused their curiosity to fever pitch."

" It's nearly finished," Rhoda told him. " One more sitting should be enough. I've done quite a lot without you but now I'm stuck."

" I might come to-morrow."

" Oh, do, Henry," said Rhoda earnestly. " Do come to-morrow. I want to get it finished."

CHAPTER TWENTY-THREE

THE next morning Henry walked over the hills to Boscath. He knew the path well by this time for unlike his mother he was fond of walking and preferred to walk rather than to risk his car upon the daft road. He had found an old drove-road which followed the line of least resistance along the shoulder of Crowthorne Hill, over a saddle between Crowthorne and Winterfell. The road was overgrown, it had not been used for many years, but it was easy enough to see. Long ago hundreds and thousands of men had passed this way driving

their beasts to market and the trail had been beaten down by
their passage. What a glorious walk it was! The trail wound
upwards into the midst of the rounded hills and the hills opened
up before you as you went. There was a tiny ruined cottage
in the middle of the hills (a shepherd's cottage of course) you
passed it on your right and walked on ... and then suddenly
and unexpectedly the hills fell back and you were looking down
into the valley where Boscath and Mureth lay on the banks of
the river, and the long green slopes of undulating pasture
swept down from your feet to Boscath Farm.

This was how Henry always came to Boscath, and this was
how he came to-day for his last sitting. In some ways he felt
sorry it was to be his last. Contrary to his expectations he
had enjoyed his visits to the studio. Rhoda was a dear, so
interesting and unusual, they had talked about all sorts of
things and had got to know one another well. He was fond of
Duggie too. As a matter of fact he had been thinking about
Duggie a good deal and had formulated a plan to help the boy.
He intended to consult Rhoda about it at the first opportunity
and see what she thought.

To-day was a little different from the other days and not only
because it was to be the last. Henry noticed that Rhoda was
not quite so natural and friendly as usual. If Rhoda had not
been such a natural, friendly person the slight restraint in her
manner would have been unnoticeable, or if Henry had been
less sensitive he would not have perceived it; but there it was.
He wondered what was wrong. Another unusual circumstance
was the absence of Duggie from his little table in the corner.
Henry would have been even more conscious of the unusual
conditions if he had known that Duggie had come and been
sent away.

"About Duggie," said Henry as he took up his pose. "I
haven't been able to talk to you about him because he was
always here but I've been thinking about him quite a lot. The
fact is I'd like to help him."

"Help him?"

" I don't mean *now*. I think what you're doing for him is perfect—couldn't be better—but later on he'll need some help. Perhaps we could arrange to send him to an art school or abroad, or whatever you think best."

" You mean you would pay for him to go? That's awfully good of you, Henry! "

" It isn't really. I have more money than I need, and no family, so I could easily afford to help Duggie. I'm interested in the boy," explained Henry. " I should have liked to be a painter but I chose medicine instead. I told you that, didn't I? Well, here's a boy who wants to paint *more than anything*."

Rhoda nodded. She understood what Henry meant because she, herself, had much the same feeling about her pupil.

" And what's more he has it in him," added Henry with conviction.

" I'm sure of it! " Rhoda exclaimed. "Duggie is worth helping. Quite apart from his painting he's a worth-while person in himself. He's intelligent and clever and he wants to learn. When he first began to come here he was a bit rough, if you know what I mean, and he took no pride in his personal appearance. His speech was rough, too; he spoke like the other boys on the farm—it was quite natural of course—but now he's improving in every way."

" That's your doing," said Henry, smiling.

" No, honestly. I don't bother him about things like that. In fact I don't bother him much about anything. I want him to develop naturally along his own lines." She paused and then added, " If you can help Duggie I'm sure you won't regret it."

Henry nodded. " That's settled then," he said. " We'll decide later what's to be done with Duggie."

Rhoda was delighted. Henry's offer was a great relief to her mind, for she had been wondering about Duggie's future. The time would come when she could teach him no more; he would outstrip her and what would happen then? She had even gone so far as to wonder whether she was doing right to encourage the boy and to set his feet upon a path which led to uncertainty and perhaps to disappointment. Now his future was assured. Henry would help him. He must go abroad of course; she was determined upon that.

The picture was almost finished now, there was little more she could do to it. Rhoda knew it was good; it was one of the best things she had done. The strong face was so sad in repose but it glowed with the light of eager intelligence when its owner was interested . . . and somehow she had caught that glow. She laid down her brush and looked at the picture with the immense satisfaction of an artist in a job of work well done.

But there was something else she meant to do (it was because of this that she had sent Duggie away) and although it was more difficult now after Henry's generous offer she was determined to do it. She had waited until the picture was finished. Now was the time.

"Henry," said Rhoda. "There was a friend of yours here the other day. She recognised your portrait."

"A friend of mine?" inquired Henry with interest.

"Yes, Nan Forrester."

"Oh!" said Henry.

"I'm very fond of Nan," Rhoda told him.

"Yes—well—I'm not surprised," said Henry in an uncertain voice. "I mean you and—and Nan are the sort of people who—who would naturally like one another."

"I thought the same about you and Nan," said Rhoda frankly.

There was a short but very uncomfortable silence.

"Look here, I can't help it!" exclaimed Rhoda. "I can't sit back and not interfere with things—with people. I expect you're angry."

"I'm not angry at all."

"You will be in a minute. I'm going to say something—unpardonable."

"You couldn't," he said in a low voice. "Nothing you could say would be unpardonable. Nothing you could say would be worse than what I've said to myself. I behaved abominably."

" But why?" cried Rhoda. " Why did you?"

He rose and went over to the fire. " I can't tell you," he said unsteadily. " I can't explain. I wanted to marry Nan and then I found it was impossible. I thought Nan would forget me. I hoped she had."

" She hasn't."

He made a helpless gesture with his hands. It was a curiously foreign gesture, very expressive. Rhoda had seen his mother use her hands like that.

" Mysteries are horrible," Rhoda said. " I know I'm being awful and I've absolutely no excuse except that I—I like you both so much—so *very* much, Henry—but honestly, couldn't you tell Nan?"

He was looking down into the fire. " You think I should?" he asked.

Rhoda hesitated and then she said slowly, " It's difficult for me to answer because I don't know what it is, and I'm not Nan, but if it were me I would rather know. I'd always rather know things even if they were—horrible."

" It isn't horrible, just hopeless," he said.

There was a moment's silence and then the door opened and James came in. He found an odd sort of atmosphere in the room, an atmosphere of tension, and he did not like it at all. His heart gave a curious twist which was actually physically painful. This fellow had no right to create an odd sort of atmosphere in Rhoda's studio; he was too vital or something.

" Hallo," James said. " Am I interrupting the sitting?"

" We've finished," Rhoda replied. " We're just going down to tea. Come and see how you like it."

He moved forward and looked at the picture. He could not say he liked it. All he could think of was that it was horribly like the fellow.

" I think it's simply marvellous," Henry declared. " The parents will be delighted—more than delighted. Not only is it a magnificent piece of work but it's a wonderful likeness. Yes, that's the somewhat cadaverous countenance I see every morning in my shaving mirror."

" I've got a clever wife, haven't I?" James said. The words were spoken in rather a nasty way and for a moment Rhoda felt chilled. This reaction was so different from his usual reaction to her work, which was one of unqualified admiration. Rhoda had got used to the unqualified admiration and was hurt when it was not forthcoming. What was the matter with James? Then suddenly she realised that the poor lamb was jealous! She was surprised and amused and glad and sorry all at the same time, but amusement predominated. If only James knew! The scene he had interrupted was far from a scene of amorous dalliance. To all intents and purposes she had told Henry he was a cad.

" It's much more than clever," Henry was saying. " It's much more than a picture of my face. It's a picture of my personality."

That was exactly what James had thought and that was why he did not like it. Rhoda knew too much about the fellow's personality.

" I was interested," said Rhoda as if that explained the whole thing. She slipped her hand through James's arm and they went downstairs to tea.

" I wish I could tell you how grateful I am," declared Henry. " It's so nice to be able to give the parents something they will really value. That sounds conceited but I know you understand."

" Of course," said Rhoda.

James's arm was like a piece of wood. She wished Henry would go away so that she could comfort James and explain matters to him but she could hardly turn the man out. She would have to give him tea. Rhoda had a feeling that tea would be a less pleasant meal than usual.

CHAPTER TWENTY-FOUR

IT was a very cold wet evening. The Forresters had had their supper and settled down beside their fire. Nan was knitting a pullover and Adam was reading *The Lancet*. Now and then Adam read out something that he thought would interest Nan and they talked about it. Although Nan knew little or nothing about medical matters she took an intelligent interest in Adam's work; she realised that it helped him to talk to her about his patients and gradually it had become a habit. Nan was perfectly safe, there was no chance of a leakage of information.

" This is nice," said Nan. " I like this time of the day best of all."

" Yes," agreed Adam. " It's a cosy time of day."

The telephone bell rang.

Nan hated the telephone; sometimes she envied Rhoda whose home was free from the plague. She watched Adam's face as he took up the receiver and said, " Doctor Forrester here."

" Yes," said Adam, his face suddenly grave. " Yes, yes, I see . . . Yes, I was afraid of it . . . No, don't do that . . . Yes, I'll come."

" Oh, Adam! " Nan exclaimed.

" Mrs. Wood," he said. " Sounds rather serious. I shall have to go up to the hospital at once. I may be there all night. Don't wait up." He struggled into his waterproof, seized his hat and was gone.

Nan had gone to the door with him. It was a wretched night, dark as pitch and raining. She heard Adam's quick footsteps going up the street, almost running. Mrs. Wood had been on Adam's mind for days. She was well over forty and she was having her first baby and the baby was not behaving as babies should. Adam had explained the whole thing to Nan.

Nan sighed and shut the door. She was very sorry for Mrs. Wood. It seemed dreadful that she should have to go through so much pain and misery and perhaps lose her baby after all, but Adam would save if it he could.

She went back to the fire and sat down. It was too early to go to bed. She took up a book which she had got from the library and at that moment the door-bell rang.

It was quite a common occurrence for the door-bell to ring, almost as common an occurrence as the telephone, and the caller was usually a patient or the relative of a patient requiring the services of the doctor. Well, they couldn't have Adam to-night, thought Nan as she opened the door.

A tall slender figure in a waterproof coat was standing upon the doorstep. The light from the fanlight above the door shone down upon his cap.

It was Henry Ogylvie Smith.

For some reason she was not really surprised to see him, perhaps it was because she had been thinking about him so much. Since she had seen his portrait in Rhoda's studio she had not been able to get him out of her mind. She had seen him at the dance but he had not spoken to her.

" Oh," said Nan. " I'm afraid Adam is out."

" May I come in? " he asked.

She opened the door wider and he came into the little hall, wiping his feet on the mat.

" Adam will be sorry," she said. " He had to go to the hospital."

" Who would be a G.P.! " Henry exclaimed.

" Adam would," said Nan, smiling. She had control of herself now and felt more confident of her ability to play the rôle he had assigned to her, the rôle of calm friendship. It was all over long ago. She had thought he was fond of her and then found he was not, but that was no reason why they should not be friends. Henry had been Adam's friend before he had become hers.

" So Adam likes it? " Henry was saying. " I'm glad of that, because I feel responsible for his being here."

" Yes, Adam likes Drumburly, and so do I. We're very grateful to you."

They were standing in the hall beneath the light and the hall was so tiny that they were very close to one another. Nan did not ask him to come into the sitting-room because he had come to see Adam and Adam was out.

" There's nothing to be grateful for," Henry said. " It's Doctor Black who should be grateful, and to do him justice he is. Adam is the best assistant he ever had. As a matter of fact he wants Adam to go into partnership with him. He asked me to sound Adam about it."

" Adam will be pleased! " exclaimed Nan.

" But should he accept, that's the question. He might do better elsewhere. He shouldn't accept without thinking about it very seriously."

" I'll tell him," said Nan.

Now that the message had been given Nan expected Henry to go away, but evidently he intended to stay for he was taking off his coat. She could hardly turn him out without offering him some sort of hospitality.

" I was just going to make tea; perhaps you would like some," she said. " I'm sorry I haven't anything stronger to offer you."

" Tea would be nice," he replied.

He looked just the same: his keen eyes beneath the delicately arched eyebrows, his dark hair brushed back from his forehead. Perhaps he looked a trifle older; she noticed new lines in the face she had known so well. His hands—Nan had always loved his hands with the long tapering fingers! Above all she had loved his voice; a deep voice with a curiously vibrant quality so that although he spoke quite softly you could hear every word. Nan had always felt sure that it was his voice which made him such a successful doctor, it seemed to go straight to one's heart and awaken a response. She had tried very hard to forget Henry's voice but now she knew she had not forgotten it and never would. If I were dying his voice would call me back, thought Nan miserably. Her hands shook as she took out the cups and saucers and filled the teapot.

When she carried in the tray she found him sitting by the fire holding out his hands to the warmth.

" What a difference you have made in this little house! " he said. " It's charming, Nan. So comfortable and cosy."

" It's a home," Nan replied. " Adam and I have never had a home before and, as you know, we always wanted one. We're both very happy." She made the statement with quiet dignity, for she had her pride, and as she spoke she met his eyes squarely.

" You're very lucky," said Henry.

For a moment Nan could not speak; then she said, " Yes, I know," but her voice was unsteady.

" People with homes are lucky," said Henry carefully. " I have my parents' home of course but that isn't the same. I shall never have a home of my own."

Nan tried to speak but her voice would not come.

" I shall never marry," he continued " I thought at one time it would be possible for me to marry and then I found it was impossible."

Nan felt her heart contract. It was as if the whole world stood still. The room was very quiet and shadowy. The only light in it came from the reading-lamp and from the fire. The whole world was quiet. There was the sound of footsteps in the street outside, they came nearer and passed and went on.

Henry had been listening to them too and it was not until the sound of them had died away in the distance that he spoke again.

" Nan," he said. " I wonder if you would like to know why I can never marry. You have a right to know if you want to.

I would have told you before but I thought it would be better for you if I just went away and said nothing. I thought if I said nothing you would—would forget me more easily. Perhaps I was wrong."

" I should like to know," whispered Nan.

" It's a long story," he said. He was sitting forward in the big chair, looking into the fire and his face was reddened with its glow. His eyes were on the fire as if he were reading the long story amongst the burning coals. " It begins—I suppose it begins when I was born, or even before that. Stories do. There's such a lot of our forebears in us. If I hadn't been the sort of person I am it wouldn't have happened, but I won't worry you with that." He paused for a few moments, thinking.

Nan was sitting far back in her chair with one leg tucked beneath her; she had pushed the chair away from the light so that her face was in shadow. She did not want Henry to see her face. She did not want him to see that she was trembling . . . shaking all over uncontrollably.

" Once upon a time," said Henry in his deep, quiet voice, " there was a boy. He was an only child and I'm afraid his parents spoilt him. He wanted to be a doctor so when he left school he went to Glasgow University to study medicine. He lived in lodgings, quite comfortable lodgings, but he was very lonely. This boy had never been lonely before. He had enjoyed the companionship of other boys at school and he had been spoilt at home by his parents. He was rather a clever boy so he didn't have to work very hard. It would have been better—safer—if he had had an ordinary sort of brain because he wouldn't have had so much time to feel lonely. It would have been safer if he hadn't had so much money to play about with. There was a girl (you see, Nan, this is a very banal story); her name was Elizabeth and she lived next door to the house where the boy was lodging. Elizabeth was very young, she was even younger than the boy, and she was a pretty, rather pathetic little creature. Elizabeth had no parents, in fact she had nobody belonging to her at all so she was lonely too. They got to know one another quite naturally. Elizabeth worked in a shop; sometimes she was very tired when she got home, too tired to do anything, but at other times she liked to go out. They were both free on Sundays of course so they used to meet and go for walks together, but Sundays in Glasgow are very dreary and these two young creatures had nowhere to go and nothing to do except to walk about in the streets. It wasn't so bad in fine weather but in wet weather it was dreadful . . . so they got married."

He paused but Nan said nothing. She could not have spoken to save her life.

"They got married," he repeated. "It seemed the best thing to do. It seemed the natural thing to do. They took a little flat and furnished it and moved in. It was a very small flat but it was comfortable and for a time they were happy. Instead of walking about the streets or going to the Pictures they could sit by their own fireside. Yes, for a time they were happy. The boy didn't tell his parents about his marriage, his idea was to keep his marriage a secret from his parents until he had trained his wife. That was his idea. The young fool!" said Henry bitterly. "The young blackguard!"

"Oh, no," whispered Nan. "He meant well, I know."

Henry glanced at her for the first time since he had begun his story and then he looked away. "Yes, he meant well. I suppose that's *some* excuse. As a matter of fact he thought he was doing a fine thing; he thought he was doing something worth while. Elizabeth had no parents and very few friends, she was lonely and was obliged to work very hard to keep herself. The boy meant to train her so that she could take her proper position in the world—in his world—and then he meant to take her to Drumburly and present her to his parents. 'Here is your daughter-in-law,' he would say.

"Elizabeth knew his plan; he had explained the whole thing to her and she had listened and agreed. She thought it would be fun. It *was* fun at first; he chose her clothes and

tried to teach her how to wear them; he made her do her hair
differently. Sometimes she remembered what he had told her
but more often she forgot. He was disappointed because he
had thought it would be quite easy to teach her parlour tricks,
but it wasn't easy; there was nothing of Eliza Doolittle about
her.

" It all went wrong. It was bound to go wrong. They
quarrelled and made it up and quarrelled again. The boy was
sitting his finals and Elizabeth was going to have a baby, so
they were both nervous and irritable and things went from bad
to worse. Quite often she wept and the boy put aside his work
and comforted her.

" Somehow or other the boy passed his exams and no sooner
had he done so than war was declared. He joined the Navy and
was appointed almost immediately to a destroyer as Surgeon-
Lieutenant. It was not until he received orders to join his ship
forthwith and discovered that it was destined for service in
the Mediterranean that he realised what a swine he had been.
He was leaving Elizabeth to have her child alone. He might
never see her again. What would happen to her if he were
killed? Obviously the right thing to do was to write to his
parents and tell them about her. He wrote the letter but
Elizabeth refused to allow him to send it. They were both
very miserable indeed when they said good-bye.

" The boy wasn't killed, in fact nothing happened to him
except that he grew up a bit and came to his senses. He was
away for more than a year and then he got leave and returned
to Glasgow to his wife and child. Things were much better
between them; he had given up all idea of training her and
although he didn't love her—and realised now that he never
had—he was fond of her and much more tolerant. Elizabeth
was good with the baby and seeing them together, his wife and
his child, he felt a great tenderness for them.

" By this time he was very anxious indeed that his parents
should be told and did all he could to persuade Elizabeth to
let him tell them. She was a soft little thing in some ways,

but she was terribly stubborn about this. She was afraid they would insist on her leaving Glasgow and going to live with them at Drumburly and she couldn't bear the thought of it. She would be miserable, she declared. They wouldn't like her. She would die of fright if he made her go. He knew she ought to go, he wanted her to go (Glasgow was being bombed sporadically and she would be safe at Drumburly); but what could he do? He couldn't force her to go against her will. The only thing he could do was to write a letter to his parents and leave it with Elizabeth so that if anything happened to him she could use it. He explained everything in the letter, he asked his parents' forgiveness and commended Elizabeth to their care. His leave was over now, and he rejoined his ship."

CHAPTER TWENTY-FIVE

HENRY rose and walked to the window; he pulled aside the curtain and looked out. He said, " There isn't a great deal more to the story. I was on convoy duty for several months and then, on the fourteenth of March, nineteen forty-one, my ship docked at Portsmouth and I heard that the Luftwaffe had bombed Glasgow the night before. I had a feeling about it —perhaps because I had been dreading it—I had a horrible, hopeless, sick feeling . . .

" I asked for leave and went north at once and my worst fears were realised. I shall never forget that morning. The street where our flat had been was gone. It had vanished completely. There was nothing left but ruins and rubble and smoke from the smouldering fires and water from the hoses. People were wandering about amongst the ruins; some of them were weeping but others were too dazed to weep. I felt it wasn't real. The whole thing was a sort of nightmare and everybody else was sharing the nightmare with me. They were all doing as I was; asking questions, making inquiries, trying to find out what had happened to their relations or their friends. I made every effort possible to discover what had happened to Elizabeth and the child. I spent my leave searching, questioning, asking everybody I met but nobody had seen them or could tell me anything about them. I was forced to believe they had been killed."

He paused for a minute and sighed. "It was a nightmare," he said. "I thought of it constantly, wondering how they had been killed, whether it had been sudden or—or whether they had been—frightened. I dreamt about it at night. And then gradually I thought of it less and less. The war was near and horribly real; the dangers and discomforts and anxieties of war filled my mind and the nightmare got buried. After the war I got that job in the hospital; it was a very responsible job and I had no time to brood over the past. Years passed, years of responsibilities and hard work. Then I met you."

He came back and sat down. "Nan," he said in a low tone. "Nan, I hadn't thought of Elizabeth for years. I was certain they had been killed. I suppose I should have told you about it, but somehow I never really thought of it. The whole episode was over and done with; it had been a nightmare (part of the nightmare of war) and both were past and gone. That was how matters stood when I met you. You know what happened, Nan. I loved you at once and more every time we met. That day at Kew . . . but the very next morning I got a letter from Mr. Murray, a young lawyer in Glasgow who had helped me in my search. Quite unexpectedly he had come across a woman who was a friend of Elizabeth's and had gone to the shelter with them; *so they weren't in the house when the bomb fell.* I went straight to Glasgow and saw the woman. She was quite certain about it, there was no doubt at all, she had been with them in the shelter and had helped Elizabeth to get food for the child. She had seen them after the raid was over.

"That morning the evacuation began and of course it was a bit of a muddle as you can imagine, hundreds of people were being sent away to places where they would be safe from bombing. This woman was sent to Ayr; Elizabeth was supposed to be going with her in the same bus, but for some reason Elizabeth didn't turn up and the bus went without her. The woman never saw her again." He stopped suddenly. "That's all," he said.

There was a long silence.

"Ten years," said Nan at last in a faint voice.

"It's a long time, isn't it? It feels longer. In fact I feel as if it hadn't happened to me at all, but to somebody else."

"You can't find her?"

"I've tried every way I can think of."

"She could find you quite easily."

"Yes," agreed Henry in doubtful tones. "You mean she doesn't want to be found? That's what Mr. Murray said."

"It's obvious, isn't it?"

"It would have been the obvious conclusion if she were like other people, but, you see, I know her. Poor Elizabeth, she's so helpless somehow."

He was speaking as if his wife were still alive and Nan realised this. He had been certain she was dead; now he was equally certain she was not. It seemed strange to Nan. How could she possibly be alive? Surely, however helpless she was, she would have had enough sense to get into touch with Henry through his parents.

"I could free myself legally," continued Henry in a level, controlled voice quite different from his usual vibrant tones. "Mr. Murray advised me to do that; he says that if a person disappears and (in spite of every effort to find them) nothing is heard of them for seven years they can be 'presumed dead.' He says it could be done quite easily."

"But you don't want to do it?" asked Nan.

He held out his hands in a helpless gesture. "I can't," he declared. "I can't bring myself to do it! To free myself without finding her—without seeing her and explaining and finding out what she wants! I just can't do it. Our marriage was a foolish mistake—we both realised that—but she's my wife and the mother of my child."

"I know," said Nan. "I understand, Henry."

"If only I could find her I should know what to do. I could put things right or at least make some amends. I failed her, you see. If I hadn't failed her—if I had made her happy—if I had insisted on her going to Drumburly and taking the child—and that's what I *should* have done! Oh, Nan, what's happened to her!" he exclaimed. "Where is she? What's she doing? Perhaps she's very badly off; perhaps she's in actual want! And what about my son? How is he being brought up? Nan, honestly, I nearly go mad when I think of it."

Nan tried to speak but she couldn't.

"It goes round and round," said Henry wearily. "There's no way out. I can't take legal action. I just can't do it. I dare say it's foolish, Mr. Murray thinks it's very foolish indeed, but there it is." He paused and added in a lower tone, "I shall never be happy till I find her."

Nan realised that this was true. He would never be happy until he found her. If she were dead he would never find her . . . which meant he would never be happy.

Somehow she managed to find her voice. "I understand," she said. "I do understand and—and sympathise. I'm glad you told me. You won't mind if I tell Adam, will you?"

"I should like Adam to know," he replied.

There was a short silence and then Nan whispered. "Henry, please go away. It sounds horrid of me but—but I can't bear any more."

He rose at once and went to the door; from there he looked back. "Forgive me," he said brokenly. "We could have been—so happy. Forget me if you can."

He went out and shut the door. He was gone.

Nan began to cry quietly, her head pressed into the cushion. They were not so much tears of grief as the reaction from the emotional tension which she had endured. Henry's voice, his tragic story, the necessity of appearing calm had upset her nerves completely. It was because she had felt the storm rising within her that she had asked Henry to go away. She was shaking all over and the tears were welling up and running down her cheeks . . . it was a relief to let them flow.

Presently the storm passed and the trembling of her limbs grew less. She dried her eyes and pulled herself together. The familiar room looked strange to Nan, it was almost as if she had not seen it before; it belonged to another world, a safe familiar world. All the little intimate things that she and Adam had bought together, and which she had dusted and polished and grown fond of, looked strange. It was as if she had been raised to a different plane where only big things mattered, things like life and death and love and pain. So far she had not really thought about Henry's story but had felt it emotionally. Now she began to think about it and to consider its implications. She knew now that Henry loved her but the knowledge did not bring happiness. She had thought it would. Often and often she had thought that if only she could know Henry loved her she would ask for nothing more. But now she had this knowledge and she was more unhappy, not less, for Henry was unhappy too and that was worse—because she loved him. His unhappiness was harder to bear than her own.

CHAPTER TWENTY-SIX

RHODA had not seen Nan for nearly a week, in fact not since the party, and as there was no telephone at Boscath she could not get in touch with her and find out how she was. Rhoda was worried about Nan, she wondered whether Henry had gone to see her and had told her his secret. If so it was at Rhoda's instigation and perhaps her advice had been wrong. She wished now that she had not meddled in her friends' affairs.

Then there was Adam. What was Adam doing? Was Holly really pursuing him seriously? The only way to answer these questions and to set her mind at rest was to go and see Nan.

Rhoda decided to go to Drumburly in the car and James admitted that the expedition was practicable. The bog would be frozen and if Rhoda were reasonably careful there was little danger.

It was a frosty morning; the ground was hard and powdered lightly with snow. The sky was grey, the land was bleak, yellow and grey, cold and sad and lonely, a landscape in acid tones. As Rhoda drove along she saw sheep all about the moor and on the road. They were seeking their food, moving about, nosing the hard ground in their efforts to find nourishment (James said the sheep did not mind the cold, but how did James know?), it made Rhoda shiver to look at them.

Drumburly was all grey this morning; a little grey town beneath the cold grey skies. There were very few people about and those were hurrying along with their coat-collars turned up, hurrying from one place to another instead of dawdling in the streets and gossiping amicably as usual.

Rhoda drew up at the green gate and ran up the path. She did not ring (for she knew that Nan disliked the sound of the front-door bell), but opened the door and shouted cheerfully.

" Rhoda, how lovely!" cried Nan, appearing from the kitchen. " Goodness, how lovely! I thought I was never going to see you again."

Naturally this was a slight exaggeration and Rhoda realised the fact, but all the same she had a feeling that her friend had been particularly anxious to see her and was particularly glad she had come.

" Well, here I am," said Rhoda. " Old Hornie froze up the bog quite nicely and as long as he doesn't start thawing it before I get home it will be grand. What has been happening in Drumburly? "

" A lot," replied Nan, taking Rhoda's arm and leading her into the sitting-room. " A lot has been happening and none of it very good. As a matter of fact the Forrester family is having a spell of rough weather."

"Tell me about it," Rhoda said.

"First of all there's Adam," said Nan unhappily. "I don't know *what* to do about Adam—at least that isn't really true because I know I can't do anything."

"Holly, I suppose."

Nan looked at her in amazement. "How did you know?"

"I saw it happen."

"Rhoda," said Nan earnestly. "It isn't that I'm selfish. I wouldn't mind if it were somebody who would marry Adam and be kind to him. I would just clear out and get a job——"

"Holly will neither marry Adam nor be kind to him."

"That's what I thought," admitted Nan. "She isn't the sort of person who would marry a penniless doctor. Listen, Rhoda, this is what I wanted to tell you: she came to supper with us last night—Adam made me ask her—and she was charming, she really was. Nobody could have been more friendly and kind and amusing. She praised my soufflé and helped me to wash up the dishes; she was just as charming to me as she was to Adam. It was a delightful evening and I couldn't help liking her."

"I told you she was attractive."

"Attractive! Adam is quite mad about her. After she had gone he began to talk as if she had promised to marry him, so I asked him if they were engaged. He said no, not really, but he was sure it was going to be all right. The only thing that was worrying him was me."

"And you told him not to worry about you."

"Of course! I couldn't do anything else. I did try to hint that Holly is an expensive sort of person but I couldn't say much because I'm in rather an awkward position if you see what I mean."

"Yes, I do," said Rhoda.

Nan sighed heavily. "I don't understand," she said. "If she doesn't want to marry Adam why bother with him?"

" It isn't a bother to her, Nan. I know it sounds catty but it's just a statement of fact. It isn't a bother to Holly to be charming."

" Can't we do something about it? "

Rhoda shook her head. The only thing she could think of was that Holly should be provided with another swain, not necessarily more attractive than Adam but with a bigger balance at the bank, and she was not going to suggest this, even to Nan. Rhoda hated to be " catty " but there was something about Holly that she could not endure, the mere thought of Holly made her feel uncharitable.

" What about the other member of the Forrester family? " asked Rhoda, changing the subject. " What has been happening to her? "

" Nothing very good," replied Nan.

" Don't tell me if you don't want to," said Rhoda quickly.

Nan wanted to tell her. It was a little difficult but she pulled herself together. " Henry came to see me," she said. " I hadn't imagined things, he was fond of me. He told me everything, so now I know. It's over."

" It's over? "

" Yes, it's quite hopeless," said Nan. " I can't tell you about it because it isn't my secret." She looked up and saw the expression of dismay upon Rhoda's face. " Oh, Rhoda! " she exclaimed with a sad little laugh. " Don't worry about it, and don't try to guess because you never could. He isn't a Mr. Rochester with a mad wife in the attic or anything like that."

Rhoda blushed. Strangely enough she had been thinking of Mr. Rochester. " You're very good about it," she declared.

" ' Shoulder the sky,' " said Nan, smiling. " Do you know A. E. Housman's poems? I think it helps a lot to find that other people have troubles, and understand what it feels like to be unhappy. Poets seem to know a lot about unhappiness. Here's something that has helped me." She hesitated for a moment and then quoted the lines:

" *The sorrows of our proud and angry dust*
Are from eternity and shall not fail.
Bear them we can and if we can we must;
Shoulder the sky, my lad, and drink your ale."

" ' Shoulder the sky,' " said Rhoda. " It's a sort of clarion
call, isn't it? He makes it sound a worth-while job."

" It's a big job, but not too big. ' Bear them we can and if
we can we must.' At first I thought he had put it the wrong
way round but the more you think about it the more you
realise that his way is right."

Rhoda nodded thoughtfully.

" ' And drink your ale,' " added Nan with a brave smile.
" Don't go moping about and making every body else miserable.
' Shoulder the sky, my lad, and drink your ale.' "

James had walked up the river, it was the path Rhoda had
taken the day she went to Tassieknowe, but James did not
intend to visit the Heddles, he intended to make sure that the
dykes which bounded the northern limit of Boscath hirsel were
in good order and to have a look at his sheep. It was nearly
time to bring the tups down from the hills and James was glad
of this, for when they were out it made a lot more work. James
had Shad out to-day and was giving him some intensive training,
sending him up the hill to round up a stray ewe, and controlling
his movements with whistles and gesticulations. Shad did his
job none too badly and came back to his master with a self-
satisfied air which amused his master a good deal. There was
a rakish look about Shad, partly due to a black patch round one
of his eyes which gave the impression that Shad had been
partaker in a debauch and had got the worst of it in the fight
that had ensued. Not a beautiful creature, thought James (as
he patted Shad and gave him a small piece of biscuit), but a
friendly, intelligent, humorous creature. He was beginning to
like Shad quite a lot.

It was frosty and cold; the hills looked bleak beneath the

grey skies, the river looked leaden and the ground was hard as iron; but James enjoyed his walk all the same. He climbed up one hill and down another, counting his sheep. At first he had found it exceedingly difficult to count a group of sheep upon the hills for they were pearly grey like the rocks and boulders but now he was getting used to it and could cast his eyes over the hills, pick out sheep from boulders and compute their numbers with astonishing accuracy.

When James reached the boundary dyke he saw Sutherland coming down the hill towards him, he shouted and waved and Sutherland came up to the dyke and took off his cap in his usual polite manner.

" Good afternoon, Mister Dering Johnstone," he said. " I was wondering if you'd be seeing a tup. I've been gathering my tups and I've lost one."

" You'd better have a look round yourself," replied James, smiling. " I'm not experienced enough to know one Cheviot tup from another. You've taken yours in, have you? "

" There's bad weather coming," Sutherland said.

To James the weather looked settled but he was not such a fool as to disregard Sutherland's prophecy. " We'd better get our tups in," said James anxiously.

" Och, you'll have a day or two," declared Sutherland. " I would give you a hand with the job if Roy would not mind."

James closed with the offer. He said, " You know, Sutherland, I'm rather ignorant about this business and I'm always grateful for advice."

" In that case you'll not stay ignorant long," remarked Sutherland dryly.

They fixed up a plan for the following day and then parted, but Sutherland's remark stayed in James's mind and amused him a good deal. It was one of those deceptively simple remarks with hidden depths of humour. The more you thought about it the funnier it was.

By this time it was after two o'clock and James was hungry so he found a sheltered spot in the angle of a dyke and sat down

to have his lunch: excellent sandwiches made for him by
Flockie washed down with clear sparkling water from a hill-burn.
The burn was full of icicles and the water was ice-cold and
tasted a trifle peaty, it was a drink fit for gods. What would
James have given for a tumbler of it when he was in Malaya?
What wouldn't he have given!

James lighted his pipe and ruminated happily (and Shad sat
down beside him with his brown eyes fixed upon his master's
face). Things were going well, thought James. Even the daft
road was behaving reasonably at the moment. The men were
taking a real interest in their work and the farm was tidied up
nicely. Best of all Rhoda had settled down. James had been
a little worried about Henry Ogylvie Smith but Rhoda had
convinced him that his worry was unnecessary . . . and anyway
the picture was finished so the fellow would not be coming to
Boscath again. He thought of Rhoda, what a darling she was!
What a perfect companion!

To-day Rhoda had gone to Drumburly to see Nan, most
likely she would have stayed to lunch with Nan, but by this
time she world be home. She would be in the studio painting.
She would be wearing her bright blue overall which was smeared
with multi-coloured streaks of paint and her golden hair would
be slightly untidy. Quite possibly there would be a smear of
paint upon Rhoda's nose—it was not an unusual decoration
when Rhoda was painting. It would be warm and bright in
the studio, the fire would be burning merrily in the grate, a
fire of logs of course. The scene was so clear in James's " inner
eye " that he could not resist its magnetism; he leapt to his feet
and set off home at a brisk pace.

It was much colder now and a chill wind had begun to blow,
rustling through the frozen grasses. The light was beginning
to fade and the hills looked bleaker and more forlorn than ever.
Scarves of mist were drifting along the lower slopes of the hills
and thickening in the hollows by the river but above the mist
the rounded tops of the hills were clear against the grey sky.

As James neared home he began to feel anxious: supposing

something had happened to Rhoda! That road—how he hated that road! It was dangerous. The bog was not the only peril, there was that horrible steep bit of hill with the hairpin bend, and the narrow corner where the surface had been swept away exposing the bare rock . . . and he had said go. He had told her to go! What a fool! If anything had happened . . .

James dashed into the house and up the stairs and burst into the studio like a tornado. It was all exactly as he had imagined: Rhoda in her blue overall with her hair standing on end painting as if her life depended upon it (a little smear of crimson paint on one cheek, not upon her nose), the bright fire burning merrily in the grate and, sitting at the table in the corner, the queer silent little boy who (according to Rhoda) was going to be a great man one day.

" Gracious! " exclaimed Rhoda, looking up in surprise. " Is the house on fire or something? "

" No," said James breathlessly. " It was just—I suddenly wondered—if you were all right."

Rhoda understood, because on several occasions she herself had suffered in exactly the same way. Quite suddenly and without the slightest cause she had felt that she must make sure if James was still alive and in reasonably good health, and there and then had dropped whatever she happened to be doing and gone out to search for him. The only difference was that, whereas she had concealed her imbecility and made some sort of footling excuse, James was unashamed. James was the nobler character.

Rhoda smiled at him. " Come and see what I'm doing," she said.

He went over and, standing behind her, looked over her shoulder at the canvas.

" It's Heddle! " he exclaimed in amazement.

" Yes," agreed Rhoda, putting her head on one side and regarding her work critically. " Yes, it's dear Nestor—from memory—and just for fun."

It was over six weeks since Rhoda's visit to Tassieknowe

when she had seen " dear Nestor " for the first time, but she had not forgotten her impulse to paint him in oriental garb bedecked with barbaric jewellery and having seen him again at the Christmas party the impulse had quickened. She had finished Henry's portrait and was at a loose end so there seemed no reason to resist the impulse. Rhoda explained this to James at some length for she saw that James was interested.

" It's funny," James said thoughtfully. " The first time I saw Heddle—no, it was the second time—I thought of him as one of the Borgias. It was Cæsar Borgia, wasn't it, who asked people to dinner and poisoned them? "

" Yes," nodded Rhoda. " And I can imagine Nestor behaving in that endearing way—nothing that Nestor could do would surprise me in the least—but he isn't a Latin type, that's the trouble."

" Adam said he was an Assyrian."

" Assyrian! " she exclaimed. " That's it, of course! I must begin all over again." She laughed and began to splash paint somewhat recklessly upon the canvas.

" Hold on! " cried James. " Don't spoil it. The face is good. You've got that baleful glare to the life. You're a clever little devil, aren't you? Nestor wouldn't be a bit pleased."

" Nor would Anna. I never told you Anna asked me to paint him, did I? "

" You told me very little about your visit to Tassieknowe."

Rhoda was aware of this. She had thought it better to tell James very little about it, for if James knew how extremely unpleasant " dear Nestor " had been it would make him very angry. The Heddles were almost their nearest neighbours and James was continually meeting Nestor Heddle so it was wiser to leave things alone.

" Tell me about it," urged James. " Come and sit down by the fire and tell me what happened. Was dear Nestor in his usual form? "

" I don't know his usual form, but—well—first he was too nice and then he was too nasty."

" The brute ! "

" Yes, he is," she agreed. " I didn't mind so much when he was rude to me but he was horrible to Miss Heddle. That riled me."

" It would," said James with conviction. " I've noticed how you get riled when people are cruel to dumb animals."

Rhoda hesitated and then she said quite seriously, " Miss Heddle isn't dumb, she's mad . . ." and she proceeded to tell James all about Miss Heddle and her amazing and alarming theories regarding the late Mr. Brown. Rhoda was a good narrator with a feeling for dramatic form and the story was sufficiently dramatic in itself to make it well worth her trouble. James listened with bated breath and they were both so enthralled by the recital that neither of them gave a thought to the third person in the studio nor noticed that for once his busy pencil lay idle upon the table.

" Mad as a hatter ! " declared James.

" Mad as the Red Queen," corrected Rhoda. " There are no straws in her hair. In fact she looks so absolutely sane that you can't help believing her—almost."

" So old Mr. Brown is still at Tassieknowe ! He wanders about and coughs but doesn't appear in person. Pity he doesn't, really," said James, rising and stretching himself. " Perhaps they'd go away and we'd get some peace."

CHAPTER TWENTY-SEVEN

DOCTOR FORRESTER was extremely busy with the after effects of New Year parties; colds and coughs and upsets due to unwise indulgence in the pleasures of the table affected the Drumburlians, though not all of them, of course. Eleanor Shaw had a touch of tonsilitis and Doctor Forrester visited her daily and had long talks with her cousin who apparently was in charge of the patient. Whether Doctor Forrester went to see the patient or the nurse was doubtful. The patient, who was in the best position to judge, was convinced that her medical adviser took little interest in her slightly swollen tonsils but a good deal of interest in Holly's charms. Eleanor thought it would be nice if Doctor Forrester married Holly and, being altruistically inclined, she did a little hanky-panky with the thermometer when Holly took her temperature at night so that the doctor should continue to call. Unfortunately Lady Shaw became suspicious; Eleanor was hauled out of bed and sent for a walk and the doctor's visits ceased.

When he could see Holly every day Adam had been happy, he had looked forward to seeing her from one visit to the next, but now that he was not seeing her daily (and indeed had little prospect of seeing her again except by some fortunate chance) he felt very unhappy indeed. He suggested to Nan that they should ask Holly to supper again and gave Nan no peace until she rang up and asked her; but apparently Holly was very busy, her engagement book was full, and she declined the invitation with expressions of regret. There was only one thing to be done, thought Adam, he must write to Holly . . . and this he proceeded to do.

Several days passed and then one morning a bulky letter fell into the Forresters' letter-box. They were having breakfast at the time but Adam had been listening for the postman. He rose at once and went and got the letter, and standing in the hall he tore it open and read it.

Nan knew what was happening of course; she toyed with her toast and marmalade and waited for Adam to return but instead of returning to finish his breakfast he went into his own room and shut the door.

For a time there was silence and then Adam came into the . kitchen with his overcoat on. "I'm off, Nan," he said.

"Adam! But you've had no breakfast!"

"I don't really want any," he replied. He hesitated and then came in and leant against the dresser. "You may as well know," he said in a level voice. " You said Holly wouldn't be happy unless she could have all the things she was used to and you were right."

" I'm sorry I was right," murmured Nan.

" I've only known her for a fortnight," continued Adam in a dazed sort of way. " It seems more. I've been an awful fool. We won't talk about it if you don't mind. Perhaps you would read her letter and then you'll know."

He put the letter on the table and went out. Nan heard the front door shut and his footsteps going heavily along the street.

Holly's letter was written upon thick hand-made paper with her monogram in the corner; her writing was very large and rather straggly, so although it was not really a very long letter it overflowed on to several sheets. As Nan took it up and began to read it she wondered whether Holly would mind but that did not matter, Adam had given it to her to read.

" MY DEAR ADAM,

I was very touched by your sweet letter and all the wonderful things you say about me. I am sure I don't deserve them but I am very glad you think them. You say in your letter ' when we are married ' but, Adam dear, you know I never said I would marry you. I am very fond of you and I admire you very much but quite honestly I could never marry a poor man—there now, I have said it straight out. You see Adam I am not clever at housekeeping like Nan and I could never be happy living in a tiny house with no maid and trying to make ends meet. I like going about and having fun. I know this sounds horrid but it is just the way I am made and I can't help it. I would not be happy and neither would you. It is better to be sensible, isn't it? I have enjoyed our friendship very very much and I hope we shall go on being friends because I don't want to lose you altogether. I think perhaps it is kinder to tell you a piece of news because you may hear it in Drumburly and I would rather you heard

it from me. The news is that I have promised to marry somebody else. He is a good deal older than I am but he is a dear.
I have known him for some time and always admired him.
He really is a dear and so very devoted to me. You are such
an understanding person—I have always told you that
haven't I—so do try to understand this as well as all the other
things. I must stop now Adam dear and go to bed. It is
very late indeed. I wish you every good wish and I send you
my love. Even if you don't want to be my friend any more
I shall always be your friend.

HOLLY "

Nan read the letter several times. She thought it was a very
good letter; it conveyed unpalatable news in the kindest way
imaginable. Perhaps Holly had had some experience in this
form of correspondence! But although this unworthy thought
crossed her mind Nan did not blame Holly severely. It seemed
to her that the letter was straightforward and sincere. Nan
understood Holly's reluctance to become the wife of a poor
man (perhaps this was because she knew so well what it was
like to be the sister of a poor man). Holly's fault lay in leading
Adam on, in bewitching Adam. Nan blamed her for that.

It was tea-time when Adam returned, for he had had to go
out into the country. He had been out all day, had missed his
lunch and had had practically no breakfast. He looked cold
and miserable, his eyes were circled with dark rings and his
face was pinched. Nan felt a little sinking of the heart. She
longed to say something comforting but he had said he did
not want to talk about Holly so she refrained.

" I'm awfully tired," said Adam as he took off his coat.

" Of course you're tired," agreed Nan. " And I expect
you're hungry too. Tea will be ready in a moment." She
linked her arm with his and they went into the kitchen together
to have their tea.

After tea they settled down comfortably. It was getting
dark outside and as Nan drew the curtains she noticed great

banks of heavy clouds coming up from behind the hills, she
shut them out and sat down in her usual place. Adam took up
a book and began to turn over the leaves in a desultory manner;
he looked better now, Nan decided, the dreadful pinched look
had gone . . . but he was very thin. She must try to give him
more nourishing food. Perhaps the butcher would let her have
a bone for soup. He must drink more milk—let it stand and
give him the top, thought Nan—and he must go to bed earlier.
He must go to bed early to-night.

But Adam did not go to bed early; the telephone bell rang
and Nan, watching Adam's face as she always did on these
occasions, realised it was an urgent summons.

"It was Mr. Heddle," said Adam, as he replaced the receiver.

"Tassieknowe!" exclaimed Nan in horrified tones. "You
can't go out to Tassieknowe to-night!"

"I'll have to. Miss Heddle has been taken ill suddenly. It
sounds like a stroke."

"Adam, surely——"

"I must," declared Adam. "You had better go to bed. I'll
be back as soon as I can."

Nan knew that it was useless to persuade him. She made
him put on an extra cardigan beneath his overcoat and a thick
scarf round his neck. When they opened the door the wind
whistled into the house like a Fury bearing with it a few stray
snowflakes.

"It's all right," said Adam reassuringly. "It's only ten
miles when all's said and done. I shall be there in half an hour.
Don't worry if I'm not back soon."

"If the storm comes on badly you should stay there for the
night."

"Perhaps I will," he replied.

"You'll put on the chains, won't you?"

"Of course I will," said Adam. "Don't fuss, Nan."

Nan said no more. She did not often fuss Adam, for she
knew he hated it, but to-night she could not help fussing. She
had a feeling of apprehension, a heaviness of spirit.

"Good-bye, Adam!" she cried as she watched him stride off to get his car.

He turned and waved. It was snowing hard by this time and as he passed beneath the street-lamp his cap and his shoulders were already powdered with white.

CHAPTER TWENTY-EIGHT

THE road to Tassieknowe was narrow and winding and there were some fairly steep gradients to be negotiated but Adam knew the road and the little car was going well, the chains bit into the powdery snow with a satisfactory crunch. Adam's only trouble was with the windscreen for he had no warming device and, as he was heading straight into the storm, the snow froze upon the glass and blocked the wiper. Every now and then he was obliged to stop and clear it away. It was very dark and the snow limited the visibility, his head-lights lighted up the driving snow and little else. He was obliged to go slowly and by the time he got to Mureth which was half-way to his destination, the snow was a good deal deeper upon the road. The lights of Mureth cheered him, they were friendly lights, Adam would have liked to stop and warm himself before continuing on his way, but already he had been delayed by various circumstances and he decided to push on. After Mureth the road was even more hilly and winding as it climbed into the hills and the snow had begun to drift and swirl in the wind, but Adam held on doggedly and at last he reached the gates of Tassieknowe and turned in.

As Adam stopped his car before the steps of the house the front door opened and a blaze of light streamed out into the darkness. Mr. Heddle had opened the door himself.

"Doctor Forrester!" he exclaimed. "I was beginning to think you weren't coming!"

It was not a very gracious welcome to a man who had come ten miles through a snowstorm, but Adam was aware that people are often selfish when they are anxious and frightened and it was obvious Mr. Heddle was both.

" I came as soon as I could," said Adam blinking, half blinded by the glare of light.

Mr. Heddle led Adam into the dining-room and offered him a drink but Adam refused. " I would rather see the patient first," he said.

" But I think I had better explain what happened before you see her," said Mr. Heddle doubtfully.

" In that case perhaps I could have something hot," suggested Adam.

Mr. Heddle rang the bell and ordered coffee. He said, " My sister has never been very strong mentally. She got a shock."

" What kind of shock? "

" A fright."

" It will be a help if you tell the whole story."

" Yes, I suppose I had better. The fact is my sister thinks this place is haunted by the old man who used to live here. To-night she thought she saw him—I must say I thought there was something—somebody—but it couldn't have been." He took up the decanter of whisky as he spoke and poured out a stiff drink. Adam noticed that his hand was shaking.

" You saw it too? " asked Adam.

" It's nonsense! " exclaimed Mr. Heddle with an odd sort of violence. " When we die we go out like a snuffed candle."

" But you thought there was something," Adam persisted. " It's important, really. If there was nothing to see Miss Heddle was suffering from an hallucination, but, if you saw something too, there must have been something to see."

" There was something," Mr. Heddle admitted. " It happened like this: Anna was just going out with her dog, she takes it for a little walk every evening after tea. She opened the front door and went out on to the steps—then I heard her scream. I ran out after her and she was standing there screaming and pointing up the hill. There was—a figure—a small man with white hair. My butler saw it too. She went on screaming and we couldn't stop her so I rang you up. Anna's maid managed to get her to bed. I sent Mason, the chauffeur, to see if he could find anything—or anyone—on the hill. He could find nothing."

"Was it snowing?" asked Adam. "If it had started to snow it might have been a bush or a small tree with snow on it."

"It didn't start snowing until later," replied Mr. Heddle. "And anyhow it wasn't a bush. It was—it was a man."

"Your butler saw it too, you said?"

"Yes. It was beginning to get dark but there was still enough light for the figure to be seen—to be clearly visible. It waved a stick in a—a threatening sort of way." Mr. Heddle took out his handkerchief and wiped his forehead. "It has upset me," he complained. "You've no idea what it has been like—for weeks—it has got on my nerves. That's why I feel—doubtful about what happened to-night. At first I was able to laugh when Anna said she could hear the old man moving about and coughing, but she kept on saying it. Even when she didn't *say* it I could see her listening—listening to—to something. It was—horrible."

"Yes, it must have been."

"Horrible," repeated Mr. Heddle. "She's unhinged of course, but—but, even so, when people keep on listening to something, you begin to think you can hear it too."

"Strange things can happen——" began Adam, who was beginning to suspect that he had two patients to deal with in Tassieknowe.

Mr. Heddle laughed mirthlessly. "Oh, yes, say it! 'There are more things in Heaven and earth, Horatio, than are dreamed of in your philosophy,' is that right? Well, never mind. The point is I happen to be a rational being and therefore I don't believe in Heaven. The whole thing is absolutely and utterly absurd."

"Perhaps I had better see my patient," Adam said.

Anna Heddle was lying quietly in bed and seemed in a sort of coma. Her maid was sitting beside her; when Adam approached she rose respectfully.

" Miss Heddle is tired out," said the maid in a low voice. " She went on and on screaming until she couldn't go on any longer. It was awful."

Adam lifted one of her thin white hands and was startled to discover she was almost pulseless. He was annoyed with himself for wasting time downstairs.

" I must give her an injection at once," said Adam.

" Miss Heddle doesn't like injections."

" She must have it all the same. Bring a clean towel and some boiling water, please."

When he had given the injection Adam sat beside his patient for some time and was relieved to find her pulse strengthening and to see the colour coming back to her lips. He had been alarmed at her condition but she was improving.

Presently she stirred and opened her eyes. She said in a faint voice, " Doctor Forrester ! "

" Yes. You were not very well so your brother asked me to come."

" It was silly of me, wasn't it ? " said Miss Heddle. " We should have asked him to come in."

" You'd like to see your brother ? " suggested Adam.

" No, I meant Mr. Brown," she explained. She was silent for a few moments and then added in a troubled voice, " It's so *bad* for him to be out in the cold—with that dreadful cough."

Adam did not know how to reply.

" It is *his* house of course," she continued in a thin whispery voice. " So of course he has every *right* to come in . . . but if he comes in I can't stay. You realise that, don't you ? I can't *stay* if he comes in. I should be too frightened. Besides, you can't stay in people's houses if they don't *want* you."

" You must go away," agreed Adam.

" It sounds unkind. I don't *mean* to be unkind."

" It isn't unkind," Adam assured her.

She gave a little sigh of relief. "You'll arrange it with Nestor, won't you?" she said sleepily. Her eyelids fluttered and closed.

Now that her mind was easier she was sleeping quietly and her pulse was almost normal. Adam sat back in the chair and watched her. He did not want to leave her until he was quite certain she would be all right.

What a queer story it was, thought Adam. What on earth was the meaning of it? Adam had seen many queer things in his life and he did not dismiss as absurd the idea of the old man's spirit returning to the house he had loved. These people had used his house badly (had used it in a way he would disapprove of), was it utterly absurd to think he might return? Of course there was another possible explanation and on the whole Adam favoured this: it was possible that the haunting was in these people's minds, that they themselves had raised the ghost that was troubling them. It was possible that the haunting of Tassieknowe was fostered by a sense of guilt, a subconscious feeling admittedly but none the less powerful. Adam knew full well that a sense of guilt, sleeping far down beneath the surface, its presence unsuspected or ignored, can do the most extraordinary things to the most unlikely people and can make them behave in a most irrational manner.

What strange people these Heddles were! So rich and yet so unhappy—so unstable! So rich! why, if Adam had had one quarter of their wealth Holly would have said yes instead of no. But somehow this thought did not stir Adam to envy, and he realised that he did not want Holly on those terms. No, thought Adam, he and Nan living from hand to mouth in their tiny doll's-house were happier and more contented than Nestor Heddle and his sister. In spite of everything, in spite of Nan's unfortunate love-affair and his own, he and Nan were happier in their little house than the Heddles in their luxurious mansion. It certainly was luxurious, thought Adam, as he looked round Miss Heddle's bedroom and noted the carpet's mossy pile, the silken curtains, the large fat cushions on the chairs and the dressing-table with its mirrors and its pots of cream and powder and silver brushes and tortoise-shell combs. The very air was luxurious—warm and scented. He thought of Nan's ascetic little room with its uneven wooden floor and the wardrobe which he had tried to mend himself . . . and then he glanced at the haggard face on the pillow and thought of Nan's face.

Thinking of Nan broke the sequence of Adam's meditations and he discovered it was half-past one. Miss Heddle was now sleeping peacefully and it was perfectly safe to leave her, so he gave the maid a few simple instructions and went downstairs.

Mr. Heddle was waiting for him and again offered him a drink. Again Adam refused. If Mr. Heddle had offered a bed Adam would have accepted it but apparently that did not occur to him.

" How is she? " asked Mr. Heddle anxiously.

" Better," replied Adam. " I've given Miss Heddle an injection and she has reacted to it as I hoped."

" Will she be ill for long? "

" A day or two in bed will be necessary and then she must be moved."

" Moved? " exclaimed Mr. Heddle. " Who's going to run the house and do all the catering if she goes away? "

Adam gazed at him in amazement.

" She must pull herself together and get over all this nonsense," added Mr. Heddle.

" That wouldn't be easy," replied Adam. " As a matter of fact it wouldn't be safe and I shouldn't like to answer for the consequences. I found Miss Heddle very much upset and if she should get another fright it might be extremely serious. Miss Heddle's nerves are——"

" Nerves! Why can't you say she's frightened out of her wits and be done with it! "

Adam reflected that he could have said exactly that, and said it with truth, but most people preferred a more professional diagnosis. " It doesn't matter what you call it," he replied. " The important thing is Miss Heddle must be moved. She is my patient. You called me in to see her and I found her in a very precarious condition. Her heart——"

" Her heart! " exclaimed Mr. Heddle scornfully. " I thought that was coming! Doctors always fall back on heart disease when they find themselves at a loss for something to say."

Adam looked at him with repugnance. The man was detestable, he was cruel and ruthless. His solicitude for his sister was not for her sake but for his own. Adam felt extremely sorry for Miss Heddle, he felt sorry for anybody dependent upon the man.

" I did not say it was a disease of the heart, Mr. Heddle," said Adam with an assumption of dignity. " It most certainly is not. In my opinion Miss Heddle's condition is due to exhaustion following a severe shock, but I shall be very glad to arrange for you to have another opinion or to fall in with your wishes if you would rather arrange it yourself."

" So you want another doctor? How utterly absurd! She was frightened, that's all."

" Fright was certainly the primary cause. That's why it's so important that she should be moved."

Mr. Heddle laughed. " You believe in running away! "

" I believe in removing a nervous patient from uncongenial surroundings."

" It's the same thing in different words."

By this time Adam was boiling with rage but he was determined not to show it for he was quite certain that the man was baiting him and he was not going to give him the satisfaction of rising to his bait. " I'll look in to-morrow," said Adam coldly. " If anything goes wrong you can ring me up, but I don't anticipate a relapse. When Miss Heddle is well enough she must be moved."

" I've told you she must remain here," declared Mr. Heddle with an elaborate show of patience. " Anna's place is here. I need her here, especially just now. Later on I might be able to arrange for her to have a short holiday but at the moment it's impossible. I'm engaged to be married and my fiancée is

coming here to stay, so Anna must be here to look after things.
I'm telling you this so that you may realise it's quite impossible
for me to do without her at present."

The absolute selfishness of the man disgusted Adam. Apparently it did not matter what happened to anybody as long as
Mr. Heddle got his way.

"Do you realise that if you keep Miss Heddle here her
brain may become completely unbalanced?" Adam inquired.

"It's that already," was the scornful reply.

"Yes," agreed Adam. "It is unbalanced. I was trying to
spare you but I see there is no need. Miss Heddle will go
raving mad if she remains at Tassieknowe. Is that plain enough
for you?"

"So that's it? You think that by using threats you can get
us out of the place!" cried Mr. Heddle, working himself up
to a sudden fury. "That's what you want. I know that
perfectly well. It's a conspiracy, that's what it is. The whole
lot of you—every man-jack in the district is against me and has
been against me from the very beginning. First it's one thing
and then it's another—you needn't think I don't see through it.
I'll show you—I'll show the whole lot of you! I'll teach you a
lesson before I've finished. You won't get the better of Nestor
Heddle as easily as you think . . . and you can tell your friends
that Nestor Heddle is staying at Tassieknowe and he doesn't
care a brass farthing for any of them."

Adam took up his bag and left the room.

CHAPTER TWENTY-NINE

WHEN Adam opened the front door of Tassieknowe and went out on to the step he was absolutely appalled by the weather conditions. The house was so quiet and warm and so brilliantly lighted that the outdoor world seemed as cold as the polar regions and as black as pitch. The wind had risen to gale force and was shrieking down the valley laden with driving snow. It had been snowing hard ever since he had arrived at Tassieknowe and the wind was piling it into enormous drifts. The sensible thing to do was to go back into the house and ask for a bed, or at least for permission to remain at Tassieknowe until the storm abated. Adam knew that was the sensible thing to do but he was too angry to go back. Go back? Go back to that detestable man and ask permission to stay in his house? Go back and say " Please Mr. Heddle, nice kind Mr. Heddle, may I stay at Tassieknowe for the night?" Nothing— *nothing* would induce Adam to go back. Adam had kept his anger in check, partly for the sake of his patient and partly because he felt it beneath his dignity to quarrel with such a man, but now anger rose in him like a flood. He got into his car, started the engine and drove off.

The snow was not deep upon Tassieknowe for the wind was blowing it off the hills and filling up the hollows, Adam's lights showed a rounded blanket of white. There was a small drift at the gates but the chains took him through it on to the road and he turned down the valley. Here the wind was stronger—fortunately it was behind him—it came in gusts, pushing the car along so that it was difficult to steer; but the road was fairly level and the wind had cleared its surface, piling the snow against the wall. Wreaths of snow stretched long fingers into the road but they were easily avoided. The car was going well, it was old but serviceable and Adam had confidence in it, he knew exactly how to get the best out of it.

A steep hill loomed up in front of him, the snow was deeper here and it clogged the wheels, he crawled up it slowly. Suddenly he was at the top and the full force of the wind screeching, whistling, incredibly fierce, caught the car and blew it sideways across the road almost overturning it. Adam clung to the wheel and managed to avert catastrophe but his heart was thumping uncomfortably when the moment had passed. It was a relief when the road sloped downwards into a dip, a relief from the noise of the wind and the buffeting. Down he went, slowly, carefully. At the bottom of the dip the snow had settled into a drift which stretched from side to side of the road. There were banks at either side so the only thing was to go straight through. After ploughing through it for a few yards the little car shuddered and came to a halt. Adam backed and ran forward again, the chains bit into the snow and he was through . . . he knew now that he had been an almighty fool to attempt the journey but it was too late to think of that now.

He went on. It was cold, so cold that his hands were becoming clumsy, fumbling for the gears; and the chill seemed to penetrate every part of his body. Even his brain was beginning to feel clumsy . . . and dizzy. He felt that he had come a long way, that he had been driving through this turmoil for hours with the wind whistling and the snow whirling.

In some places the road had been swept bare, in others it was covered by the smooth whiteness; only the posts, which had been placed at intervals to mark it, showed where it lay. On either side of the road there was bare moor or ditches or perhaps a dyke, waiting to trap the unwary. Several times Adam found himself slithering into a ditch and was obliged to stop and back on to the road before he could proceed upon his way. Presently he came to the top of a steep hill which snaked down into a little valley. He remembered the hill and the twists in it so he put the car into bottom gear and crawled down . . . and here in the valley was another drift of snow piled high by the eddying storm.

Adam stopped and looked at it. The snow glistened in the light of his head-lamps; it was perfectly smooth so it was impossible to tell how deep it was or how far beneath that rounded innocent-looking blanket lay the solid safety of the road, but there was nothing for it but to go on, or at least Adam could see no alternative. He put the car into bottom gear and went on; he went on until the snow, piling up in front of the car, brought it to a standstill. This time he could not back out of the drift.

The engine had stopped and as he was in a deep hollow the noise of the wind had abated. He could hear it whistling over his head but here in the hollow it was comparatively calm. It was still snowing. All round him was snow, rising, falling, swirling in the eddies of the wind, but always getting deeper. Already the bonnet of the car was white.

It was a long time since Adam had experienced physical fear; he had encountered it in the war of course (who had not?) and here it was again, clamping down upon his spirit, drying up his mouth, fluttering like an imprisoned bird in his bosom. It was so lonely. There was not another human creature within miles; there was only the dark and the screeching wind and the whirling snow.

Suddenly Adam was reminded of a glass ball which he and Nan had treasured when they were children; inside the ball there was a tiny figure of Santa Claus standing knee-deep in snow. When you shook the ball the snow rose and swirled and whirled round the little figure in a miniature blizzard. Adam could remember Nan's childish face looking down at the ball and her thin, childish voice saying, "Isn't he brave? Look Adam, he's still smiling." Nan had always admired courage more than any other virtue. She still did. " ' Shoulder the sky,' " thought Adam. The sky was a pretty heavy burden at the moment (in fact there was no sky to be seen, only darkness and snow), but the thought of Nan's courage fortified him, roused him to action.

It was no use sitting here waiting to be buried. The only thing to do was to get out and walk. He must have come about two miles—which meant he was half-way to Mureth. Should he go back to Tassieknowe or struggle on to Mureth? He considered the alternatives carefully. On the one hand he knew that the road back to Tassieknowe was open and well marked with posts and he had no idea what lay ahead, but on the other hand he would have the wind behind him if he decided to make for Mureth. The advantages or disadvantages of the two courses of action seemed fairly equal and Adam's feelings decided the matter. Mureth of course. He took his electric torch and got out. Somehow he hated to abandon the little car, she was a good friend. " It's all right," he said, laying a hand on her bonnet. " I'll be fetching you, old lady." He laughed at himself and turned off the lights.

Now that Adam was actually in the midst of the storm and without any shelter he found it even worse than he had expected, colder and darker and fiercer. He stumbled through the drift and up the hill on the other side. His trousers were soaked through and clung to his legs; his shoes were filled with snow and clogged, so that his feet slipped and were so heavy that he could hardly put one before the other. At the top of the hill the wind seized him and buffeted him, hurling him from side to side as if he were a dry leaf in an autumn gale; the chill of it struck through to his very bones, the noise of it screaming in his ears deafened him. The snow was all round him, there was nothing to be seen but snow, his torch showed him the madly whirling flakes and little else. It was difficult now to find the posts, which were his only guide to the road, for his torch was far less powerful than the head-lamps. Here was one! He leant against it for a moment to get his breath and shone his torch ahead searching for the next.

The temptation to stop—just for a few minutes—was very strong; it was strongest when the road turned the corner of a hill and he found himself in comparative shelter. Here was a boulder to break the force of the wind, why not stop just for a few minutes—to rest, to get his breath, to ease his laboured breathing—but he had heard about people being lost in the snow and was aware of the danger. If he sat down he would never get up again.

Adam battled on. He fell. He got up and went forward. The wind was behind him, pushing him on. Suddenly he found himself struggling through deep heather, buried beneath the snow, and knew that he had lost the road. He turned and went back, pushing against the wind, fighting against it as if it were a live thing, a malignant beast. It tore at his clothes and filled his mouth with driving snow, it blinded his eyes . . . by some miraculous chance he stumbled against a post and clung to it. He had found the road again.

Now he was so cold and so exhausted that he had lost all power to think. He only knew that he must go on—on to Mureth—that he must not stop, he must go on. He went from post to post, counting them as he reached each one and struggled on to the next: five, six, seven . . . eighteen, nineteen . . . twenty-four, twenty-five. Surely it couldn't be much farther . . . Mureth . . . he was going to Mureth . . . was that the next post. It looked different, somehow.

As he groped his way towards the post he realised that it was not a post, it was a tree. He was off the road again— which meant he must go back. He turned and floundered back; his feet slipped from under him. He found himself sliding into a ditch . . . sliding down the bank. He grasped at a rock and tried to draw himself up but his hands were numb; his feet slipped and slithered and he fell sideways on to the rock with his face in the snow. For a few moments he lay there exhausted, almost sick with the pain in his side, then somehow or other he dragged himself up, got on to his feet and staggered on. The pain went with him; it was like a knife in his side when he breathed.

Another tree loomed out of the darkness, and then a wall and a gate. It was Mureth.

Adam had arrived at Mureth but he was too far gone to feel any lift of spirit. He turned in at the gate. The house loomed up before him, a darker shadow in the enveloping darkness.

He struggled through a heavy drift in the drive and blundered up the steps, he found the bell and pressed it. Far off in the distance he heard the tinkle of the bell, but nobody came. He waited, but nobody came. He tried again and again. He kept his finger on the bell.

It was still snowing heavily; the wind was whistling past the corner of the house and now that Adam had stopped moving he was freezing cold—cold to his very heart—his teeth chattering, his knees weak with exhaustion.

Adam leaned against the door. His hand grasped the handle and turned it. The movement was instinctive; Adam's hand turned the handle without orders from his numbed brain. He almost fell when the door opened at his touch. He remembered now, in a dazed way, that James always said Mureth door was seldom locked. He knew, in a dazed way, that this circumstance had probably saved his life.

Adam went in and closed the door and switched on the light. It was a most extraordinary feeling to be out of the wind and the driving snow, to feel the warmth of the house, to hear the old grandfather's clock ticking peacefully. Adam took his arms out of his sodden overcoat and let it drop on to the floor. He leant against the closed door. The hall was going up and down in a curious way ... up and down ... the staircase seemed to be slipping sideways. Adam gazed at the staircase, trying to steady it, and he saw Mamie coming down. Mamie was wearing a blue dressing-gown and her long fair hair was in two plaits, hanging down on either side of her face. To Adam her face was the face or an angel.

196

" Adam Forrester ! " she cried. It was the last thing he heard before he slid quietly on to the floor.

When Adam regained consciousness he found himself in bed, swathed in blankets and surrounded with hot-water bottles. He came to himself slowly, as if he were groping through a fog. He could hear movements in the room and the sound of voices.

" Here's the tea," somebody was saying in a deep bass voice. " If we could only get him to take some ! Maybe a wee drop of whisky in it would help."

" I think he's coming round," said another voice.

Adam opened his eyes and Mamie's face swam into view, bending over him, full of pity and kindness and anxiety. It was the last thing he had seen before he fainted and it was the first thing he saw when he opened his eyes . . . Mamie's face.

" Jock, he *is* coming round ! " cried Mamie.

Adam could not speak. He felt a strong arm raise him from the pillow. " Come away now," said Jock's voice wheedlingly. " Just a wee drink, laddie, a nice hot drink. I'll hold it for you."

The cup was put to Adam's lips and he drank; it was weak tea with lots of milk and sugar in it and a dash of whisky. The warming liquid revived him; he felt a tingling all through him as his chilled body thawed, a painful tingling. His side pained him in a different way, it hurt when he drew a deep breath. He felt pretty certain it was a broken rib—possibly more than one.

" Another wee sip," suggested Jock encouragingly. " That's fine . . . look, Mamie, he's smiling. He'll be all right now. Gosh, I thought he'd gone ! "

" Kind," said Adam weakly. " Sorry—so much—trouble."

" Wheesht," said Jock firmly. " You're not to talk."

" Unless you can tell us anything more we can do ? " said Mamie anxiously.

There was nothing more they could do. They had done everything. Adam shut his eyes, he felt himself sinking into sleep. He let himself sink.

CHAPTER THIRTY

TWO whole days had passed and Adam was still in bed at Mureth House. He was ill, but not too ill to appreciate the care and the kindness which was being lavished upon him. The road to Drumburly was blocked completely by drifts of snow so it was impossible for Nan to come and see him or for Doctor Black to visit him and set his broken ribs. Fortunately however Jock knew a little about first aid and under the direction of the patient had managed to strap them into place. Adam could not help smiling when he thought of the scene; when he remembered the anxious faces of Jock and Mamie and how they had got themselves entangled in the roll of adhesive bandage. It was agony to laugh, so he hadn't laughed, but some day when his ribs had mended he intended to have a good hearty laugh over it.

They had put him to bed in the room which was known as " James's room " and very pleasant it was, large and square with coloured rugs upon the floor and a comfortable arm-chair standing beside the fire-place. The room had a solid old-fashioned atmosphere about it, only the bed was modern (and, incidentally, luxurious). Adam was in clover and he knew it; he liked the room best when the light was put out and the flickering flames of the fire-light gleamed on the polished oak furniture. He liked it in the morning, too, because the window faced east across the river and, lying in bed, he could see the sky redden and the sun come up from behind the snow-covered hills.

Adam did not worry. It was no use worrying because he could do nothing at all about anything . . . and he was so tired.

He did not read nor listen to the wireless which his kind hostess had provided for his entertainment; he just lay and thought and dozed a little and let the long hours drift past in idleness. Oddly enough he was not unhappy about Holly. Perhaps he had not really loved her but had only been enchanted by her charms, or perhaps he had loved the person he thought Holly was, and finding that Holly was not that person had ceased to love her; or perhaps . . . but what did it matter? Holly was not for him and to his surprise Adam did not greatly care. He wondered a little about Miss Heddle: what were they doing with the poor creature? He hoped that when the road was opened they would make arrangements to send her away from Tassieknowe. But there again he could do nothing. He had given his advice and could do no more.

Sometimes he felt uneasy about Nan. It was lonely for Nan all by herself in the little house. Mamie rang up every day to give news of Adam's progress and reported that Nan was perfectly safe and happy. Safe perhaps, thought Adam, but not happy. She was going through a bad time, he knew. She had told Adam the whole story as revealed to her by Henry and together they had discussed it thoroughly.

In one way Adam felt differently from Nan. The story had taken a weight off Adam's mind. He had always admired H.O. tremendously and it had been a grief to discover that his idol had feet of clay (he had treated Nan abominably); but now Adam could admire him again though perhaps in a slightly different way for the story had shown a different side to his character. Like Nan, Adam felt sure that Henry was mistaken in thinking his wife was still alive for surely if she had been alive she would have got into touch with the Ogylvie Smiths (she knew where they lived and she had Henry's letter which he had written to them), but apparently Henry was convinced she was alive and was unwilling to take the necessary steps to free himself from his marriage—or at least he was unwilling to do so without finding out his wife's feelings upon the subject. Some people might think this quixotic, Adam himself thought it quixotic but he knew Henry and therefore was aware that this quality was characteristic of the man. Henry felt he had behaved badly and wanted to make amends. Idiot! thought Adam, half in irritation and half in affectionate admiration. His friend's quixotry was both irritating and admirable. It was irritating —much more than irritating—to reflect that he was messing up his own life and Nan's, it was admirable to be possessed of high principles. Adam knew that when you got up against H.O.'s principles there was nothing on earth to be done about it.

" If she could be found . . ." Nan had said. Yes, but how could she be found? Adam was convinced that the woman was dead, and, that being so, it was hopeless. Nan was wonderful, of course. She was not only brave, facing the facts squarely, she was actually cheerful. It was only sometimes when she sat silent and thoughtful with her knitting-needles idle that one saw the look of sadness upon her expressive face.

Adam did not worry about himself. He had got off lightly and well he knew it. If things had gone otherwise: if he had lost his way, if he had twisted his ankle when he fell, if he had missed Mureth gate in the darkness he would be lying out there buried beneath the blanket of snow instead of safe and warm in James's bed. The injury to his ribs was not serious and it was merely a question of time before they would mend and be as good as new; in addition he had contracted a slight bronchitis. The cough bothered him a bit and hurt his ribs, and his temperature went up at night. He could neither sound his chest nor take his temperature, for his thermometer had been broken when he fell, but his quickened pulse denoted fever and he felt weak and shaky when he got out of bed. If the road had been open he would have insisted on being removed to hospital in the ambulance, and so relieved the Johnstones of the burden of looking after him, but as Mureth was completely cut off from the outside world there was nothing for it but to lie in bed until he was better.

" We like taking care of you," declared Mamie. " We're

rather proud of ourselves for being so clever and doing all the right things. It was Jock, really. Jock is used to finding half-frozen lambs in the snow."

" Don't make me laugh," pleaded Adam.

" No, of course not," said Mamie repentantly. " As a matter of fact I didn't mean to make you laugh. I say things without thinking, sometimes, and I was just trying to make you under-stand how glad we are that you're here. Lizzie is in her element. There's nothing Lizzie likes better than to have somebody ill in bed to look after. Unfortunately Jock and I are never ill."

Adam smiled. It was difficult not to laugh but he managed it. He was beginning to understand his hostess very well and to appreciate her unique flavour.

" I'm not worrying," Adam told her. " I know I should be worrying about all sorts of things; about all the trouble I'm causing and about poor old Doctor Black having to do all the work himself and about the wretched Miss Heddle snowed up at Tassieknowe with that blue-pencil brother of hers, but to be perfectly honest I'm not worrying at all. I'm just lying here peacefully and chewing the cud like a cow."

Adam had realised already that Lizzie enjoyed looking after him. Lizzie had the instincts of a born nurse though unfortun-ately not the mentality. She was a curious mixture and Adam who had little else to do was interested in the mixture. In all practical matters Lizzie was capable; she was an excellent hand with pillows, arranging them deftly so that they supported his head and shoulders at exactly the right angle; she heated his milk to exactly the correct temperature and brought it up to him punctually; his meals were punctual too, well cooked and daintily served. She would come up and peep in at the door and if he were sleeping—or pretending to be asleep—she would close it softly and go away . . . or she would tiptoe across to the fire and make it up noiselessly so that he should not be disturbed. All this was perfect and showed consideration and sound common sense; it was when Adam tried to talk to Lizzie that he discovered her limitations.

As has already been mentioned Adam was interested in the simpler forms of psycho-analysis; he decided to try out Lizzie and to discover her mental age. This was not difficult for she came every morning to dust his room; he talked to her as she worked.

"Lizzie," said Adam. "Here's a riddle for you: there are three boys sitting on a bench, facing you, and their names from left to right are Tom, Dick and Harry. Who is in the middle?"

"Dick," replied Lizzie after a moment's thought.

"Good," said Adam. "And who is on Dick's right hand?"

Lizzie thought this over. Obviously she suspected a trap. "That would depend whether he was left-handed," said Lizzie. "Greta's left-handed," she added as if this proved the matter conclusively.

Adam tried her with several other questions of the same nature, questions which were designed to measure the intelligence. He tried her with the one about the man who set out to walk four miles and when he was half-way to his destination turned round and went home.

"How far did he walk?" inquired Adam.

"Two miles of course," said Lizzie. "That's easy, that is."

"But he had to walk home," Adam pointed out.

"Och, away! You never said that," declared Lizzie in reproachful tones. "He might have taken a bus."

"Here's another one," Adam said. "A man had six children and he gave them each a sweetie, but he gave the youngest two sweeties. How many sweeties did he give them altogether?"

"Eight," replied Lizzie after a moment's thought.

"Are you sure?"

"Six and two make eight," replied Lizzie firmly.

These little experiments proved that according to Professor Woodhead's admirable treatise upon the subject Lizzie's mental age was ten; but no child of ten years old—or for that matter

precious few grown-up women—could have looked after
Adam so capably or so kindly as Lizzie.

The fact was Lizzie had lost her heart to Doctor Forrester
when she saw him lying upon the floor in the hall. She had
thought he was dead but Mrs. Johnstone had assured her that
he was not dead and Mr. Johnstone had picked him up as if he
were a child and carried him upstairs. Lizzie had helped to take
off his wet clothes, to rub his chilled limbs and to wrap him in
blankets; Lizzie had filled every hot-water bottle in the house
and helped to pack them round him. All this time he had lain
like one dead . . . and then he had opened his eyes and lo and
behold he was alive! No wonder Lizzie loved him.

Lizzie was very fond of Mr. James. He had stayed at Mureth
and had slept in this very room. Mr. James had been fun, he
had teased Lizzie and had jokes with her and she had enjoyed
it, but Doctor Forrester was different. The more she saw of
Doctor Forrester the more she realised how different he was
from Mr. James. He was not so amusing of course; he was
softer and more gentle . . . and he was so grateful for everything, so appreciative of all that was done for him! Lizzie
loved to do things for him; to bring water for him to wash in,
to brush his hair, to settle his pillows comfortably; before
he had been in the house twenty-four hours she would have
laid down her life for him. Fortunately no such major service
was demanded of her and she was able to work off her feelings
quite comfortably in minor services.

As a rule Lizzie did not like snow, it was messy stuff, people
brought it into her kitchen on their boots and it melted. The
children could not go to school so they were under her feet
all day, they went out and got wet and dirty and she had to
dry their clothes; but on this occasion the snow was her friend,
for when it thawed and the road to Drumburly was opened
Doctor Forrester would go away. Every morning when
Lizzie awoke the first thing she did was to look out and see
whether the snow was still there, and every morning the snow
was there, white and shining in the sunshine.

Mamie's feelings were exactly the opposite; as a rule she liked the snow and it amused her to be snowed up and cut off from the outside world. Her store-cupboard was full, there was milk and butter and eggs on the farm; Mureth could have withstood a siege of several months' duration quite comfortably; but on this occasion the snow was her enemy for it had severed all communications with Boscath. It was not the river this time, the river was low and easily fordable, for the springs higher up the valley were frozen, but on the other side of the ford there was an enormous drift, a miniature mountain. And Boscath had no telephone so it was completely isolated; there was no way of getting in touch with Boscath. What were they doing, Mamie wondered as she gazed in the direction of Boscath (the chimneys of which alone were visible above the drifts of snow). Were they all right? Had they enough food? Every morning when Mamie awoke the first thing she did was to look out of her window and see whether her prayers had been answered and a thaw had set in . . . and every morning she was disappointed to find that it had not. There lay the snow, great drifts of it, white and shining in the sunshine.

CHAPTER THIRTY-ONE

MAMIE need not have been anxious about Boscath for Boscath was perfectly safe and happy, perfectly capable of looking after itself, and Flockie was well prepared. The great freeze-up did not disturb Flockie's equilibrium. It was God's weather so Flockie neither worried nor grumbled. Of course she had taken care that it did not catch her out. As she tore off the leaf from her daily calendar and as usual studied the text with reverent attention she was a little surprised to read the words: "Take therefore no thought for the morrow: for the morrow shall take thought for the things of itself."

How queer! thought Flockie, as she sliced the rashers from the side of bacon which she had cured when the pig had been killed, and fished for eggs in the crock of water-glass and dug into the well-filled bin of oatmeal. It really was *very* queer . . . but then she remembered that Palestine was a hot country (you could tell that from the sort of clothes they wore), so of course they never got snowed up.

It was a new experience for Rhoda to be snowed up and Rhoda enjoyed new experiences. The landscape was completely changed by the snow, even the contours were different. There were no walls to be seen, no hedges nor ditches; it was as if some giant with a puckish sense of humour had taken his tablecloth and laid it lightly over the whole countryside . . . and what a gorgeous tablecloth it was! How it gleamed and glittered in the dazzling sunshine! Rhoda took her painting materials and went out to make a picture; it was too cold to sit for long of course but she could not resist the lure. She had intended her picture to be a study in Chinese white and sepia but she found that would not do; there were all the colours of the rainbow latent in the giant's tablecloth. Rhoda splashed about happily for about an hour and then went home with frozen fingers. She propped her canvas on the mantelpiece in the sitting-room and looked at it critically. It was impressionistic—much more so than any of her other pictures—and it certainly looked a bit strange, and exceedingly colourful; but all the same Rhoda liked it.

When James came in he saw it at once of course; nobody could have failed to see it. " Oh! " exclaimed James.

" The snow," explained Rhoda.

" Awfully good," declared James with admirable loyalty. " I mean it's marvellous. I mean your eyes must be quite different from mine if you see *that*. Snow looks white to me."

" You don't look at it, that's all."

" My eyes are different," said James with conviction.

Flockie's reaction was surprising; instead of being shocked or horrified she was entranced by the picture. " So gay," said

Flockie. " So cheery. Much nicer than white. I once saw a wee snowflake under a microscope—Mr. Brown showed it to me—and it was all colours of the rainbow. Mind you," said Flockie putting her head on one side and regarding it admiringly, " it would make an awful nice calendar."

Rhoda was aware that this was high praise indeed and was suitably impressed.

There was only one aspect of the great freeze-up that worried Rhoda: what were the poor sheep doing in the midst of all that snow? She was feeding the birds with crumbs and fat, but apparently nothing could be done for the sheep.

" What could we do? " said James. " You don't suggest that Roy and I should take them a basket of crumbs? "

" They'll all die," declared Rhoda. " I know they will. How can they possibly survive? Look at the hills! "

" They won't die," said James reassuringly. " Roy says they'll weather it unless it lasts too long and I remember Dan told me the same thing. They're hardy mountain sheep. The snow covers them and keeps them warm and the heat of their bodies makes airholes so that they can breathe. Each sheep is living in a sort of Eskimo igloo—at least we hope so. We can't do anything to help them, that's certain."

No letters and no papers arrived at Boscath; the only link with the outside world was Rhoda's portable wireless. She and James—and Flockie of course—listened to the news twice daily and discovered that the world was still there beyond the snow-covered hills. Things seemed to be going on much as usual; politicians were making speeches, committees were making reports. They learnt without surprise that many parts of the country were snow-bound, that trains were delayed and communications were upset and football matches had been cancelled . . . and the Automobile Association warned its members to beware of icy roads. They learnt from the reports of the Meteorological Office that the anti-cyclonic conditions were likely to continue unless they were interrupted by a change. It was all very interesting indeed.

" But it doesn't seem real, somehow," said Rhoda as she switched it off.

" I know," agreed James.

There was very little to be done on the farm except to feed and milk the cows, so Rhoda saw more of James than she had seen since their honeymoon. James found an old toboggan stowed away in the rafters of the barn. It was a particularly large one with iron-shod runners curving up in front. James spent some time mending it and when it was ready he and Rhoda took it up the hill behind the house and had a lot of fun. They came in to dinner warm and happy, their faces glowing with the swift rush through the cold air. Flockie, who had watched them from the window with indulgent smiles, had a good solid meal awaiting them. James offered to take Flockie on to toboggan but Flockie refused; that sort of thing was not in her line.

" I wonder what Mureth is doing," remarked Rhoda as they went to bed.

" We'll find out," replied James. " I thought I'd put the men on to digging a path to the ford; I could give them a hand and it wouldn't take us long. If the road from Drumburly to Mureth has been cleared we could at least get our letters."

The weather remained dry and frosty with a cloudless sky. There was no sign of a thaw. James and his two men armed themselves with shovels and attacked the drift which was blocking the path to the ford and Rhoda went to watch them. The drift was deep and, as they cut into it, the sides of the cutting were so high above their heads that it was difficult to throw out the snow. Occasionally Rhoda took a turn to give one of them a rest and found the work less arduous than she had expected for the snow was light and powdery. They knocked off at half-past twelve for dinner but at two o'clock when James and Rhoda went back to the cutting they found Wanlock finishing the job.

" I thought I'd just get it done," said Wanlock looking up

and smiling. " I thought maybe if you were not wanting me this afternoon I'd go over to Mureth myself."

" Of course," agreed James with a knowing look at Rhoda.

" It's a neat job, mind you," added Wanlock surveying the work with satisfaction.

It was a very neat job. They had driven the cutting straight through the drift; it was three feet wide, the sides were perpendicular and in some places ten or twelve feet high. It was like a narrow corridor with white walls and the sky made a blue roof overhead. Coming out of the corridor they looked across the river and saw Mureth and the snow-covered hills beyond. The river was low and as they had put on their rubber boots there was no difficulty in crossing the ford. James and Rhoda crossed it hand-in-hand and went up the path to the house.

" We'll go in quietly," said James with a grin. " They'll be in the drawing-room having their coffee. We'll creep in and give them a surprise."

But unfortunately the plan miscarried. Jock, emerging from his library with a sheaf of forms in his hand and his spectacles balanced precariously upon the tip of his nose, saw the front door opening in a curiously furtive manner and immediately flung it open.

" Gosh! " cried Jock in surprise and delight. " Gosh, it's you! Where have you sprung from? " and before they could reply to this somewhat unnecessary question he started bellowing for Mamie at the top of his voice.

Although Mureth had suffered only three days of complete isolation it seemed a good deal more and the visitors were welcomed as if they had come from the North Pole.

" My poor darlings! " cried Mamie. " You must be frozen! How did you get through? Come and warm yourselves at the fire and I'll get some fresh coffee for you. Goodness, how lovely to see you! I've been thinking about you and wondering how you were getting on."

There was a lot to tell. Mamie had to tell the story of Adam's arrival at Mureth in the middle of the night, of how he had found the door unlocked and stumbled into the hall and fainted.

" The door's never going to be locked again as long as I'm alive," said Jock gravely.

" As long as *any* of us are alive," added Mamie. Then she went on to tell about poor Miss Heddle's sudden illness (for somehow the story of Adam's adventures was coming out back to front), and Rhoda interrupted to say Miss Heddle was like the Red Queen and James chipped in to say, " Great Snakes, so Mr. Brown *did* come back! I said he ought to," and then it was Mamie's turn again. Rhoda had a lot to tell too; she told them about Flockie and how wonderfully she had prepared for the snow and Mamie asked if they were short of any household commodity and was informed that Boscath had everything it required. James told about the toboggan and Mamie said she had loved tobogganing when she was a child and she would come over to Boscath to-morrow morning (if she were invited of course) and take part in winter sports. Then Rhoda said, " What about Nan? She's all alone, I suppose? " and Mamie said yes, but she was well and happy so no anxiety need be felt on her account. Then James chipped in and told them about Wanlock finishing the cutting instead of having his dinner and they all said, " Daisy, of course! " and Mamie said, she hoped he was *really* nice because Daisy was such a nice girl and James assured her that Wanlock was not a bad fellow at all and would probably make quite a good husband. It was all a bit of a muddle as conversation so often is when everybody tries to talk at once. Only Jock did not contribute to the babble; he sat back in his big chair and smoked his pipe and listened with indulgent smiles. Here were the three people he loved best in the world enjoying themselves and having a good time.

Of course the visitors had to go up and see the invalid and they found him very comfortable and peaceful, lying in James's bed and gazing out of the window at the white hills which were now glowing pink with the reflection of the sunset.

They talked to him, but not for long because his temperature was apt to go up in the evening, and then they said good-bye and went home.

Jock and Mamie walked down to the ford with them to speed them on their way.

"Come to-morrow, Mamie," said Rhoda. "Don't forget, will you? And bring Duggie; I expect he would enjoy tobogganing." She put her hand through James's arm and they crossed the ford together and disappeared into the cutting on the other side.

"Well?" said Jock, in a questioning tone of voice, smiling at Mamie as he spoke. "They're all right, aren't they? No need to worry about that marriage, is there, Mamie?"

"They're almost as happy as we are," Mamie agreed. She slipped her hand through her husband's arm and they went home to Mureth.

"No need to worry," repeated Jock.

"Not about *them*," agreed Mamie. "I mean not about their happiness together. The only thing is they're terribly isolated. James isn't very happy about *that*. You know yourself that when the snow melts and the river rises they may be cut off for weeks. Jock, isn't there anything we could do? You talked of building a bridge across the river."

"I've thought of it often," replied Jock. "It would cost a lot of money, but maybe we'll need to do it. If there was a decent bridge from Mureth to Boscath we could leave the daft road alone. We'll see," added Jock. "We'll think about it, Mamie. I'll get a surveyor to come and have a look at it one of these days."

CHAPTER THIRTY-TWO

BY this time all the main roads about Drumburly had been opened with the snow-plough. In some places where there were drifts the passage was only wide enough for single line traffic, in other places the whole road had been cleared. In Drumburly itself the streets had been cleared by the burgh workmen aided by volunteers. Huge piles of snow which had become a trifle dirty were lying at the street corners waiting for the dust-cart to take them away. Blackthorn House was soon liberated, for its gates opened on to a main road, and Henry, who was taking a few days' holiday, cleared the drive himself. Blaikie had been detailed to help him but Blaikie disliked work and was imbued with the idea that shovelling snow was beneath his dignity so he took care not to emerge from his cottage until the work was done.

"You've finished, Mr. Henry!" exclaimed Blaikie in well-feigned surprise.

"Yes, Blaikie, you're too late," said Henry. "It's a pity, isn't it? But I tell you what, you can clear the back drive. That will be a fine job for you and it'll give you an appetite for your dinner."

Henry smiled when he had said it, not only because Blaikie's face of consternation was enough to make anybody smile but also because he had used "Flockie's phrase" as Rhoda called it. Rhoda had caught it from Flockie and Henry from Rhoda; it was as infectious as measles.

The portrait had arrived and was a tremendous success. The "parents" were entranced with it. They had spent several days trying to decide where it should be hung, whether in the dining-room where they could see it when they were having their meals or in the drawing-room where it would be visible to them at other times. Each wanted to hang it exactly where the other wanted it hung which made the choice of position exceedingly difficult. Henry had taken no part in the arguments, it was his part to get the steps and hang the picture and then to take it down and hang it somewhere else. Eventually an exceedingly fine Constable was removed from the wall and Rhoda's masterpiece hung in its place. Henry intended to tell Rhoda about the removal of the Constable; it would amuse her, he knew.

"Dear Rhoda!" said Mrs. Ogylvie Smith when at last the matter was settled. "She has done it so beautifully and so understandingly. It is you, Henry, your very self. When you are not here in person I shall still have you here to look at. Yes, that is where it shall hang, where we can both see it from our chairs. You may put away the ladder, Henry."

Mr. Ogylvie Smith said less but was equally pleased with the portrait; it was an exceedingly good likeness and also a very fine piece of work—quite remarkable for a young unknown painter. Mr. Ogylvie Smith knew a good deal about art; he had inherited a taste for good painting from his father and his grandfather, both of whom had been connoisseurs. It was his grandfather who had bought the displaced Constable when few of Constable's contemporaries appreciated his beautiful interpretations of the English countryside.

"I hope Mrs. Dering Johnstone has allowed you to pay her a good price for the portrait," said Mr. Ogylvie Smith to his son.

"We're still wrangling about it," replied Henry, smiling. "Her idea of the value of her work is absurdly modest. I must go over to Boscath one of these days and fix it up."

All that had happened several days ago and to-day, when Henry went into the drawing-room glowing all over after his work in the cold air, he found his mother standing before the portrait gazing at it.

"I like it more and more," she said with a sigh. Then she turned and smiled at the original.

Henry threw himself into a chair. "I've cleared the drive," he said. "It was grand exercise and it has given me an appetite like a horse. Of course Blaikie appeared when I had finished."

"But I told him to help you!"

"I told him to clear the back drive, and if looks could kill I'd be as dead as mutton," said Henry cheerfully.

"Listen, Henry. We will talk of the idle Blaikie later (though what use it will be to talk of him I do not know). There has been a telephone message for you from the sister of your nice Doctor Forrester."

"Oh," said Henry casually.

There are all sorts of different ways of saying "Oh," and Mrs. Ogylvie Smith was a discerning woman. She had a feeling that Henry's exclamation was rather too casual to be true. Mrs. Ogylvie Smith had tried very hard to find a young woman to suit Henry's requirements; it was time—nay, more than time—that Henry arranged himself and produced some grandchildren for her to spoil.

"I did not know you knew Miss Forrester," said Mrs. Ogylvie Smith craftily.

"Of course I know her; she's Adam's sister."

"Of course! How foolish of me! It never occurred to me that you knew her. I have seen her in church and admired her; she has such a very interesting face, so full of spirituosity."

"Yes, she is—interesting," agreed Henry.

"I must ask her to tea," declared Mrs. Ogylvie Smith. "I should like to meet her. Interesting people are few and far between . . . but I have not told you her message. She is troubled about her brother. It appears that the young doctor went to Tassieknowe to see that very strange Miss Heddle and coming back he was caught in the snowstorm and lost his way. Now he is laid up at Mureth with bronchitis and a broken rib."

"Good Heavens!" cried Henry in consternation.

" Mamie telephones daily and her reports are reassuring but Miss Forrester is not altogether reassured; she suspects Mamie of concealing the true state of affairs and is afraid her brother may be seriously ill."

Henry nodded. Adam's chest had never been very strong and Nan always worried about it.

" Mureth is snow-bound," continued Mrs. Ogylvie Smith. " Doctor Black cannot go to see him and Miss Forrester begs you to telephone to Mamie and find out the truth."

She paused but Henry remained silent. " Mamie might give more detailed information to you," added Mrs. Ogylvie Smith.

" What's the good of speaking to Mamie on the phone? " Henry exclaimed.

" You will not speak to her? "

" What's the good? " repeated Henry. " Somebody should see Adam. He ought to be having treatment."

" Those little pills, I suppose," said Mrs. Ogylvie Smith with a sigh. " Those dreadful little pills that you forced down my throat when I had pneumonia. They made me feel so exceedingly ill and so excessively miserable—as if my best friend had died and nobody loved me any more."

" But they cured you," said Henry, smiling.

" So you said. I believe I would have recovered more quickly without them."

Henry thought not but he did not argue the matter. He walked over to the window and looked out. " I'll have a crack at it," he said.

" But you cannot go! The road is blocked completely. I have just telephoned to the Police Station and the sergeant told me."

" So you had the same idea! " said Henry, looking round and smiling.

" Naturally," retorted his mother. " Surely it is not a very strange idea that you should want to go to Mureth and see your friend! Unfortunately you cannot go. They are trying

to clear a passage with the snow-plough but so far without
success."

" I might do it on skis," said Henry.

Mrs. Ogylvie Smith looked at her son with pride and affec-
tion. She admired loyalty and courage above everything. If
she had realised the danger of the proposed expedition she
might have tried to persuade him not to attempt it, but danger
never entered her mind. She had watched Henry ski-ing,
flying gaily down the slopes which surrounded Blackthorn
House, and she imagined him flying gaily over the hills
to Mureth to see his sick friend and to take him a bottle of
those dreadful little pills which would make him feel so
miserable. Oh, to be a man—and young! thought Mrs.
Ogylvie Smith.

" I'll have a crack at it," repeated Henry. " It's too late to
go to-day. I'll start early to-morrow and give myself plenty
of time to get there and back before dark. I'd like a few
sandwiches and a Thermos of coffee, just in case . . ."

" In case of what?" asked his mother with dawning anxiety.

" In case I'm hungry, of course," replied Henry, laughing.

" We will prepare your haversack," nodded Mrs. Ogylvie
Smith. " And I will give you a pound of tea to take to Mamie
for fear she has run short. Her cupboard will be well stocked,
I have no doubt, but tea is strictly rationed. One cannot hoard
tea."

" How is it that you can hoard tea?" inquired Henry.

" That is a thing one does not ask," retorted his mother.

Henry was fond of ski-ing but it is one thing to fly gaily
down a well-known slope and execute an elegant telemark at
the bottom and quite another thing to set off across country,
up hill and down dale, with no idea how deep the snow may
be nor what snags may lie beneath the surface. Henry was not
looking forward to the expedition (in fact the more he thought
about it the less he liked it) but all the same he was determined
to go. He was very fond of Adam not only for his own sake
but also because Adam belonged to Nan . . . and here was

something he could do for Nan. It was not much, but it was something. Henry thought it most probable that Adam was seriously ill. Mamie knew very little about illness, her temperament was optimistic and she disliked worrying people. Mamie would argue that it was useless to worry Nan since nothing could be done—oh, yes, Henry knew what Mamie would be thinking.

Having decided to go early to-morrow morning Henry began to make his preparations, he went to Drumburly and procured the necessary assortment of drugs at the chemist and then he returned and looked out his skis and the ski-ing suit which he had worn when he was in Switzerland. He would take boots as well, climbing boots would be the best. When he had collected the various articles he laid them out on the bed and looked at the little pile and thought it over carefully; he was aware that he must take everything he would need and he did not know in what condition he would find his patient. It was more than possible that he would find lobar pneumonia as a complication. The pile consisted of adhesive strapping, a sling, gauze, cotton-wool and scissors, sulphonamide tablets, ampoules of penicillin, ampoules of distilled water and ampoules of morphine. There was a hypodermic syringe and several needles of different sized bores. There was a stethoscope, a thermometer, a bottle of aspirin tablets and a bottle of Friars Balsam. After gazing at the pile for a few moments Henry added forceps and a flask of brandy. He packed them up carefully—very carefully indeed for he did not want to risk anything getting broken if he happened to take a toss on the way.

When Henry went down to dinner that evening he found an atmosphere of tension in the room.

"Henry!" cried his mother. "You cannot go. I have been speaking to Ian Shaw on the telephone and he says your idea is madness. The snow has drifted, some parts of the hill are bare and others but lightly covered. Ian says you will fall over a rock and break your ankle and then you will lie there and freeze."

Henry was annoyed. He was all the more annoyed because this eventuality was exactly what he feared. He had far too vivid an imagination to have overlooked the possibility of falling and injuring himself.

" What has Ian Shaw to do with it? " Henry inquired.

" Ian knows the danger," replied Mrs. Ogylvie Smith excitedly. " I was talking to Lady Shaw on the telephone and happened to mention what was in your mind. Ian said it was madness."

" He said that, did he? " remarked Henry.

" And he knows! " she cried. " He has been to Switzerland every winter and is an accomplished skier. He says he would not dream of attempting such a thing."

" Nobody has asked him to attempt it," Henry replied. " I'm not going for fun, I assure you. I'm going because Adam is ill and may need professional attention."

" Henry, I implore you——"

" My dear," said Mr. Ogylvie Smith quietly. " Henry is determined to go, so it's no use saying any more. He will take every precaution and I think it will be a good plan if he will ring us up from Mureth when he gets there."

" You are both mad," she declared, spreading out her hands in a gesture of resignation. " If Henry is lost upon the hills it will be useless to send Blaikie to look for him; I shall have to go myself."

CHAPTER THIRTY-THREE

ALTHOUGH Lizzie enjoyed having Doctor Forrester to
look after it made a good deal more work and she was
surprised and pleased to find her son quite helpful and kind.
At one time, and not very long ago, Duggie had been most
unwilling to take any part in domestic duties. Now he carried
coal and washed dishes and did all sorts of little chores with a
good grace—and of course he had plenty of time for he could
neither go to school nor to Boscath.

Duggie seemed different and he felt different as well. He
had felt frustrated and restless, going from one thing to another,
"taking notions" as his mother put it, but never sticking to
anything for long. Now he had found his *métier* and had scope
to develop. Now he knew what he wanted and, because he
was on his way to achieve his heart's desire, he was contented.

"Shall I take up Doctor Forrester's tray?" asked Duggie at
breakfast time.

It was the morning after the visit of Mr. and Mrs. James.
The way to Boscath was open and Duggie had been invited to
go over with Mrs. Johnstone and take part in winter sports.
He was so extraordinarily happy at the prospect that he felt
charitable to all the world and had made up his mind to help
his mother as much as possible before he went. There was
another reason, not quite so altruistic, for Duggie's offer to
take up Doctor Forrester's tray. He was anxious to see Doctor
Forrester and to ask him something, it was something that was
weighing rather heavily on his mind.

"Well," said Lizzie in doubtful tones. "Maybe I'd better
take it myself."

" I could take it for you."

" Would you do it *nicely*? "

Duggie received this as permission to perform the service, which indeed it was, and taking the tray carried it up forthwith.

The patient was lying down when his breakfast arrived upon the scene. Duggie propped him comfortably with pillows, brought the bed-table and placed the tray before him. He then proceeded to rearrange the dishes in a convenient manner upon the tray.

Adam was amused and touched at the boy's thoughtfulness and somewhat surprised at his dexterity; he watched the slender brown hands moving over the tray, putting the cup straight upon the saucer and a spoon near the marmalade jar. Adam had seen hands like that before, slender brown hands with long tapering fingers, larger hands than Duggie's but exactly the same shape. Often and often Adam had watched those hands and admired them as they took a syringe to pieces or performed some other delicate operation with grace and precision.

" Your hands, Duggie! " exclaimed Adam impulsively.

" They're quite clean, Doctor Forrester," declared their owner in alarm.

" I meant—they're—well-shaped hands."

Duggie smiled with relief. He was proud of his hands, so he held them out for Doctor Forrester to see . . . and then with a sudden mischievous impulse he bent the top joint of his third finger backwards in a most peculiar way. He had discovered that he could perform this trick and that other people could not; he had also discovered that other people disliked seeing the trick performed; in fact they were usually horrified at the sight. They screamed (if they happened to be of the female sex) and covered their eyes.

Doctor Forrester reacted quite differently. He seized Duggie's hand and examined it; then he looked at Duggie's face.

" When were you born? " demanded Doctor Forrester.

It was an unexpected question but it did not disturb Duggie for long ago he had made up his mind that grown-up people were queer. " The eighteenth of November, nineteen thirty-nine," said Duggie without hesitation.

" Yes, that's it!" exclaimed Doctor Forrester, waving his arms excitedly. " Yes, of course! Good heavens, yes! It all fits in. How amazing!"

Duggie seized the tray which was in danger of being upset and gazed at the patient in alarm.

" How amazing!" repeated the patient, gazing back at Duggie. " How absolutely staggering! Here you were—all this time—and nobody knew! Listen, Duggie—no, that won't do. Goodness, I don't know what to say! Never mind—I'll have to think about it——"

" Are you feeling well enough?" inquired Duggie (in the peculiar idiom of the district, where to be well enough simply means not to be unwell). For now it seemed to Duggie that the trick he had played with his unusually constructed finger-joint had deranged the patient's wits.

" I'm perfectly well," replied the patient untruthfully. " I'm on top of the world. I'm as fit as a fiddle. You cut along now, Duggie, or you'll be late for school."

" But I can't go to school," said Duggie in surprise. " You know I can't, Doctor Forrester. We're snowed up. That's why I brought your breakfast. If I'd been going to school I'd have gone *long* ago."

" Of course," agreed Doctor Forrester beginning to laugh and then remembering his ribs and stopping rather hastily. " Of course! What a fool I am! I'd forgotten we were snowed up. You can thank your lucky stars we're snowed up and you brought up my breakfast. Now cut along, I've got some thinking to do."

Duggie hesitated. There was something he wanted to ask. Maybe Doctor Forrester was not in a fit state to be bothered with questions. Maybe he should wait.

" What's the matter?" asked the doctor. " Why are you hovering like that? Don't worry about me, I'm as right as rain."

" I was wondering," said Duggie. " I was just wondering if you could tell me something, Doctor Forrester."

Adam smiled. " It's your turn to ask."

" Well," said Duggie in doubtful tones. " It's just something I'm wanting to know and I thought maybe you could tell me."

" Fire away, I'll answer if I can."

Duggie stood first on one leg and then on the other. " It's just—I was wondering—supposing a person gave a person a fright and they got very ill, would the person be put in prison? "

Adam considered the matter. " No, I don't think so," he said. " It would depend a good deal on circumstances; whether the person meant to frighten the—the other person, I mean."

" The person meant to frighten the other person but not to make her ill," explained Duggie carefully. " The person meant them to go away from Tassieknowe, that's all."

" Duggie! " exclaimed Adam gazing at him in consternation. " Duggie, you don't mean—no, I don't want to hear another word."

" You don't want to hear—— "

" Not another syllable," said Adam firmly. " There are some things which should be locked in the secret cupboard in the deepest recesses of the bosom and never exposed to the light of day. I'm deaf," declared Adam. " I didn't hear a word you said, but other people might not be so deaf. Be dumb, Duggie, and all will be well."

Duggie nodded. His question was answered; he went away with an easy mind.

When the door had shut, and not before, Adam exclaimed aloud. He felt a trifle giddy to tell the truth for he was not in a fit condition to withstand shocks and he had received two shocks one after the other in the space of ten minutes. He had solved two mysteries. The second was over, it was past and done with. Be dumb, he had said and this was the right advice ... but the other mystery ... quite a lot would have to be done about that.

I must think, said Adam to himself as he began to eat his

porridge (for the porridge was before him upon the tray and, although the skies fall, porridge must be eaten and should be eaten hot). I must think . . . but he could not think clearly. It was too amazing. *Could* it be true? But it *was* true. Adam was certain of it. Those hands! That curious freak formation in the joint of the third digit, a freak formation which he had noticed in the second finger of his chief! And now that his eyes were opened he saw Duggie's resemblance to Henry so clearly that it seemed incredible that he had not seen it before and that apparently nobody else had seen it.

But he must think what to do, whether to keep the secret to himself until he could get into touch with Henry or to tackle Lizzie and so make assurance doubly sure. He was still swithering when Lizzie came up to remove his breakfast tray and clean the room.

" It's still freezing," said Lizzie cheerfully. " You'll not win through to the hospital yet awhile." She said the same thing every morning in exactly the same words. Lizzie had a one-track mind, she thought the same thing every morning and every morning she said it.

Adam tried to find a new answer every morning and to-day he said, " The Man Who Came to Dinner, that's me."

The allusion meant nothing to Lizzie but this did not worry her for she was used to her limitations. If she did not understand a thing she left it alone.

" Did Duggie bring up the breakfast nicely? " she inquired.

" Very nicely," replied Adam.

By this time Lizzie was on her hands and knees, dusting beneath the book-case, and quite suddenly Adam decided what he should do.

" Lizzie," he said casually. " Do you know where your husband is? "

For a minute or two there was no reply and then she said, " Mr. Johnstone tried to find him."

" Yes," agreed Adam. " But you told him the wrong place to look. People can look long enough in the wrong place and never find what they're looking for. Shall I find him for you, Lizzie?"

She sat back on her heels and gazed at Adam in consternation.

"I know," said Adam nodding.

"You'll not tell!" she exclaimed.

"Why don't you want to go back to him?"

"It was a silly thing. We never ought to have got married at all, him and me."

"Why did you let him think you had been killed?"

"We nearly were," explained Lizzie. "If Duggie and me had been in the house we'd have been killed right enough, but Mrs. Crow came up and said we'd best go to the shelter. We didn't always go to the shelter—only sometimes."

"How did you come to Drumburly?"

"In the bus, of course."

"But why Drumburly, of all places?"

"Oh, that was funny, really. By rights we should have gone to Ayr with Mrs. Crow and the rest of them, but there was another woman wanting to go to Ayr."

"So you changed places?"

"She gave me a pound for my seat," said Lizzie nodding. "Her brother lived at Ayr . . . and then somebody said there was a bus going to Drumburly so Duggie and me just got in. I thought maybe I'd go and see his mother like he said I was to."

"But you didn't go and see his mother?"

Lizzie shook her head.

"Why didn't you?"

"How could I?" Lizzie said. "You see we all came to Drumburly in the bus and they told us to go into the school and wait. I just went in with the other ones."

"You could have told somebody."

"I thought of it," admitted Lizzie. "But—— Och, well, I was awful dirty and untidy and miserable and Mrs. Johnstone looked kind. When the other lady said I was to go with her and she would take care of Duggie and me, I just went. That was the way of it."

" So that's how you came to Mureth? "

Lizzie nodded.

How simple things were when you held the key, thought Adam. He sighed. It was hard work screwing information out of Lizzie (not so much because she was unwilling to answer questions but more because she found it difficult) but there were several other matters to be cleared up before he could let her go.

Lizzie was continuing her work; she was dusting the mantelpiece with her usual careful attention so Adam was obliged to talk to her back.

" Why didn't you write to him? " Adam inquired.

" I thought of it," admitted Lizzie. " But I was ill and I put off writing and then Greta was born and . . . Och, what was the use? I knew fine he'd be better off without me and I was better off without him. The whole thing was a silly mistake, that's the truth of it."

She was right, of course, the marriage had been a mistake, but still! " He might have married somebody else," Adam pointed out. He brought up this point because it was a point that had caused him some concern; the thing had so very nearly happened. Henry had so very nearly married somebody else.

" I wouldn't have minded," declared Lizzie.

" But that would have been wrong," explained Adam, trying to put it simply and to make her understand.

" He would never have done nothing *wrong*," said Lizzie warmly. " He was good—real good, he was. I never knew him do wrong all the time I was married to him."

" You're still married to him, Lizzie."

" In a way, I suppose," admitted Lizzie. " But he could have married somebody else if he'd wanted."

" A man can't marry somebody else when he has a wife already," said Adam patiently.

" But he thought we were dead—and we nearly were."

" He was very unhappy about you," Adam told her.

" Och, I dare say he was a bit upset," admitted Lizzie. " He was fond of us in a way, but it was better in the long run."

" Of course he was upset!" exclaimed Adam. " It was cruel of you not to write to him."

" It was better in the long run," repeated Lizzie.

" You ought to write to him, Lizzie. Duggie and Greta are his children."

" They're his children right enough," agreed Lizzie. " But he doesn't know nothing about Greta. I never told him there was another on the way."

" You ought to write to him," repeated Adam.

" Now!" she cried. " That's the last thing! It's years and years! He's forgotten all about us, I wouldn't wonder. He's better without me and I'm better without him. I'll not leave Mureth and Mrs. Johnstone for nobody—let well alone, that's what I say."

Adam was too tired to continue the argument; Henry would have to see her himself. Adam understood Lizzie's attitude perfectly and to a certain extent he sympathised with it. There was a sort of sense in what she said—a sort of crazy common sense. She had so nearly been killed that to all intents and purposes she was dead. That was what she had been trying to tell him.

She had finished her work and come over to the bed. " You'll not tell, will you, Doctor Forrester?" she said earnestly. " It wouldn't be a bit of good, for I'll not go back. I'm fine here and I like it. I'm in my right place. I'll not leave Mrs. Johnstone for nobody."

He smiled at her. " Mrs. Johnstone couldn't do without you, Lizzie."

" That's true enough," she agreed. She gathered up her dusters and the tin of polish and went away without another word.

Adam was glad to see her go. He was surprised that she had not tried to wring a promise from him (perhaps she thought a promise unnecessary) and he was even more surprised that she had not asked how he had acquired his information about her private affairs. Surely it would have been a natural question! But as he had no intention of telling Lizzie how he had discovered her secret it was just as well she was not of an inquisitive nature.

He knew everything now and he saw how naturally the whole thing had happened. Adam, working at the big London hospital, had come across much stranger stories. There was the Polish couple, for instance, who had lost touch with one another during the war; they had spent years looking for one another and then, suddenly and unexpectedly, had met face to face in the hospital waiting-room and fallen into one another's arms. That was strange, if you like! Lizzie's story was not strange when you knew Lizzie and understood the working of her mind. It had all happened quite simply, one event leading to another with the inevitability of a Greek drama.

The discovery of Duggie was in a different category. Lying back upon his pillows and thinking about it Adam saw the events of the last few weeks like beads upon a thread. It had begun with Shylock. He remembered Nan sitting by the fire struggling with that wig; sewing it together; holding it up and laughing at it; taking it to pieces and starting all over again. Nan little knew she held the key to happiness in her hand. Yes, the thread began with Shylock's wig which had given Duggie his brilliant idea, and the beads upon the thread were Miss Heddle's illness; his own visit to Tassieknowe; his rage and fury with the egregious Nestor; his wanderings in the snow; his arrival at Mureth; his illness and his recognition of Duggie's hands. At any moment and at many places the thread might have snapped and the beads been scattered to the four winds but the thread had held and led him to Duggie. You could call it Fate, he supposed. He preferred to see the guidance of Providence in the thread . . . and he was unutterably glad to feel that he was the instrument Providence had used.

There was no selfishness in Adam, no thought of his own future, all his thoughts were of Nan and of his best friend.

They could be happy now, everything could be arranged, the old foolish mistake undone. It could be undone, Adam knew. Lizzie had deserted her husband deliberately and had no intention whatever of returning to him (" I'll not go back," she had said). It would take time, of course—anything to do with lawyers took time—but that did not matter if happiness lay at the end of the road. Happiness instead of hopelessness!

Adam thought of Duggie. He had been deprived of his birthright by his mother's foolishness. That was the worst wrong of all, but fortunately it was not too late to right the wrong. Adam had told the boy to thank his lucky stars that Mureth was snowed up and that instead of going to school he had brought up the breakfast tray. He had spoken without thinking seriously, but now he saw the truth of his impulsive statement.

Adam was happy. He lay and looked at the snow-covered hills. There was only one thing he wanted now, he wanted to see his friend.

CHAPTER THIRTY-FOUR

HENRY left home just as it was beginning to get light and long before his parents were awake. He put on boots with nailed soles for the first part of the trip and strapped his skis on his back; with his haversack and his ski-sticks he was fairly heavily laden but there was no need to hurry. He had decided to go to Mureth by way of Boscath (the idea had come to him just as he was going to bed and it seemed to him a brilliant one). He would go by the old drove road, which he knew well, and once at Boscath he would have no difficulty in crossing the river. Having settled this he felt a good deal happier and more confident about the success of his expedition.

It was dry and cold and windless; the sky was red with the

glow of sunrise and the reflection of the glow shone upon the billowing coverlet of snow. The forest trees looked dark, their branches a delicate tracery of brown; the patches of conifers looked almost black; here and there an outcrop of rock broke through the coverlet and a steep scree made a purple patch upon the hill.

It was very quiet, not a sound broke the stillness of the morning, and not a creature was to be seen ... but the snow at the sides of the road was marked by the tiny tracks of rabbits; and branches of trees, which had been broken off by the storm, had been stripped bare of bark. Henry trudged on, looking about him as he went and presently he reached deep snow and stopped to put on his skis.

Quite suddenly the sun came up from behind the eastern hills, it rose in a little cloud, a dove-grey cloud with a lining of purest gold. First a golden line appeared above the hills, it was like the edge of a golden guinea ... it rose and grew larger and the light from it poured down the snow-covered slopes in a golden flood. The whole land was transformed from glowing half-tones to a brilliance of light and shadow, dazzling to the eyes. Every little mound had its brilliance and its shadow; every rock and tree had a long blue finger stretching out towards Henry upon the gleaming snow. Henry gazed at it spellbound, he had never seen anything so beautiful, so dramatic, in all his life.

But he could not stand and gaze at the sunrise for long—it was too cold. He picked up his boots and tied them round his neck and continued on his way.

Henry had learnt to ski from a friend, Jack Briggs, who was an accomplished skier. Together they had been to Switzerland on three occasions. They had gone in February, which is an unfashionable time of year, and they had avoided fashionable resorts. Jack's idea of ski-ing was not to stay in a crowded hotel; to be taken to the top of a five-mile slope in a train and to come gliding down in company with a horde of Winter Sports fiends. Such artificial conditions had no allure for him.

What he liked was to live at a small inn and to start off early in the morning with a sandwich in his pocket; to ski through woods and over deserted hills finding his own trail. Henry had enjoyed this too. They had been good companions, not saying very much but happy to be silent together. Now that Henry had put on his skis he thought of Jack and wished that he were here. Good old Jack, this was the sort of expedition which would appeal to him! " I like to go to a place under my own steam," Jack was fond of saying. " Skis were invented for use, not for the amusement of a herd of swine." Well, Henry was using skis for a purpose to-day, using them to go to a place under his own steam.

The snow was dry and powdery and his skis ran well. Once he had got the feel of them he began to swing along at a good pace but he had to be very careful for it was impossible to tell what lay beneath the snow. In some places the snow was shallow, a mere covering over stones and heather; in other places it had drifted into heaps. The well-known path looked completely different, mounds and hollows had been levelled out, dykes and ditches had disappeared, but fortunately there were landmarks to guide Henry on his way. He remembered that the path ran through a group of wind-blown trees; he steered a course for the trees and found them without difficulty. From thence the path took a bend and skirted a pile of curiously shaped boulders . . . and there was a wooded cleft in the hills where a burn ran down.

Several times Henry strayed from the path and once he found himself in thick heather; the woody stems caught his skis and upset him head over heels. The experience, though very unpleasant, did him no physical harm, but it frightened him considerably. A sprained ankle or indeed any small injury, which would be of no consequence if he had a companion, might prove an extremely serious matter for a lonely man.

Presently the path swung westwards and steepened as it rose to the saddle between the hills. There was less snow here and Henry was obliged to change back to his boots. The path was slippery with ice ... he toiled up laboriously, his breath made a cloud in the sharp cold air. The sun was warm now; he could feel the warmth of it on his back and his shadow went before him, a curious ape-like shadow upon the snow.

It seemed hours before he reached the top but at last he reached it and paused and looked back. The sun dazzled his eyes; it had risen well above the hills and was blazing in a cloudless blue sky. He found a flat rock, spread his mackintosh cape upon it and sat down to eat his sandwiches and drink his coffee. The climb had given him an appetite and he could have eaten twice as much.

While Henry was sitting there a sheep came round the corner of the rock, stepping delicately, scraping the snow away and eating the grass beneath. It was not frightened of Henry (perhaps it was too hungry or too dazed to be frightened). It was the first living creature he had seen and it awakened a curious feeling of fellowship in Henry; he and the sheep were the only two warm-blooded creatures in this waste of snow! What frightful privations this creature had suffered and was suffering! It seemed miraculous that it had survived. He watched it for a few moments and noticed it was lame.

Henry knew nothing whatever about sheep but he decided to have a look and see what was the matter, so he rose and went towards it. The sheep moved away and Henry went after it. The sheep moved faster, it leapt from rock to rock. Although it was lame it was extraordinarily agile and it took Henry a good ten minutes before he managed to grab hold of it by its wool; even then his difficulties were not over for it struggled and kicked and he had no idea how to hold it. Finally however he managed to turn it over on its back and wedge it between two rocks so that it was helpless. By this time Henry was extremely hot, he was also extremely annoyed with his patient; he had had trouble with patients before but the sheep was the most recalcitrant patient he had ever had.

" You *are* a fool," said Henry. " You really are an unmitigated fool. I'm only trying to help you." The sheep kicked its legs feebly in the air but made no sound whatever. Henry examined its feet carefully and discovered a hard ball of mud and ice packed tightly between its toes; he decided that this was the cause of the trouble and removed it carefully, swabbing the place with disinfectant. He then turned the sheep right side up and released it. The sheep bounded away; it was still lame, he noticed, but that was not to be wondered at.

All this had taken time but the worst part of the trip lay behind him and a few hundred yards took him up to the saddle between the two hills. Here Henry stopped again and put on his skis and went forward quickly and easily; he passed the ruined cottage (which to-day was unrecognisable as the one-time home of a man but was merely an irregular mound of snow) and then suddenly the hills fell back on either hand and he was looking down to Boscath and Mureth.

This sudden view of the valley always surprised him and to-day it surprised him more than ever: at one moment he was surrounded upon every side by the hills and the next he was through them and the valley lay before him. There before his eyes lay the two farms of Mureth and Boscath like two outposts of civilisation in the wide wastes of snow. They looked very small from the vantage point of the hill, small and somehow deserted, but their chimneys were smoking bravely in the still morning air. The rays of the sun caught one of the windows of Mureth House and glittered and winked like a heliograph. The river was low (Henry noticed that at once). The river was a mere trickle, half blocked with ice.

Henry had been so intent upon the farms and the river that he had not noticed what lay nearer at hand, but now he heard the sound of voices—which was a very curious sound to hear—and looking down the gentle slope which lay between him and Boscath he saw a group of little figures upon the shoulder of the hill. Who were they and what on earth were they doing, he wondered.

Suddenly a toboggan shot away down the slope and Henry realised that Boscath was amusing itself upon a miniature

Cresta! It was a huge toboggan laden with human freight and it seemed to be going at a terrific speed and gaining impetus every moment. Henry was not surprised when he saw it overturn at the bottom and its occupants scattered in a flurry of snow—their screams of excitement came to his ears a few moments later and made him smile. And now, as they picked themselves up and gesticulated wildly, he was able to recognise the figures: James and Rhoda and—yes, it was Mamie, and the small figure was Duggie of course.

Henry coo-ed to them and, launching himself forward, sped down the slope as gay and graceful as a flying bird. He swooped round in a wide circle and with a telemark turn stopped within a few yards of the little group.

It was worth all the toil and trouble of the trip just to see their faces for they had been far too concerned with their own avocations to hear his call. To their astonished eyes the tall, slender figure in the well-fitting, grey ski-ing suit seemed to have fallen from the heavens or materialised from the air.

Duggie was the first to recover from the shock. "Oh, Doctor Ogylvie Smith!" he exclaimed in tones of admiration and delight. "You're just like the picture on the poster in Drumburly Station!"

The picture was known to Henry and he was by no means displeased at the comparison (besides he liked Duggie and spontaneous admiration is heartening) so he smiled at Duggie in a very friendly manner indeed.

"It's true," declared Rhoda, laughing. "But what a surprise you gave us! Where have you come from?"

"You don't mean to say you've come over the hills!" Mamie exclaimed.

James said nothing. He was busy righting the toboggan and clearing off the snow.

"Over the hills," said Henry, nodding.

"Goodness! How marvellous!" cried Rhoda. "It *was* nice of you, Henry. We're delighted to see you."

"I really came to have a look at Adam."

James turned and smiled with relief. " The doctor drops in ! " he suggested.

" Yes, this is a medical mission rather than a social call." He looked at Mamie as he spoke and Mamie took the hint.

" You weren't worried about him, were you? " she said. " He's getting on splendidly. Jock and I strapped up his ribs and he says they're fairly comfortable except when he laughs, or coughs. But the cough is better too. Of course he'll be delighted to see you."

Henry realised that his medical mission had been unnecessary and for a moment he felt rather a fool, but his welcome was too cordial for the feeling to last long. Even James, who for some reason had always been a little cold in his manner, thawed into cordiality and wanted to hear all his adventures; which way he had come and how he had accomplished the arduous journey.

" Over the saddle! " exclaimed James incredulously. " I shouldn't have thought it possible. And to attempt it alone! " For James knew the terrain, it was mostly Boscath ground, and he knew more about ski-ing than the other members of the party.

" I met one of your sheep on the way," said Henry, smiling. " At least I suppose it was one of yours . . ." and he told them the story of the operation he had performed upon the reluctant animal.

" Very decent of you," declared James. " That's what starts foot-rot. We'll have to look out for foot-rot when the snow melts."

Henry was unwilling to break up the tobogganing party and assured his friends that he was capable of continuing upon his way alone but Mamie insisted upon accompanying him.

" Of course I'm coming with you," said Mamie earnestly. " It would be awful if you were drowned in the river after coming all that way across the hills."

This was such a Mamie-ish remark that the others laughed.

" You know what I mean *quite well*! " declared Mamie. " It's the sort of thing that *does* happen to people; they come through the most frightful dangers without a scratch and then get killed by a tile falling off a roof."

Rhoda smiled. She was aware that this fate had befallen some well-known hero of Ancient Rome—or was it Greece?—and she had a shrewd suspicion that Mamie knew all about it, but that her innate modesty prevented her from mentioning the fact.

While they had been talking Henry had removed his skis, and now that he was ready he and Mamie set off together down the hill. They crossed the river without mishap and walked up the path to Mureth.

"It was *very* good of you to come," declared Mamie. "I was anxious about Adam at first and of course there was no possible way of getting a doctor. He's getting better now but all the same it will be a great relief to my mind for you to see him and perhaps you'll be able to suggest something we can do for him. I'll ring up your mother and tell her you've arrived safely while you go up to Adam. It will be a lovely surprise for him when you walk in."

So Henry went up the stairs and, guided by the directions of his hostess, he opened the door of Adam's room and walked in.

"Well!" exclaimed Henry. "What have you been doing to yourself, you young ruffian?"

"Henry!" cried Adam joyously. "How marvellous! I've been simply panting to see you, wondering how on earth I was going to *bear* it until I could get hold of you. Shut the door and come here. I'm simply bursting with news."

Adam's eyes were so bright and his face so flushed with excitement that his visitor believed him to be in a high fever and after shutting the door obediently he went over to the bed and took Adam's hand in his.

"It's all right," declared Adam. "There's a little fever but nothing to bother about. You can sound me afterwards if you like. First I want to tell you what I've discovered. Listen, Henry . . ."

234

CHAPTER THIRTY-FIVE

THE story which Adam had to tell was so unexpected that at first Henry did not believe it (it was all the more difficult to believe because Adam was too excited to tell it in proper order) but after a few minutes Henry began to get the gist of it and to realise that it was true. Elizabeth was found. He got up and walked about the room struggling with a dozen different emotions, trying to adjust himself and to be calm . . . he must be calm for Adam's sake, it was obvious that Adam was not in a fit state to be further excited and disturbed.

" I feel—quite dazed," declared Henry.

" Of course," nodded Adam. " Anybody would feel dazed."

" I can't think. I don't know what to do."

" Do nothing at all until you've thought it over quietly. There's no hurry about it."

" It's difficult to believe! "

" Yes, but it's true. You know, Henry, the boy is so like you that it seems strange nobody noticed it before."

" That boy—yes, I've always had an odd sort of feeling about him. As a matter of fact I told Rhoda I'd be responsible for his future. That's funny, isn't it? Why on earth does everybody call him Duggie? "

" Do you mean that isn't his name? "

" His name is Henry. I mean he was christened Henry," said Henry still in that vague, bewildered voice.

" So he's Henry Ogylvie Smith? "

" Yes." Henry walked over to the fire and then walked back. He said, " And he feels it too. I mean he likes me . . . my son! I wish I could see what to do about it all."

" It will work out."

" Elizabeth is the problem," said Henry. " I've been looking for her for years, but now—now I almost wish she hadn't been found. I don't feel as if I could cope with it, somehow. I feel helpless."

" But don't you see it's the best thing that could possibly have happened! You've been worrying yourself silly about her, haven't you? Well, here she is, perfectly safe and sound."

That was true, thought Henry. At least he was free from anxiety as to Elizabeth's fate. She was safe and well. All this time when he had been searching for her she had been here within a few miles of his home. He walked over to the window and looked out unseeingly. Anger rose in his heart.

" Why on earth didn't she write to me! " he exclaimed.

" She just drifted——" began Adam.

" Drifted! " cried Henry, seizing on the word. " Yes, she just drifted along comfortably, never thinking about me at all. It was cruel! "

Adam had used the same word. " Yes," he agreed. " But she didn't mean to be cruel, you know."

" It was cruel," repeated Henry. " It was cruel and wicked. You don't know—nobody knows what I've suffered." He thought of all the nights he had lain awake agonising over Elizabeth and the baby, of how he had blamed himself for allowing them to remain in Glasgow, of how he had imagined them frightened, trapped in the blazing house, of how he had imagined them starving in the gutter . . . and all the time they had been here at Mureth safe and happy.

" Silly people are often cruel," said Adam. " You know that yourself. People with no imagination are cruel because they don't realise what other people are suffering." He stopped suddenly, surprised to find himself making excuses for her.

Henry did not reply in words; he threw out his hands in a foreign gesture, a gesture with shades of meaning which it would be difficult to convey in words.

After that there was silence in the room for several long minutes. Henry was still gazing out of the window so only his back was visible. What was he thinking, Adam wondered, was he brooding over the past or trying to make plans for the future? He was angry, that at least was obvious, and Adam was glad he was angry. Adam had interpreted the gesture as a casting off of all responsibility—that was all to the good. There was less chance of any quixotic ideas arising in Henry's mind to spoil the prospect of future happiness.

" One thing is certain," said Henry at last. " She has made it very obvious that she doesn't want to have anything more to do with me, hasn't she? "

Adam found this difficult to answer.

" Hasn't she? " repeated Henry, swinging round and looking at his friend.

" Well—yes," agreed Adam. " She said nothing would induce her to leave Mrs. Johnstone. She's happy here."

" I suppose I had better see her and find out——"

" No, don't do that! " exclaimed Adam, raising himself from his pillows in his earnestness. " You must see your lawyer first. Don't see her *whatever* you do, especially just now when you're angry with her."

" I'm not angry! "

" You're furious," Adam told him. " And you've every right to be furious, but you mustn't speak to her when you're feeling like that. Don't mention it to anybody until you've seen your lawyer and asked his advice—not anybody——" implored Adam, beginning to cough. " Promise, Henry! You'll go and wreck everything—if you begin dashing about —like a bull—in a china shop——" He was coughing uncontrollably now, shaken to pieces with the paroxysm, gasping for breath.

Henry came over to him and held him tightly until he was better and then laid him back upon his pillows. He was crimson in the face and his forehead was wet with beads of sweat.

" It's all right, H.O.," he whispered. " Bad for the ribs,

that's all. Damned painful. You promise not to do anything silly, won't you?"

"Yes, yes," said Henry soothingly "I'll promise anything you like. I'll promise to do nothing and tell nobody until I've consulted Mr. Murray. Does that satisfy you?" Now lie still and keep quiet; we'll have a look at that chest."

Adam managed not to smile while his chest was being sounded but when he turned over for his back to be sounded he hid a smile in the pillow. The fit of coughing, though exceedingly unpleasant and painful, had come at an opportune moment. H.O. was first and foremost a doctor.

"H'm," said Henry, as he folded up his stethoscope. "I think we'll——"

"No," said Adam firmly. "I'm having no sulphonamide, Henry. I'm better. I don't care what you found in my chest. I'm better, I tell you. I've been lying here for four days comfortable and warm, fed on eggs and cream. Mother Nature is curing me in her own sweet way. As a matter of fact I've been thinking a lot about a number of things (including drugs) and I've decided to go a bit easy on drugs in the future."

"Isn't that nice?" said Henry, smiling. "As a matter of fact I wasn't going to mention sulphonamide. Your chest is clearing nicely. I think I could improve upon the strapping and give you more support."

Adam had the grace to feel ashamed. "That would be grand," he said. "Don't think I'm ungrateful, will you? It was most awfully good of you to come and see me, but—by the way how on earth did you come?"

Henry burst out laughing.

While Henry was upstairs an exciting event had occurred at Mureth: the small red post office van had arrived to deliver four days' mail. Mamie saw it from the window and could scarcely believe her eyes. (Noah could not have been more pleased and surprised when the dove returned to the ark with the olive branch in its beak.) Mamie ran out to welcome the van and, as most of the cottagers had felt the same impulse, the van was surrounded by an admiring throng. Everybody wanted to know how the postman had managed to get through, and everybody was eager to offer him refreshment. In normal times the little red van was a daily visitant and the postman, Tom Tod, was an old friend. That he was also a second cousin once removed of Mrs. Couper's made him kin to Mureth and a sort of free-man of the place.

" Tom Tod! " exclaimed Mamie breathlessly. " Is the road open, then? "

" Aye, it's opened this morning," replied Mr. Tod. " They've been going at it hammer and tongs for the best part of three days. I'm not saying it's a joy-ride, ye ken, but I won through." He gave the impression that it would take more than a perilous road to hinder the distribution of His Majesty's Mail.

" It's marvellous! " Mamie declared. " I feel as if we'd been snowed-up for weeks."

There was a murmur of agreement from the cottagers. Everybody had felt the same.

Tom Tod distributed letters and parcels, most of which were for Mamie (he had also brought a parcel of groceries for his cousin) and having finished his business at Mureth he inquired whether it would be possible to continue up the valley. " There's a wheen of letters and parcels for Tassieknowe," explained Tom Tod. " The van's full of them. I never saw such an amount of stuff as comes for Tassieknowe in all my life. It's like Christmas Day every day of the year for them."

" I can well believe it," said Willy Bell with a grim smile. " They get the most of their stores by post from London. Drumburly shops are beneath the notice of grand folks like them."

" All but their mutton," said Tom Tod with dry humour.

The others laughed.

" Well, they'll need to wait," declared Willy Bell. " There's some things no amount of money can buy. I went up the road a bit this morning and I can tell you for certain you'll not win through to Tassieknowe till the thaw comes. The doctor's wee car is still buried, there's nothing to be seen of it but the roof and not much of that. Dear knows what like it'll be when we can get it out."

Tom Tod nodded. He had heard of the doctor's adventures of course, everybody in Drumburly had heard about them. " I'll just need to go back then," he said. " That's all about it."

It was while Tom was turning the van that Mamie remembered her visitor and decided that here was an excellent opportunity for Henry to go home in comfort. She broached the subject to Tom and found him willing to oblige. So Tom went in to have some refreshment at the Coupers' while Mamie ran back to the house to find out whether the idea of a life in the post office van appealed to Henry or whether he would rather stay to lunch.

By this time Henry had finished with his patient and was coming downstairs; coming down very reluctantly if the truth be told. He was wondering whether it would be possible to escape from Mureth before lunch. Could he possibly escape without being rude? He was feeling so upset that he wanted no lunch, nor did he feel in a fit condition to sit through lunch and discourse politely with his host and hostess. All Henry wanted at the moment was to creep into a deep, dark hole and remain there until he recovered from the shock. The mail van was not exactly a deep, dark hole but it was the next best thing and Henry accepted Mamie's suggestion with alacrity.

" Now that the road is open I could send the ambulance for Adam," Henry suggested.

" Would it be better for Adam to be in hospital?" asked Mamie.

" No," replied Henry, smiling at her. " He's doing well and obviously he's being well looked after. I'm all against moving a patient who's doing well."

" Then he must stay," declared Mamie. " He must stay until he's better. Is there anything we can do for him?"

" I've given him a cough mixture and I should like him to inhale—that's all, really."

Mamie nodded. " That's easy," she said.

Henry took up his skis which were standing outside the front door and they walked down the drive together.

" Of course we should love to have you to lunch," said Mamie. " It's dreadful to let you go without any lunch, but Tom Tod can't wait and it does seem a good chance."

Henry assured her that he was not hungry.

" Not hungry! " exclaimed Mamie, looking at him in sudden anxiety. " You haven't got a chill, have you, Henry? You ought to be hungry after coming all that way across the hills."

" No, I'm perfectly all right."

" It was splendid of you to come," she continued. " You mustn't think we don't appreciate it. Even if it wasn't absolutely necessary it was just as kind. It might have been necessary, if you see what I mean."

Henry saw what she meant. His hazardous trip across the hills had been unnecessary because Adam did not require his services and also because the road was now open and he could have come quite easily in his car, but Mamie in the goodness of her heart was trying to assure him that his act of friendship was just as valuable as if it had been urgently needed. Henry did not agree with this comforting view. He felt that he had dramatised himself in a ridiculous manner. He had felt rather pleased with himself for braving the perils of the frozen hills but it had been quite unnecessary and therefore useless. That was Henry's view of the matter. And it was not only this small act of service which had proved unnecessary—and therefore useless—but also the anxiety which he had suffered for years. Henry's mind was in a turmoil and it seemed to him that the two follies were alike and he, himself, the world's biggest fool.

" It was just as kind as if it had been necessary," Mamie told him.

" Kind! " he exclaimed. " It wasn't kindness at all, it was sheer stupidity."

Q

They had reached the gate and the little red van was waiting, so it was time to say good-bye.

" You'll go and see Nan, won't you? " Mamie said.

Oddly enough this had been in Henry's mind. He had been wondering whether or not he should see Nan. But how on earth did Mamie know anything about it? He gazed at Mamie in astonishment.

" You must," declared Mamie urgently. " She'll be so happy when she hears your news."

" My news! "

" About Adam being so much better."

" Oh, of course! " agreed Henry. He hesitated and then laughed. " Yes, I'll see Nan! " he exclaimed.

He waved good-bye, climbed into the van beside Tom Tod and they drove off. Mamie was left standing at the gate slightly bewildered. How queer Henry had been! So vague and *distrait*! Mamie *did* hope he had not caught a chill.

CHAPTER THIRTY-SIX

THE drive to Drumburly was somewhat adventurous and not particularly comfortable for there was still a good deal of snow upon the road. The little van bumped and slithered and lurched over the obstacles and once or twice it very nearly ended its career in a ditch.

" You're not frightened, are ye? " inquired Tom Tod.

" No," replied Henry . . . and it was true. There was a numb sort of feeling in him which precluded fear.

" I'll get ye there," said Tom Tod through clenched teeth.

Apart from this exchange the drive was accomplished in silence for Tom Tod had his hands full and Henry was busy with his thoughts.

Henry realised that he must see Nan, and see her at once, so that he could put her mind at rest about Adam. And if he saw her about Adam it would be difficult to refrain from telling her about the new development in his own affairs. He had promised Adam to tell nobody until he had seen his lawyer, but he knew Adam would not mind his telling Nan. Nan knew so much already and she was perfectly safe. . . . Henry felt he must talk to somebody about it.

At first he thought he would go and see Nan. Then, when he had thought about it for a few minutes, he decided that he would not go to her house. He had a feeling that it would be better to meet Nan upon neutral ground; he could ask her to come to the Shaw Arms. He did not know why he felt this, but the feeling was quite definite. So, having said good-bye to Tom and thanked him for the lift, Henry went to the hotel. First he rang up his mother and told her he was safely back at Drumburly and arranged for Blaikie to fetch him after tea, then he rang up Nan and told her Adam was better and asked her to come to the Shaw Arms.

" Now? " asked Nan in surprise.

" Yes, if you don't mind," replied Henry. " I'd like to see you if it isn't a bother."

There was nobody staying at the hotel and the lounge was deserted; Henry sat down near the fire. He was very tired and he had no lunch but he had forgotten about lunch and he did not feel hungry. He tried to think about his problems and decide what to do but it was difficult to think, his brain felt woolly. In a few minutes the door opened and Nan came in.

Henry had been watching the door so he saw her before she saw him. She looked worn and pale, her eyes seemed larger than usual . . . and rather frightened. Henry's heart went out to her, he felt an almost uncontrollable impulse to spring up and take her in his arms and comfort her, but he knew he must not. It crossed his mind suddenly that he had never kissed Nan, never made love to her, never said anything to her that all the world might not have heard!

"Nan," said Henry, rising as he spoke. "Come over near the fire. It's cold, isn't it?"

She came across the lounge quickly. "What is it?" she asked. "Is it something you want to tell me about Adam? Don't hide anything from me, Henry."

"But I told you," Henry said. "I've seen Adam and he's getting better. You needn't feel anxious about him."

"I thought perhaps—I mean why did you ask me to come?"

"I'm sorry I frightened you. Honestly there's no need to worry about him, Nan."

She sat down in the big chair by the fire and Henry sat down opposite to her. He told her exactly how he had found Adam and how he had restrapped the ribs; he told her how Adam looked and how well he was being looked after.

"It was awfully good of you to go," Nan said.

"Nonsense," replied Henry. "I quite enjoyed the expedition. I went on skis over the hills and I took a large consignment of drugs. Fortunately it was quite unnecessary."

Henry went on talking about his expedition for now that Nan was here he found it impossible to tell her about Elizabeth —he realised that he had no right to bother her with his private affairs.

"Henry," said Nan, looking at him with her clear frank eyes. "You meant to tell me something . . . something has happened . . . something unexpected."

"Yes—and I felt I had to see you, but now I realise I shouldn't have bothered you. I've no right to ask you to advise me what to do."

"We're friends, Henry," she told him. "I don't know whether I could advise you what to do but we could talk it over couldn't we? Sometimes it helps to talk things over." She hesitated and then added, "You've heard something about —about Elizabeth."

"Adam has found her."

"Adam!"

" Yes, she has been here all these years within a few miles of Drumburly."

" Here! " cried Nan. " But how amazing! Where is she—and how did Adam find her? "

Henry explained and, now that the subject had been opened, he found it easy to go on and tell Nan the whole story, for Nan was easy to talk to and she had thought so much about Henry's affairs that her mind was clear. She loved Henry so dearly that her understanding was intuitive. Before Henry had finished explaining Nan had understood—it was as easy as that.

" It seems incredible," said Henry at last. " I mean I can hardly believe she has been at Mureth all these years and I never found out."

" How could you have found out? You weren't at home very often were you? And even if you went over to Mureth it would be easy for her to keep out of your way. I mean I've been to Mureth several times myself but as far as I can remember I never saw her. Mrs. Johnstone told me that Lizzie was shy and kept in the background when anybody came to the house. No," said Nan. " No, the surprising thing is that we didn't realise Duggie is so like you. I can see it now, of course."

" Mother realised it," said Henry, smiling a little at the recollection which had crossed his mind. " Or at least she noticed that he is like *her*, which comes to much the same thing. It was in this very room, after the entertainment at the school. ' Shylock is like me,' she said. Of course we all laughed and thought it one of her jokes . . . Oh, Nan! " exclaimed Henry in sudden consternation. " Oh, Nan, what am I going to do about the parents! They'll be so terribly upset and miserable. How am I going to tell them about it? Shall I ever be able to make them understand how it happened! "

Nan sought for something to say but found nothing.

" It's a terrible thing," continued Henry in a low, strained voice. " You do something, and that leads to something else and it all piles up like a snowball . . . bigger and bigger."

" If I were you I should tell your father to-night," said Nan
gently.

" Oh, Nan! "

" I'm sure he'll understand. I've seen him in church and
he has an understanding face. Tell him to-night, Henry. Tell
him the whole story—just as you told me."

" Yes," said Henry. " Yes, I believe you're right. I'll tell
him."

There was silence for a few moments.

" About the children," said Henry, at last. " I wonder what
Elizabeth will want to do about them."

" I think she would be glad to let you take the responsibility
of the children," replied Nan thoughtfully.

" You think so? "

" She doesn't understand Duggie. She has no patience with
him. I'm quite sure something could be arranged."

" I should like that. Yes, I should like to—to make myself
responsible for the children . . . but all that must wait until
I find out what Elizabeth wants to do."

" I thought you said she wanted to stay at Mureth? "

" Yes, that's what she told Adam, but perhaps she would
rather have a house of her own. I could arrange that for her.
She made it quite clear that she didn't want to come back to
me, but she might like a house of her own . . . in that case she
might want to keep the children with her. Don't you think
so? "

Nan did not think so but she saw it was no use arguing with
Henry, he was too upset to keep to the point and make plans.
She encouraged him to talk for she thought it was the best
thing to do. Henry had never been able to talk about himself
and his troubles to anyone, his troubles had been bottled up for
years. He was talking now, talking at random, saying everything that came into his mind. He talked about Elizabeth and
about the children, he told Nan a lot more about his unavailing
search for them . . . and Nan listened and pieced everything
together in her mind. Presently she discovered that he had

had nothing to eat since his picnic at sunrise upon the hill so she rang for tea to be brought at once.

Henry did not want tea but he ate and drank to please Nan and began to feel better.

" It's awfully good of you to listen to all this," he told her. " It has cleared my mind talking about it and I'm beginning to get things straight. I don't like the idea of divorce, but in this case . . ." he hesitated and looked at Nan doubtfully.

Nan nodded. She did not like the idea of divorce, but what was the alternative? Was Henry to be tied for life to a woman who did not want him? (And this would be quite unlike the usual sort of divorce case. Henry and his wife had not seen each other for ten years. Their marriage was a thing of the past. Time and separation had dissolved the marriage and a legal divorce was merely a form to regularise the dissolution. This was Nan's view of the matter. Perhaps it was a slightly prejudiced view of the matter but most people are slightly prejudiced where their deepest feelings are concerned.) Nan thought Henry had suffered enough and deserved a little happiness. She found it easy to pardon the follies of his youth.

" Yes," said Nan. " I think you should consult your lawyer about a divorce."

" You really think so?"

" What else can you do?" asked Nan. " If she doesn't want to come back to you it's the *only* thing to do."

He nodded thoughtfully. " It ought to be cleared up. Even if neither of us wants to remarry it's the right thing to do. It's—it's untidy to—to leave it."

Nan was silent.

" Nan," said Henry in a low voice. " I've made a complete hash of my life. I've been such a fool—such a failure as a husband—I could never ask another woman to take the risk."

Nan turned her head and smiled at him.

" You understand, don't you?" he asked.

" Yes," said Nan. " But I don't think you understand. Perhaps another woman might be willing to take the risk."

" Nan——"

" No, Henry," said Nan quickly. " Don't say anything now. Let's leave it, shall we? "

" You understand everything," Henry told her. " You're so wise and good . . . you're a wonderful person, Nan."

CHAPTER THIRTY-SEVEN

THE sunny arctic conditions lasted exactly a week and then the Weather Clerk decided to make a change. Certainly if variety be the spice of life the inhabitants of the British Isles, and especially the inhabitants of the northern kingdom, have spice in abundance; sufficient spice to make their lives, in a meteorological sense, the equivalent of a Scotch Bun. On this particular occasion the Drumburly folk had just settled down to the snowy and icy conditions, had looked out their curling-stones and resurrected their sleighs, when a fresh wind from the south-west began to sigh gently across the hills and the snow began to melt. At first it melted slowly, disintegrating into grey slush, but twenty-four hours of warm rain hastened the process considerably.

Various things happened: Henry went to Glasgow to consult his lawyer; Adam recovered and went home; the road to Tassieknowe was cleared and Adam's car was rescued and towed into the garage at Drumburly. Soon everything became normal—or nearly normal—except at Boscath of course.

Boscath was completely isolated now. The daft road was a quagmire and the ford was impassable. There was no way of getting to Boscath except by walking five miles across the moor.

Mamie felt very unhappy about it. She had known this would happen but that did not make it any less disastrous—and this was not an exceptional occurrence by any means. This would go on happening every time the river rose. She went down to look at the river and there it was, a rushing roaring torrent, brown as coffee and flecked with foam, full of branches and sticks and pieces of wood which had been swept down from the hills; they were being hurled along at an incredible speed, tossed in the air and swept over rocks, they were turning over and over as they went.

Oddly enough Rhoda had had the same impulse at exactly the same moment and was standing upon the opposite bank. Mamie waved to her and Rhoda waved back and made signs to show that all was well, but somehow Mamie had a feeling that Rhoda looked a trifle dejected. No wonder, Mamie thought!

They stood and looked at one another for some little time—and waved. There was no other means of communication possible for the river was making a noise like thunder.

It won't do, thought Mamie miserably as she walked back to the house. It isn't right. I can't bear them to be cut off like that. I must talk to Jock again; we'll have to build a bridge.

Jock was out all day; he had gone to Drumburly on business and had not returned to lunch; by the time he returned Mamie was absolutely determined upon a bridge. It would be expensive of course and probably it would be extremely difficult to obtain material for its construction but somehow or other all the difficulties must be overcome and a bridge must be built.

Mamie was just sitting down to tea in the drawing-room when she heard Jock come in. He did not at once shout for her (which was his usual habit upon entering the house) but closed the front door quietly and went into the dining-room. Was it Jock? wondered Mamie, listening intently. Could it be somebody else? She rose and crossed the hall and opened the dining-room door and there was Jock standing by the table.

"Is anything the matter?" she inquired.

"Er—no," replied Jock. "Nothing's the matter. I was just—er——"

"Jock," said Mamie earnestly. "I can't bear it. I'm miserable about Boscath—simply miserable. We can't go on like this. I went down to the river this morning and Rhoda was standing on the opposite bank. We waved to each other—it was a wretched business—we stood and looked at each other for quite a long time. Oh, Jock, we must have a bridge, no matter what it costs; either that or the road must be remade."

" No," said Jock, shaking his head firmly.

" No? " she asked in surprise.

" No, Mamie, there's going to be no bridge and I'm not pouring any more good money into that bog on the daft road."

" But Jock! What are we going to do? "

" We're going to sell Boscath."

She gazed at him speechless with amazement.

" Just that," said Jock, nodding. " We'll sell the place for what we can get. We'll turn out James and Rhoda neck and crop. Throw them out, that's the thing to do. I'm sick of wasting money on Boscath."

Mamie gazed at him and Jock gazed back with an expressionless face.

" I'm the wicked uncle," said Jock solemnly. " I'm throwing the two poor children out of their home. You didn't know I was so cruel, did you, Mamie? Maybe we'll give them a wee tent to live in—we could pitch it on the lawn—or, wait a moment, maybe we could put them into Tassieknowe. How would that do? "

He had been making superhuman efforts to keep his face perfectly serious but he could manage the feat no longer and a beaming smile spread across it from ear to ear.

" Jock, you old ruffian! " cried Mamie, rushing at him and throwing her arms round his neck. " Tell me—tell me at once what have you been up to? "

" Buying Tassieknowe, that's all," declared Jock, laughing. " I bought it from Heddle this afternoon. I'll tell you the whole thing if you'll stop choking me for a moment."

" Jock, it's almost too good to be true! "

" I know," he agreed. " I keep on pinching myself to make sure I'm not dreaming . . . but here are the title-deeds! " and he showed her the bundle of documents yellow with age, which were lying on the table.

" The title-deeds of Tassieknowe! " exclaimed Mamie, looking at them in delight.

" I've been gloating over them," declared Jock. " I couldn't bear to let them out of my hands and I knew you'd want to see them. Of course they'll have to go back to Mr. Skene's office, I'm not keeping them here. It's a silly thing to keep title-deeds in the house."

Mamie nodded.

" But just for to-night," continued Jock. " Just for to-night I thought I'd like to put them in the drawer." He went across to the tallboy as he spoke and pulled out the top drawer. " This is where old Brown kept them. Many's the time I told him he was a fool to keep them there," added Jock with a somewhat sheepish grin; for Jock always pretended he was a hard-headed Scot and here he was being sentimental over a handful of old papers.

Of course Mamie understood perfectly. " I remember," she said. " Mr. Brown got them out one day when we were at Tassieknowe to clear up some point about the marches. I can see the old man standing on tiptoe and fishing them out of the top drawer."

" He was a wee man," nodded Jock, who had no need to stand on tiptoe.

" Tell me more," demanded Mamie. " Tell me everything. Did you go to Tassieknowe to see Mr. Heddle about it?"

" Not me. I fixed to meet him in Drumburly at Mr. Skene's office for I knew perfectly well I was no match for Nestor Heddle in business matters. Heddle appeared with his own lawyer in tow so you can imagine it was a solemn enough affair. When I bought Boscath it took me five minutes; I said to Sinclair I'd buy and he said he'd sell and we went and had a drink at the Shaw Arms ... but it took me long enough to buy Tassieknowe, and there were no drinks going I can tell you."

" Why did Mr. Heddle change his mind, I wonder. Adam said he was determined not to leave the place."

Jock smiled. " Miss Heddle walked out on him, that's why. He went to Glasgow on business and when he got back she had gone. I must say I was surprised to hear it for I thought she'd do anything for that glumphy brother of hers, but apparently there *are* limits to her submission, and as she does all the house-keeping, and is necessary to his comfort, he can't stay on without her. He explained all that—he was very hurt about it—but I didn't pay much heed. I wasn't caring why he was going so long as he'd made up his mind and go."

" But he's getting married, isn't he? Couldn't his wife look after him? "

Jock chuckled. " She doesn't care for housekeeping. She likes having a good time (that's what he said) and I wasn't surprised to hear it when he said who it was."

" Who? " breathed Mamie.

" Who do you think? You know the young lady. I wouldn't exactly say she's a friend of yours. It's Holly Douglas, that's who it is, and I wish her joy of her man."

" Jock! " exclaimed Mamie in horrified tones. " Oh, Jock, how could she? "

" Och, don't worry," said Jock. " She knows well enough what she's doing. There's no need for us to bother our heads about her."

They went into the drawing-room and sat down, for Jock wanted his tea. As he ate and drank he continued to talk, between the mouthfuls, and to tell Mamie all that had happened in Mr. Skene's office. Jock had been looking forward to this all day, to telling Mamie the story, for there was no audience on earth so appreciative as Mamie.

" There was an awful lot of talk," said Jock. " It went round and round without getting anywhere; I began to think we'd be in the place all night. Heddle's lawyer kept on saying that Mr. Heddle had spent seven thousand pounds putting Tassieknowe in order, over and above what he paid for it. So then I said it was a sheep-farm, and no farmer could pay that money for a house. I said it was the hirsel that mattered and the hirsel had been neglected. So then Heddle asked what I meant by that and I said the dykes were in a bad condition . . . and I asked if the ewes had been well tupped. None of them knew what I meant."

" That was rather naughty of you," declared Mamie.

" M'h'm," said Jock. " Maybe so, but the man is by way of being a farmer. Skene backed me up of course; he said the place was too far out for a luxury house and they'd have difficulty in finding a buyer. It was just what I'd said myself in different words."

" And it's true," said Mamie, nodding. " Only a farmer would want it and he wouldn't be able to afford an enormous price."

" So then," continued Jock. " So then Heddle asked why I wanted the place and I said it would suit me because it adjoined Mureth. Then Heddle's lawyer said it was a beautiful place and Mr. Heddle was very sorry to have to part with it. He was parting with it because the high altitude did not suit Miss Heddle. ' Is that so?' says Skene. ' Then there's nothing in the rumour going about Drumburly that Tassieknowe is haunted?' He said it in the most innocent way imaginable, just as if he was asking for information on the subject. Heddle was absolutely furious. He lost his wool completely and began storming about the wee office like a mad bull. Skene sat tight with a sort of grim smile on his face but Heddle's man got into a fine old flaughter; he was jumping about like a flea, trying to calm Heddle down before he said anything actionable. ' Oh, my dear sir!' he kept saying. ' Oh, my dear sir!' " Jock laughed. " It was awfully funny," he declared. " It really was as good as a pantomime. I wished you'd been there."

" I'm glad I wasn't," said Mamie with feeling.

" Well, finally he quietened down, and he signed the thing and I signed it, and it was all fixed. He's moving out immediately."

" Immediately! "

" I bargained for immediate possession," explained Jock. " I'm every bit as worried as you about those two young creatures at Boscath. We'll get them out of it straight away as soon as the river falls. They could come here for a wee while, couldn't they? You see, Mamie, we'll need Flockhart to do a bit of painting at Tassieknowe before they move in; I can't abide that blue paint on the doors and windows. The inside of the house can be painted too if Rhoda wants it done, but once the Heddles have taken out all those mirrors and carpets and what not it won't look so garish. They'll need more furniture of course, but I thought the stuff we bought at the sale might go back to Tassieknowe. What do you think, Mamie?"

" I'm quite breathless," said Mamie, laughing. " Oh, Jock, when once you get going you *do* cover the ground!"

Jock grinned. " That's true enough. I'm a slow starter but once I get a move on I'm all right. Of course we're lucky in a way," he continued. " It's been done up from attic to cellar; they've put in a plant for electricity and new plumbing all over the house. It's a lot bigger than Boscath, but maybe James and Rhoda will be needing a bit more room one of these days. We'll hope so anyway." He smiled at Mamie and Mamie smiled back. She hoped so too.

" Well, there it is," said Jock. " The thing's settled and I'm as pleased as a dog with two tails, and as full of plans as a charthouse. We'll get Sutherland back and the dykes sorted; Mureth and Tassieknowe will be farmed together."

" Mr. Brown would be pleased if he knew!"

" He knows," said Jock somewhat shamefacedly. " I mean I've had a queer sort of feeling all day. Old Brown knows we've got Tassieknowe!"

THE END